Ryan was s̶[illegible] wide-eyed look of horror on Krysty's face

"What?" he whispered.

"Oh, Earth Mother! Back. Must turn back now. Feel desperate danger behind us. Turn back." She pushed past Ryan, running clumsily past the others, nearly knocking over Abe.

Krysty grabbed at Trader's sleeve. "Stop!" she hissed. "We have to go back, Trader. I can feel it. Very, very strong. Behind us."

"Feel what?"

The woman stared behind her, into the dark bank of fog that was all around them like an encircling wall. "Something's gone triple-wrong, Trader. Mebbe they know we're coming. I can't tell what it is."

Ryan started to go back toward where they'd left the ten sec men, but Trader called to him.

"Goin' somewhere, Ryan?"

"You heard her. Krysty gets a feeling as strong as this one, then you take note of it."

"She doesn't know what it is, but she *feels* something might've gone wrong." Trader laughed and shook his head. "We keep goin'."

For a moment nobody moved.

Then the sound came from behind them, to the east, a terrible piercing scream of soul-tearing pain and despair.

Also available in the Deathlands saga:

JAMES AXLER

DEATH LANDS®

Shadowfall

A GOLD EAGLE BOOK FROM
WORLDWIDE®

TORONTO • NEW YORK • LONDON
AMSTERDAM • PARIS • SYDNEY • HAMBURG
STOCKHOLM • ATHENS • TOKYO • MILAN
MADRID • WARSAW • BUDAPEST • AUCKLAND

This book is dedicated to the memory of the enormously
talented filmmaker, gardener and humanist,
Derek Jarman (1942-1994), who carried the definition
of courage as being grace under pressure to quite
extraordinary frontiers. His name will not be forgotten.

First edition May 1995

ISBN 0-373-62526-X

SHADOWFALL

Fare thee well, no more, let us clasp our hands
And swear no tears shall mar our manly cheeks.
Now we must part, to go to distant lands,
Each of us alone, through valleys, o'er peaks.
Yet in the dark, when my last breath shall end,
My final thought will be of you, my friend.
>   —From "A Wessex Boy,"
>   LJ Priv Prntd, 1742

Chapter One

Ryan Cawdor closed his eye and entered the darkness.

He had lost count of the number of times in the past couple of years that he'd gone through this experience—entering the gateway chamber of one of the long-buried military complexes, known as redoubts, to make a mat-trans jump. The process utilized the lost technology from the predark days, before the ultimate nuclear holocaust that had effectively destroyed civilization around the globe.

The present jump was beginning in the heart of what had once been Acadia National Park, in the area of the old United States that had been called Maine. None of the group of nine companions had the least idea where the jump would take them. Knowledge of how to control the gateways had been lost in the nuke-tainted years of the long winters. All they knew was that they would arrive in a similar gateway, elsewhere.

The one control element that they'd stumbled upon was that gateways had an automatic thirty-minute reset, enabling you to jump back to where you'd just been. As well, there was a setting, generally the coded buttons *L* and *D*, that would also take you to the last destination.

Ryan's final sight, before the swirling mists closed his good right eye and his mind down, had been his eight friends.

Next to him, holding his hand in hers, was Krysty Wroth, the great love of his life. In her mid-twenties she was about ten years younger than Ryan, and three inches shorter than his six feet two. The green-eyed, red-haired Krysty had the "mutie" power of being able to "feel" when danger threatened. She was also able, in the direst of straits, to call on the power of Gaia, the Earth Mother, taught her by her own mother back in the ville of Harmony, where she'd spent her childhood. This power brought Krysty way beyond the edge of total exhaustion but gave her, briefly, an almost supernatural strength.

On Ryan's other side was his eleven-year-old son, Dean. Ryan had been totally unaware of the boy's existence—the result of a fleeting relationship—until a year or so earlier. Now he would have given his own life for the lad. Dean was meeting the jump sitting with his back against the dark gray walls, clutching his turquoise-hilted knife in his lap.

Next around the circle was Mildred Wyeth. The stocky black woman had been a doctor, specializing in cryonics, or the medical effects of freezing. Born in 1965, Mildred had gone into a hospital in late December of the year 2000 for minor exploratory abdominal surgery, but she had never gotten that far. A freak reaction to the anaesthetic had necessitated her comatose body being frozen. The world blew apart less than a month later, and she rested on in dark silence, forgotten, her life-support system powered by an undamaged nuke plant. She had finally been awakened from her long sleep by Ryan.

Other than her medical talents, Mildred also had an even more useful skill for survival in the wasteland that had once been the United States of America.

In the last-ever Olympic Games, held in Miami in 1996, Mildred had represented her country in the free pistol shooting, winning the silver medal. Now, with her ZKR 551 6-shot Czech revolver, chambered to take the Smith & Wesson .38 round, she was probably the finest shot in Deathlands.

In the past few months Mildred had begun a relationship with the person next around the circle.

John Barrymore Dix, known as J.B. or as the Armorer, was about the same age as Ryan and had been his closest friend for the past dozen years or so. J.B. was the greatest living authority on firearms and weaponry in general. Despite his appearance—five feet eight inches and one-forty pounds soaking wet, with glasses—his combat experience was almost unrivaled.

He sat next to Mildred, his sallow complexion even more pale than usual, his 9 mm Uzi and Smith & Wesson M-4000 scattergun lying at his side. In his lap he held his beloved fedora hat.

Squatting next to J.B., and holding a battered Armalite, was a lean, grizzled man in his fifties. Known throughout much of Deathlands simply as the Trader, he was the person who'd originally brought Ryan and

J.B. together, enlisting them as young bloods and training them until they became his right- and left-hand men.

Trader had found two massively powerful war wags up in the Appalachians and used them in his trading and traveling until he was one of the most feared men in Deathlands. Even the barons of some of the largest villes were wary of upsetting the uncertain temper of Trader.

The diminutive figure next to Trader, with a drooping mustache, was Abe, once the gunner on War Wag One. When Trader had vanished, many many long months ago, it was widely accepted that he'd gone off alone into the woods to chill himself, as he was known to be suffering from a painful and probably terminal rad cancer.

Then the whispering started. Trader had been seen down in Yuma; had chilled a whole ville in Peoria; was running a frontier gaudy with twenty beautiful girls, somewhere east of Taos.

It got so that Abe couldn't stand the rumors and had set off to try to track down his old leader.

Eventually he had succeeded in his quest, locating the grizzled veteran close to the ruins of old Seattle, Washington.

Ryan had mentally ticked them all off, as the disks in floor and ceiling began to glow and the white fog wraiths appeared in the gateway chamber: Krysty, Dean, Mildred, J.B., Trader, Abe.

And Jak and Doc.

Jak Lauren looked as comfortable as if he were relaxing on a goose-feather mattress. Sixteen years old, he was the finest acrobat that Ryan had ever known, as well as being murderously accurate with any of the half dozen leaf-bladed throwing knives that he kept concealed about his skinny person.

He came originally from West Lowellton, near Lafayette, in the swamps. Ryan and the others had met him when they became involved with Jak's battles against the evil Baron Tourment. The albino teenager, with a mane of stark white hair and ruby eyes, had traveled with them for some months, until he'd met and married Christina Ballinger. They had lived happily on a spread in New Mexico, with baby Jenny coming along to cement their love for each other.

Then tragedy had struck, and the woman and child had been butchered. Jak had come to the very brink of suicidal madness, but Ryan and Krysty and the others had helped him through the darkness and out once more into the light.

Last, and certainly not least, of their party was Dr. Theophilus Algernon Tanner.

None of the nine could have been called "normal" by any acceptable standards, but Doc Tanner was less normal than any of them.

The date of his birth was February 14, 1868, in a white frame house in the pretty hamlet of South Strafford, Vermont.

On June 17, 1891, he had married Miss Emily Chandler. A daughter, Rachel, had blessed their union two years later, followed by their ever-smiling little baby boy, Jolyon, in 1895.

Doc, whose degree was in science from Harvard, backed with a doctorate in philosophy from Oxford University, England, had the whole world in his hands.

But the American military scientists in the unknowable future had other ideas.

First, there was the Totality Concept, which spawned Overproject Whisper, of which Project Cerberus—dealing with gateways—was an integral part. Another subdivision of the Totality Concept was Operation Chronos.

The slang name for their experiments was "Trawling." It meant seeking out individuals from the past and using a complex and unreliable variant on the mat-trans system to pluck them from their own time, to the cold research laboratories of the late 1990s.

There were many failures.

The results of some of the failures were hideous beyond human imagining. There was really only one clear-cut success in all of Operation Chronos.

Dr. Theo Tanner.

One moment he was in mid-Victorian times with his wife and children and then, a heartbeat later, he was dragged more than a hundred years into the future.

But the whitecoat experimenters came to regret their single success.

Having Doc Tanner loose in their organization was like having a panther running loose in a tornado.

He made himself so difficult and obstructive that they eventually resorted to trawling him forward, dumping him nearly a hundred years into the Deathlands future and leaving him there to fend for himself.

Had that not happened, he would have died a scant month later when the skies darkened and the missiles ravaged the world and a civilization passed away.

Now he was one of the exclusive members of the group who traveled with Ryan Cawdor.

Doc had survived experiences that would have turned most men stark mad, but he had paid a high price. Though he was reasonably well balanced most of the time, there were occasions when the pressure of what had happened to him tipped a part of his acute mind sideways.

Now he lay sprawled flat on his back, his mouth sagging open, showing his peculiarly perfect teeth, snoring gently. The huge gold-embossed commemoration Le Mat blaster protruded from its holster on his belt.

Ryan slipped away into the brain-churning blackness of the jump, surrounded by his son and his friends, ready to waken elsewhere.

He closed his eye.

Chapter Two

Ryan blinked his eye open.

His nostrils were immediately filled with the bitter smell of sickness, and he looked down, taking care not to risk moving his head, to see that Dean had puked during the jump. Fortunately it hadn't gone on the boy's clothes. More fortunately, it hadn't gone on Ryan's clothes, either.

Seeing the small yellow puddle, Ryan felt his own guts heaving in sympathy.

He closed his eye again, trying to breathe through his mouth to minimize the stench.

His only other observation was that the armaglass walls of this particular redoubt gateway were brown, flecked with white, markedly different from the dark gray of the chamber walls back in Maine.

Using the techniques that Krysty had taught him, Ryan slowed his breathing and pulse. He concentrated his imagination on a wall of untouched blue, using the color to blank his mind, taking away a significant proportion of the barely tolerable stress of making a jump.

Doc and Mildred had once had a bitter argument about what precisely happened during a mat-trans jump, going into abstruse scientific theories about reassembled molecules and neutron displacement.

All that everyone in the group agreed on was that jumping left you feeling like you'd just gone eight rounds with a jolt-crazed stickie.

Feeling a little less nauseous, Ryan risked opening his good right eye. His left had been missing since he was a young boy, back in his home ville of Front Royale, up in the Shens, courtesy of his cold-heart brother Harvey.

The chamber swam mistily back into focus.

Now there were signs of life from some of the other members of the group.

J.B. was carefully unfolding his glasses from an inside pocket and replacing them on his sharp nose. He moved so slowly it looked as if he were sitting on broken eggshells.

Mildred was also recovering, using her sleeve to wipe a thread of spittle from a corner of her mouth. Seeing Ryan watching her, she managed a watery grin. "Best fun you can have lying down," she said quietly.

Dean coughed, doubling over, bringing up a little more bile. He pulled a disgusted face and tried to wriggle sideways, hoping to disassociate himself from the vomit.

"Hi, lover."

Ryan smiled at Krysty and gripped her hand tightly. "How's it going?"

"Been better. Been worse." She shook her head, the sentient mane of flaming crimson hair still pressed tightly to her nape. "On balance I been better." Her face was as pale as wind-washed bone. "Yeah, I have definitely been better."

Trader shook his head like a dog emerging from icy waves. "I'll be hung, quartered and dried for the crows!" He coughed up a mouthful of phlegm and looked for a moment as if he were going to spit it across the chamber. He caught Krysty's eyes and changed his mind, swallowing it. "I don't reckon I'll ever get used to these bastard jumps. Not ever."

"Amen to that, Trader," Abe agreed weakly. "Mouth feels like a skunk crapped in it."

"Sorry about bein' sick, Dad."

"Happens to the best of us, son. Just sit still and take it easy until you feel like standing up. Don't try it too quickly."

On the other side of the six-sided room, Jak uncoiled himself with the effortless grace of a prairie rattler, steadying himself for a moment on the armaglass walls. Ryan noticed there was a worm of blood seeping from the albino teenager's nose.

Looking across at Doc, generally the last to recover from the rigors of a jump, Ryan noticed that the old man was still unconscious. Like Jak, he was bleeding from his nose. Only in Doc's case there looked to be about a pint and a half staining his grizzled cheek and coagulating on the floor.

As if he felt Ryan staring at him, Doc coughed and opened his pale blue eyes, gazing sightlessly at the ceiling. "Give me a few more seconds, gentlemen of the fancy, and I shall soon be up to scratch." He touched his nose and peered at the red smears on his fingers. "I perceive that the redoubtable John L. Sullivan has tapped my claret."

"What's he droning on about now?" Trader asked.

Mildred shook her head. "John L. Sullivan was the world heavyweight boxing champion back around Doc's time. Looks like the old goat imagines he's just been knocked down by him."

Doc struggled into a sitting position. "Imagined! Did I hear you right, Dr. Wyeth?"

"Yeah, you did, Doctor of Philosophy Tanner."

"I will have you know that I once had the honor…" He reconsidered. "The dubious honor of testing my pugilistic skills against the great man himself. Though truth forces me to admit that he was a little the worse for imbibing of the grain and was in a bullying, hectoring mode."

"And he beat the shit out of you," J.B. concluded.

Doc considered the question. "I managed a few shrewd blows that caused him to blink. Then he hammered home seventy or eighty lucky blows, and I measured my length on the floor of the restaurant where the altercation had taken place."

J.B. grinned, adjusting his fedora to a more jaunty angle. "Like I said, Doc. He beat the shit out of you."

BY THE TIME EVERYONE in the group felt ready to stand without the world spinning around their ears, about ten minutes or so had passed.

"Usual red alert," Ryan said, the SIG-Sauer drawn in his right hand, the Steyr rifle across his shoulder. "Everyone ready to go?"

They all had their blasters out, lining up behind Ryan as he reached to ease open the door of the gateway.

The lock clicked, and he pushed gently at the counterbalanced weight of reinforced armaglass.

It swung open, revealing the familiar sight of a small, cramped anteroom, barely eight feet square, totally bare of any furniture.

The first thing Ryan noticed was that the floor of the room was surprisingly dusty.

Most of the redoubts that they'd visited had been in near-perfect running order, with just an occasional failed light or a small malfunction in the circuitry. The original comp-controlled nuke power sources had been working reliably for close to a century, maintaining temperature and humidity as well as circulating the air and keeping all the rooms and corridors of the complex relatively free from dust.

"Dirty," J.B. observed from over Ryan's shoulder. "And there's marks in it."

"Yeah. Everyone just wait a minute. Jak, can you come take a look?"

The young man ghosted past, stepping carefully from the chamber. He squatted, head on one side, staring at the marks, reaching out after a few seconds with delicate finger and thumb, like surgical pincers.

"Here." He held a frail shred of material to Ryan, who took it and held it to the bright overhead light. "Silk," he pronounced after examining it carefully.

It was only a dozen threads, but each seemed to be of a different color—turquoise, scarlet, aquamarine, cobalt and amethyst.

"Beautiful," Mildred said, taking it from Ryan's hand. "Looks foreign."

"Foreign?"

"Oriental. Japanese or Chinese. Funny thing to find here in the middle of a redoubt."

Doc took it from the woman. "It is beautiful. You know what it reminds me of?" He shook his head. "Silly, though."

"What, Doc?" J.B. asked.

"Well, an old friend of mine who lived up in the Pacific Northwest was a collector of militaria. Specifically he was most interested in Oriental armor and swords. You know, the samurai swords with a narrow, very slightly curved blade to them. Lovely things."

J.B. nodded. "I know what you mean, Doc. Always thought I'd like to own one, but you don't see many of them lying around in Deathlands."

"But what's Chinese swords got to do with this pretty bit of rag?" Trader queried.

"Japanese, not Chinese," Doc corrected. "Well, they sometimes have braids of silk at the hilt, like a tassel. It's just that these threads reminded me of that." He grimaced. "Sorry. Told you that it wasn't going to be relevant. Silly. Not many samurai warriors making jumps in Deathlands.''

Ryan rubbed at his chin. ''Well, now, remember we've started hearing these strange rumors. Gangs of what they called yellow-skinned killers. Only rumors.''

''Don't get bubbles without water,'' Trader said.

''Doesn't seem likely,'' Krysty argued. ''All the way from China or Japan. How would they have gotten here?''

''No?'' Ryan looked at her. ''You forgotten about Major-Commissar Gregori Zimyanin?''

''And that lovely sniper's rifle,'' J.B. added, eyes brightening behind his spectacles. ''The long Dragunov. Reworked Kalashnikov. Yeah, he got here from old Russia.''

''And we got *to* old Russia,'' Ryan said. ''We still have no idea how many mat-trans gateways there are in Deathlands. Never mind anywhere else in the world.''

''Can't be any Japanese down here,'' Abe said. ''Wherever 'here' is.''

Jak straightened from examining the faint scuff marks in the layer of fine powdery dust. ''Could be wrong, Abe. About ten or dozen feet. All of them real small. Like woman. Or child. Japanese supposed to be small.''

J.B. had stopped and run his finger through the sandy dirt. ''Tell you something else,'' he said. ''I don't reckon this is dust from Deathlands. Not like anything I've seen, and I've been to most places.''

"And seen most things," Mildred added. "Sorry, poor joke at the best of times. This isn't the best of times."

"That was Mae West," Doc said, beaming delightedly. "I recall she once said something about—"

"Shut it, Doc," Ryan ordered. He rubbed the dust between his fingers, realizing what J.B. had meant. It was far finer than most dirt he'd ever seen, almost like milled flour. He touched the tip of his tongue to it. There was an unusual bitterness, and something that was faintly aromatic and foreign.

"What do you think, lover?" Krysty asked.

"J.B. could be right. Who knows? I guess one bit of dirt's a lot like another...." He hesitated. "But, there's something odd about it."

"Think it comes from inside the redoubt here?" Dean asked. "Or brought in from outside?"

Jak answered, pointing out something that none of the others had spotted. "Small feet brought it with them. In from gateway. Dust's thicker right by chamber door and gets thinner across floor."

Ryan checked his wrist chron. "Let's get moving. Been close to half an hour since we jumped."

"Hope this place has some food and drink cached away," Mildred said.

"I would personally settle for a comfortable bed to take my ease and rest my weary bones," Doc stated.

What happened in the next fifteen seconds was never totally clear in anyone's mind.

Everyone had come out of the gateway chamber itself, crowding into the cramped little room. With nine people there, it wasn't possible for anyone to move, and Ryan was already waiting by the closed door that should open to reveal the control room.

"Don't push," he said.

But Abe jostled Trader's arm, loosening his grip on the Armalite. As the blaster started to fall, Trader began to stoop to retrieve it. His hip knocked into Doc, who dropped the sword stick from under his left arm.

It landed awkwardly, somehow wedging itself between Mildred's ankles.

She stumbled into Krysty. Jak neatly dodged her, but then got in the way of J.B., who had seen the cane drop and was about to try to pick it up.

He backed into Dean, who was totally off-balance, trying to peer down at the small footprints in the alien dust. The boy tripped backward, sprawling flat on his back on the metal disks in the floor of the mat-trans chamber, the back of his head landing with a sickly crack that stunned him for a few moments.

The confusion made Ryan turn, so fast that the SIG-Sauer cracked into Mildred's wrist. She yelped in pain and took a step backward, bumping into Abe.

The little gunner had been trying to stop himself falling in the opposite direction, as well as keeping out of the Trader's line of sight. The impact of the stocky black woman took him completely by surprise, and he began to fall toward the gateway chamber.

At the last moment he wriggled sideways, but his own impetus took him into the open door, slamming it shut.

Chapter Three

With everyone falling over everyone else, it was a few startling heartbeats before anyone realized what had actually happened.

Abe was the first, raising his voice above the general chaos and confusion. "Door's closed itself!" he shouted. "The kid's inside."

Ryan had heard the yell, but he didn't immediately take in the dreadful significance of it. Krysty heard it and was quicker to react, pushing Trader to one side, elbowing Doc out of the way as she fought to get to the armaglass chamber.

"Dark night! Boy's jumping!" J.B. called, trying to reach the sec lock.

Then Ryan realized what was going on. He could just see the gateway over everyone's heads, see the closed door and just make out, very dimly, the shape of his son inside, through the speckled glass. Dean was up on his feet, pounding with his bare fists on the armored door.

"Everyone out the way!" Ryan roared, heading across the cramped little room toward the trapped boy.

Jak and J.B. had gotten to the door first, and both were pulling on the release mechanism. "No," the

Armorer panted. "Sec lock's activated. Take a missile to break it open."

Ryan stopped by them. "Thing's started." he said. "See the mist through the glass. Look at the ceiling disks starting to glow."

"Quiet," Mildred called. "Dean's shouting."

"Dad, please.... Dad...help...me...."

"He's going," Trader warned.

"Shut up," Ryan snapped. He pressed his mouth close to the ice-cold, brown-and-white armaglass, shouting as loudly as he possibly could. "Dean! Lie down flat for the jump. Now! I'll come after you. Hear me? Stay where you end up, and I'll come after you." He drew a breath and tried again. "Dean! Wait and I'll come." Krysty touched him gently on the shoulder, but he shrugged her off. "Wait and—"

"He's gone, lover."

"Gone?"

"I regret that it is true, old friend." Doc patted him on the arm.

Ryan took a step away, trying to keep himself together. The sudden disappearance of his son had been truly devastating. It was as though he'd been walking through a summer meadow and found himself flat on his back, looking up at the sun with a bullet in his spine. No warning.

Gradually all of his fighting skills and senses came seeping back to him. "Right," he said, glancing at his wrist chron. "It's inside the half hour, so he should simply have jumped directly back to Maine. I'll use the LD control and try to follow him. Long as he hasn't wandered away from the gateway, then we can both jump back here."

"You'll feel like death," Trader cautioned.

"Sure. But we'll still be alive, and we'll all be together again."

Krysty touched him on the arm. "What if you don't get back here within thirty minutes, lover?"

"Then I'll come and find— Fireblast! 'Course. We don't know where we are right now."

"Set a meeting place," J.B. suggested. "We'll wait here in the redoubt for... for let's say twelve hours from now." Both men checked their chrons. "You and Dean haven't shown, then we'll go out and find where we are."

Mildred had been thinking deeply about the logistics of it. "If we're right, you'll be in Maine. Don't yet know where we are. So, we should set a meeting place and time that we can all likely get to."

Krysty looked again at the chron. "Time's speeding by," he said worriedly.

"Main bridge over the Sippi at Memphis," Trader suggested. "Four weeks from today at noon."

"Agreed. Four weeks from today, noon at the big bridge at Memphis."

Krysty put her arms around Ryan, holding him tightly. She kissed him on the cheek, whispering in his ear. "Come back safe, lover. I don't have anything if I don't have you."

He kissed her on the lips, returning the hug. "Same for me, lover."

Ryan shook everyone's hand, looked at his chron. "Twenty-seven minutes since our jump. Four minutes since Dean went."

"What if the lad didn't hear your warning, comes around back in Maine and has the intuitive sense to simply press the Last Destination code on the door? That would bring him back here anytime in the next half hour."

Ryan looked at Doc. "So?"

"I don't believe that you can use the Last Destination code twice."

"Meaning I'd be stranded in Maine?"

The old man nodded. "It is indeed a sorry thing to be lost, so very far away from all your friends and loved ones, Ryan."

"I know it. But we still got us a date and a place if things go wrong."

There was nothing more to be said.

With a final glance around, Ryan tugged at the door of the chamber. For a single piercing moment he thought that it wasn't going to open. The time would quickly elapse for a jump after the boy. Dean would be totally alone and lost.

He tried the door again, and this time the sec lock clicked open. Ryan stepped inside and pulled the heavy armaglass door closed behind him.

The last thing he saw was Krysty Wroth, her emerald eyes brimming with unshed tears.

Ryan sat, laying the rifle at his side and tucking the SIG-Sauer snugly into its holster. He rested his back against the brown-and-white wall and closed his eye.

He struggled to compose himself for the second jump in thirty minutes, knowing from previous experience that this wasn't going to be a pleasurable experience.

The silvery disks above his head and by his feet began to glow, and the ghostly wraiths of white mist gathered near the top of the gateway.

But Ryan saw none of that. He was preoccupied with the sickening swirl within his brain that told him the jump was irreversibly on its way.

THE WALLS OF THE CHAMBER were a dark gray, the same color of the mat-trans unit up in Acadia National Park that they'd only just left.

Ryan fought against the nausea, swallowing hard, sliding down to lie on his back to try to recover more quickly. He knew that time was now the remorseless enemy, ticking away the speedy seconds and minutes until he would no longer be able to use the Last Destination control on the coded console by the door.

The headache was ferocious, spreading from his nape, erupting like agonizing molten lava over the top of his skull, behind both eyes. Despite the pain and sickness, Ryan was able to make the clinical observation that his missing eye hurt just as much as his good eye.

He could actually smell or taste the rancid bitterness of vomit, but he couldn't face trying to find out where it was. Or whose it was.

Squinting, Ryan could see that the door of the chamber was closed, which it would have to have been for the mat-trans unit to have functioned at all.

He also saw that the chamber was empty.

Dean wasn't there.

"Two possibilities," he whispered, conscious of how dry his mouth was and how wonderful a mouthful of crystal-clear spring water would be.

The first possibility was that Dean had ended up somewhere else. The second was that he'd been there a little earlier but had already left.

A third thought occurred to Ryan; perhaps he'd jumped to a different gateway himself, to one that happened, by grim coincidence, to have the same color of armaglass walls as the redoubt in Maine.

Three possibilities, but only one possible course of action—to get up on his feet and go and see if he could find his son outside the unit.

Standing up was a major accomplishment.

Ryan managed it only with the aid of the Steyr SSG-70, climbing up it, leaning his shoulder against the cold armaglass.

Only when he was finally upright did he dare risk a glance at his wrist chron.

"Fireblast!" To his horror he saw that fourteen minutes had already elapsed since he had commenced the jump from the other redoubt.

If Dean wasn't close by outside, then it was going to mean tracking him down, then a dangerous trip overland to meet up with the others.

Ryan lurched to the door, pushing at it and nearly falling as it opened easily. He looked at the control panel, as though there might be some clue as to what had happened in the past few minutes. But the numbers and letters, in their recessed boxes, stared blankly back at him.

The anteroom was also empty.

"Dean." It sounded about as loud as a mouse farting behind a brick wall.

Ryan, feeling a little better, stepped out of the chamber and tried again.

"Dean! You there?"

"The only sound was the whirring of the huge banks of control consoles, each linked to the hidden master computer. Ryan stood a moment in the small room, licking his dry lips, pausing longer to wipe his sweating palms down the legs of his pants.

There was a feeling of cool fresh air, which had probably resulted from their own entry into the redoubt, only a couple of hours ago.

Ryan sniffed, trying to catch some scent of his only child. But there was nothing.

"Dean! It's me, son."

With an effort he slung the Steyr over his shoulder and drew the SIG-Sauer, stepping out into the control area.

At a first glance, it was totally deserted, except for the chattering machines and the flickering lights.

Ryan looked again to check the time.

"Nineteen minutes," he said quietly.

The floor of the redoubt was totally clean, with no hint that anyone might have passed that way.

The massive sec door that opened onto the rest of the complex was still closed, the green control lever in the down position. Ryan had the overwhelming certainty that his son, only eleven years old, couldn't possibly have managed to open and then close the door, which meant either that he'd somehow jumped to some other gateway or he was still there.

Ryan walked slowly up the first row of desks. They were too high for him to see over, but it suddenly occurred to him that if he climbed up...

He nearly passed out, swaying dangerously, overcome with vertigo.

But he could see the whole room, see Dean lying huddled in a corner, as pale as ivory and still as death.

Only eight minutes remained.

Chapter Four

A pulse, as faint as a tiny bird's, barely fluttered against the man's index finger.

Ryan had run along the desks, his heavy combat boots splintering delicate comp keyboards. He jumped down, clumsily, the butt of the Steyr smashing a vid screen into a noisy implosion of silver-and-crimson sparks. A thread of dark smoke began to crawl toward the ceiling.

"Dean." He lifted the boy's head from the floor, wincing as his hand encountered a great bump on the side of Dean's skull, which happened when he fell into the other gateway chamber.

The boy's eyes were closed, and when he pushed back one of the lids, Ryan could only see bloodshot whites.

Dean's mouth was open, his breathing so shallow that it was hardly there. His skin was sallow and cold to the touch, slightly sweating.

"Come on, lad. Wake up." He chafed the limp wrists, trying to rouse Dean by slapping him hard across the cheeks. All that happened was that the marks of Ryan's hands stood out like livid scars on the boy's face.

There was a crackling sound that made Ryan spin quickly, seeing that the sparks had turned into flames and that the worm of smoke had become a great dark, curling python, wreathing toward the bright overhead lights.

Ryan glanced again at the wrist chron, having to waste a vital second or two tugging back the sleeve of his coat while still holding Dean.

Five minutes and forty seconds were left before the Last Destination option expired.

There still seemed no sign of his son reviving so Ryan stood, managing to pick him up in his arms, awkwardly fumbling for the strap of the rifle.

The comp voice boomed out from the speakers in the corner of the room, nearly making Ryan drop the boy.

"Fire in Matter-Transfer Computer Control Center. Fire in Matter-Transfer Computer Control Center. All personnel immediate evacuation. Download all comp programs onto security disks and evacuate soonest by main exit."

Simultaneously the sprinklers in the ceiling of the room began to operate.

Water poured out, stinkingly rancid, soaking Ryan and his son. The sprinkler system probably hadn't been activated for most of the century that the redoubt had stood empty, and its clotted contents had become unspeakably vile.

After less than twenty seconds, the sprinklers became clogged and stopped operating, long before they'd done anything useful to control the fire that was spreading fast through the complex, the ancient plastics catching all too easily.

The smoke roiled along the ceiling, as though it were seeking some route of escape from the control room. As it grew thicker and darker, it started to fill the whole space, dark yellow flames lapping sulkily at the desk tops.

Despite his youth, dean was a solidly built boy, and Ryan was seriously weakened by the second jump. He ducked his head beneath a wave of flame and battled on toward the gateway.

"Emergency fire crews both active and standby immediate move to matter-transfer unit. Gateway evacuation grade-one priority. B12 clearance is waived for this emergency. Serious malfunction with cont—"

The voice stopped dead in midword.

Ryan was halfway toward the anteroom, the stock of the rifle jolting at every step, but he couldn't stop to adjust the sling without putting his son down in the pools of stinking, green-yellow water.

The fire was racing at incredible speed, consuming everything in its path, filling the whole large room with impenetrable choking smoke.

Ryan had peeled back his sleeve, and he blinked down at the chron. It was becoming difficult to see, but it looked like he was inside four minutes.

The liquid from the sprinkler supply didn't just have a foul stench. It was also oddly thick and slimy, making every surface slippery to the touch, making the floor itself like an ice rink for Ryan and his burden.

"Can walk, Dad," mumbled a faint voice in his ear, but he ignored it.

He could hear the swelling hum from the air-conditioning, struggling to overcome the smoke. Fortunately he was now close enough to the anteroom to be able to slip inside, heeling the door half shut behind himself, gaining a little ease in both breathing and seeing.

Then the lights all went out.

For a single moment he froze in midstride, his mind racing as he considered the awful possibilities. The sprinkler and the comp-warning voice had both malfunctioned. Now the lighting was gone. How long before some key part of the mat-trans unit controls also went down?

If that happened, then he and Dean were both off on the last train to the coast.

The fire was now so intense that they had no chance at all of making it to the sec door to try to get it open. In those few static seconds, Ryan had already made the decision to shoot his son and then himself if the end was inevitable and there was no way out for them.

Better that than burning alive.

Best was making the jump out of the place before it crumbled to ashes around their ears.

"Put the lights on, Dad." The boy started to wriggle as though he wanted to be put down on the floor, but Ryan simply held him more tightly.

One foot at a time, he carefully walked across the little room, feeling the step into the gateway with the toe of his right boot. Ryan stepped up and into the chamber, stooping to lay Dean quickly down, dropping the rifle alongside him. He turned to grab for the edge of the door and slam it shut behind him, missing it first time, in the pitch darkness.

The only sound was his son, still barely conscious, whimpering at his feet, and the growing roar of flames. He could see the brightness of the fire through the half-open door of the anteroom, giving him just enough light to also make out the heavy gray arma-glass door.

It finally closed with a firm, satisfying click, and Ryan flung himself onto the floor, reaching out and grabbing hold of Dean's wrist.

"We'll be all right," he shouted.

"Not another—"

"Be sick and bad, but we'll live."

The smell of burning plastic seared his throat, and the smoke was making his eye water. The disks had started to glow in the ceiling and all across the floor.

"So far..." he whispered.

Ryan snatched a last glance at his chron, in the light from the metal disks.

It showed that twenty-nine minutes and fifteen seconds had elapsed since the last jump.

"Close," Ryan muttered, before the darkness oozed up from the center of his brain and swallowed him.

DEAN DREAMED, but he didn't know that it was just a dream. Every last detail was etched too finely across his brain for it to be anything but reality.

He was underground, crawling through soft warm mud. Movement was made more difficult because his legs were tied together at the ankle. No, that wasn't quite right. They weren't exactly tied together.

They were actually *joined* together, the flesh and bones fused into a single clumsy, flapping limb.

The boy knew that he was hunting something or somebody who was in the dark, winding tunnels around him, ahead of him, to both sides of him, above him, below him.

Behind him?

Dean had been down in the ancient catacombs for all of his eternal life. Though he spoke little or no Spanish, an old proverb came to his mind. *Al vivo la hogaza, y al muerto, la mortaja.*

The boy heard it very clearly, as though someone were speaking it in a lisping Catalan tongue, somewhere deep inside the vault of his skull.

"A large loaf of bread for the living, and for the dead, a shroud."

His own voice was soundless, though Dean knew that he had moved his lips.

Somewhere far ahead was the salvation of a wine-dark ocean, braking ceaselessly on a shingled shore where discarded needles lay, mountain-high.

There was a ledge on the right, where squatted an ancient man in stained frock coat and cracked knee boots, clutching a cane of polished ebony, its handle carved from silver in the shape of a lion's head.

"I disremember the source, dear boy, but it is better by far to dwell on your knees than to die on your feet. It is not so, dear boy?"

"No, Doc, it isn't."

But his mouth was filled with the warm mud, sulfurous and bitter, and Dean made no sound.

RYAN WAS ALSO LOCKED into the heart of a whirling, bright nightmare.

But it wasn't seeming like a nightmare—no gibbering phantoms in dusty corridors, no terror swimming up from the deeps of some half-remembered horror.

Just a profound sense of unease.

There was a threat of violence hanging in the air, like an unspoken promise.

Ryan was walking through a large predark house, filled with wonderful paintings and ornate statues in gold and silver and bronze, horsemen spearing snarling lions and dying warriors, slipping from life, artistically posed.

The furniture was covered in large white sheets of spotless linen, and the windows were veiled in the same material, giving a strange, muted quality to the light, like wandering in an undersea cavern.

Ryan was conscious of clocks ticking in every room. One was ormolu-and-blue porcelain, topped with the placid bust of a serene Roman emperor wearing a laurel wreath. As he passed it, the clock began to chime, a high, thin, pure sound.

It chimed seventeen times.

In the corners of the corniced ceilings there were huge spiderwebs, spun from fine silvery filaments that floated in the ceaseless currents of air. Jaundiced mirrors, blotched with green mold, framed in warped mahogany, distorted Ryan's face as he walked slowly by them.

There were high double doors that opened into the oppressive heat of an orangery, the leaded panes of glass smeared with moisture and golden lichen.

The sense of unease was deepening, and Ryan kept looking back over his shoulder. Lush foliage, dank with condensation, filled the enormous room, and it seemed that someone had just that moment moved out of sight, timing their disappearances to coincide perfectly with his turning.

He stepped out onto a long terrace, dotted with large stone jars, taller than a man. The sky was totally overcast, with not a trace of sun, though the yew hedges left odd, sharply angular shadows.

Ryan saw a copper statue of a child, stooped as though in fear, hands raised to ward off a blow. The name on the plinth simply read: Lazarus.

There was a lake just visible at the bottom of a rolling expanse of lawn. And a domed monument, stark against the hillside beyond.

He was feeling sick, and he walked to sit on a wrought-iron bench, doubling over. He coughed and brought up a tangled mass of raw bloody meat and thin red worms.

DEAN HAD SUNK into the mud, feeling it suck him down, like soft hands that brushed against him, then clung and pulled, dragging him into the warm darkness.

It was comfortable to slip into the dark, away from all worries, no longer any need to fight against it.

The only thing stopping him was a tiny bright bead of light, like a dazzling eye, searching him out in the black sludge, homing in on him like a missile seeking its target, becoming larger and brighter.

Dean pushed his hands out, as though warding off a blow, trying to hinder the swelling light from preventing him from enjoying the bliss of restful sleep.

It felt as though someone were shaking him hard, an angry giant mutie that dwelled within the silent depths of the thick, welcoming ooze, squeezing his wet body.

RYAN HAD RUN AWAY from the bench, leaving the wriggling mess behind him on the raked gravel walk, the taste horrid in his dry mouth.

He entered the maze of dark, bitter yews, boxed around him, twenty feet high, a fear of the demiurge pursuing him, driving him deeper into the heart of the riddle.

It was beginning to snow. The large, soft white flakes settled on the trodden ground and on the hedges, on his own dark curly hair and across his broad shoulders, soaking through him.

There was painful pressure in his chest, across his temples, behind his eyes, holding him from the rest he

desperately wanted, probing at his nape, squeezing his
wet body.

MILDRED STRAIGHTENED, smiling at the anxious faces
around her in the control room of the mat-trans unit.

"They're both coming around now," she said.
"Father and son recovering together."

Krysty sighed. "Good." She shook her head. "One
thing I don't understand is why they both smell of
smoke and why they're both soaking wet."

Chapter Five

Recovering consciousness was only a part of getting to feel better.

The triple jump had taken a grave toll of both Ryan and his son, weakening them both physically and mentally.

As soon as they'd appeared together in the gateway, almost exactly a half hour after Ryan had made his jump, Mildred had gotten to them, throwing open the door before the disks had ceased glowing. She wrinkled her nose at the stink of burned plastic that hung in the chamber and was puzzled at the water that dripped from their clothes.

She helped Trader, J.B., Abe, Krysty and Jak to haul them out and lay them on the floor of the control area.

"They chilled?" Abe had asked, staring down at the two unconscious figures.

"They'll be fine." Mildred had turned them both onto their sides, probing with her finger to make sure neither swallowed his tongue. "Pulse and respiration are about what you'd expect after what they've been through."

Twelve worrying minutes passed without much sign of returning life.

Then they had both come around together.

"FEELING BETTER? Krysty asked, sitting on the floor beside Ryan.

"Some. How long since we finished that last jump? Guess I must've dozed off again."

She checked his chron. "Closing in toward two hours."

He sniffed. "What I need is a hot bath, some food and then sleep for a couple of days."

"That's all, lover?" She touched him on the thigh.

Ryan managed a smile. "Nice try, Krysty. Thanks, but no thanks. Not just yet."

"Can't blame me for trying."

"I don't, lover."

"How's Dean?"

"Better than his old man, if you want the truth. Resilience of youth, and all that."

"He ready to go out and explore the redoubt?"

Krysty thought about that for a few moments, then nodded. "Guess so. How about you?"

Ryan pressed his hand to his temple. "Can't remember feeling so wrung-out. Times that I curse those predark whitecoats for not making jumps easier to take."

Doc had wandered over to join them. "There are few waking hours in my life when I *don't* curse the whitecoats for what they've done. But credit where it's due. The work on matter-transfer systems had been going on in ultrasecret for some time. One of the scientists told me that it was triggered back in the 1950s by a horror film called *The Fly*. There was matter-transfer jumping in that."

"Did it work, or did the hero finish up with a real bad headache?" Ryan queried.

"My recollection, dear friend, is that the hero ended up with a real bad fly's head, when the actual jump went more than a little awry. The inevitable cinematic consequence of trying to tamper with the works of the Almighty."

Dean's face, the stark planes like polished ivory, peered over Doc's shoulder at his father. His voice sounded hoarse. "How's it going, Dad?"

"Better by the minute, son. You ready to go and start a look around this redoubt?"

"Sure. Just as long as we don't have to go anywhere near a gateway for... for at least another hundred years."

Ryan grinned at the boy. "You and me both, Dean. Yeah, you and me both."

THE PONDEROUS SEC DOOR rose smoothly into the air as J.B. threw the green lever up. He stopped it when it was only a scant few inches off the concrete floor, so that Jak could flatten himself and peer beneath it with his shrewd ruby eyes.

"Nothing."

The door continued its upward progress, almost silently.

Ryan leaned his hand against the wall while he waited, aware of his own weakness. Krysty saw the movement and moved closer. "Want a shoulder to lean on, lover?" she asked.

"All the time," he replied, then lifted a hand. "No. I can make my way. Tell you what, though."

"What?"

"Wouldn't mind if you took the Steyr for a while."

"Sure." Ryan unslung the rifle, taking care not to knock the Starlite night scope and laser image enhancer against the wall. He handed it to Krysty, who took it and put the strap across her own back.

Trader glanced around him. "Ready to go?"

"Sure. J.B. take point, and you cover our asses, Trader. I'll just sort of stumble along somewhere in the middle."

There was a biting, nagging headache at the back of his skull, but Ryan pushed it away and joined in the skirmish line with the others, Dean walking at his side.

"SMELL," Jak said.

Everyone stopped, sniffing the air.

"I fear that I have my usual snuffling cold," Doc announced after a few moments.

"Sulfur," Mildred said.

They'd gone only a few dozen paces along a typical redoubt corridor. To the left of the gateway entrance had been a blank wall of concrete. The corridor to the right was about twenty-five feet wide, with walls that sloped slightly until they became the arched roof. Strip neon lighting kept it well illuminated, though some of the tubes had, not surprisingly, burned out over the past century. Miniature vid sec cameras placed near the tops of the walls kept their ceaseless vigil, tiny red lights showing when they were actually functioning.

Ryan could smell it now, faint, at the back of consciousness—the smell of rotten eggs.

"Hot springs?" Trader suggested. "Could mean we're near that place north of the Shoshone Forest. Damn, but my memory gets worse every damn day!"

"Yellowstone?" Abe suggested cautiously, knowing that Trader got even more angry if an attempt to prompt turned out to be inaccurate.

"Yeah!" Trader slapped Abe on the back. "Ace on the fucking line, buddy. Yellowstone. All those bubbling pools and steam and shit."

"Could be." Ryan sniffed again. "But there's another smell, as well. Kind of salt. I reckon we might be out in the western islands. Hot springs and volcanoes and every kind of wrong thing you can think of."

"What're the western islands?" Mildred asked. "I don't think I've heard that name before."

Ryan answered her. "Probably because we've never jumped out that way since you've been with us. Which, in its turn, is probably because it was worst hit during the nukecaust and I doubt that many redoubts survived."

"Not close to the coast, anyway," J.B. agreed. "What was California in your day, Mildred."

"Oh, right. I know you told me some of the changes in the old U.S. of A. during the last war. You said that the West Coast was particularly badly hit by the missiles."

"Nearly wiped clean away," Trader said. "Couldn't find a speck of beach for a thousand miles."

Doc coughed. "My belief is that the San Andreas and all the other associated tectonic fault lines were struck and opened up. All of their energy was released, and the consequent quakes stretched out far beyond the coast. Is that not the correct scenario, John Barrymore?"

J.B. nodded. "Apart from the long words, it sounds right to me, Doc. The Cific just poured inland for hundreds of miles in some places."

"Tsunamis... monster tidal waves," Doc said. "I would speculate that the loss of life along the entire California coast was total. A flat one hundred percent."

"So, what's there now?" Mildred asked, looking at J.B. "Islands?"

"We never went there very often," he replied, glancing, in turn, to Trader.

"Hot spots and the worst muties in Deathlands. Human and fucking animals." He lifted his Armalite to his shoulder and mimed opening up with it. "Best if the whole place was chilled."

"Well," said Ryan, "that's my guess."

"Must be open if smell outside air," Jak stated. "Could be anyone in here."

"Or anything," Trader suggested.

THE END OF THE CORRIDOR came more quickly than any of them expected, less than fifty yards around a slight curve, beyond where Jak had caught the whiff of sulfur.

"Not another elevator!" Krysty said. "I really hate the trapped-in feeling."

"Look on the bright side." Dean grinned. "Might not be working, and we can all go back and make another jump. Wouldn't that be a hot pipe?"

"No," his father said angrily, "it wouldn't."

They hadn't passed any other corners or doors, so this single elevator represented the only way out. It was larger than usual, wide enough to take a small armawag.

"Not coded," J.B. observed. "Just the standard arrows for up and down."

"I guess we want to go up." Ryan was feeling better, but his original desire for a hot bath, food and a bed was still there. His wet clothes had virtually dried on him, with a faint smell of mold.

"Want to come back onto the point?" J.B. asked, gesturing to Ryan with the Uzi.

"No. You stay there. 'Better' isn't the same as 'well.' Everyone keep alert."

The Armorer reached out and pressed the silver arrow that pointed upward.

Nothing happened.

"How do we know we want to go up?" Mildred asked, smiling nervously as everyone turned to look at her. "Well, it's just a question. How do we know the gateway isn't at the top of the redoubt instead of at the bottom?''

"Because they've almost always been at the lowest level," J.B. replied, his glasses flashing in the stark neon light. "Security, I guess."

"Why not press 'down,' just in case," Ryan suggested.

J.B. did, but nothing happened.

"All right," Mildred said. "All right. Just a thought, that's all."

"Force the doors," Abe offered.

"Agreed," Trader said loudly. "Over, under, around or through. Let's go through."

"Wait!" Ryan had to shout to stop Trader and Abe from ramming against the locked doors of the elevator.

"Why the fuck not?"

"Take it easy, Trader. Might be we'll try breaking them down. Best to stand off and think a little first. Could easily be the controls have jammed up."

The older man shook his head, turning away and farting noisily. Sniggering at his own wit, he said, "Let's have a thinking, stinking time?"

"If you work real hard, Trader, for a few years," Mildred said, "I reckon you might eventually be able to become a pure half-wit."

The insult simply made him laugh longer and louder.

During the exchange, J.B. had been working patiently at the elevator controls.

"Got it," he called. "I can hear machinery." He placed his hand flat on the mat-finish metal door. "Yeah, I can feel the vibration of it."

"Double red," Ryan said into the sudden stillness. "Get ready for when the doors open."

They fanned out into a half circle, each gripping his or her favored weapon. A white strip above the door was lighted from behind, a maroon pointer showed the progress of the car toward them.

"Over halfway," Dean said.

"Three-quarters," Doc stated.

"No more talk," Ryan warned. "Don't want to give any warning that we're here."

The pointer slowed as the elevator neared the bottom of the steep shaft. Ryan had been counting, and he calculated that it had to be around one hundred and fifty feet to the top.

There was a faint but audible jolting noise as the car finally stopped.

Nothing happened for several long moments.

Ryan took a quick look at the faces of his companions.

Krysty's green eyes were blazing, her hair tightly knotted at the back of her neck.

Mildred stood in the classic pistol-shooter's pose, right arm extended, both eyes open, the 6-shot ZKR 551 as steady as a rock.

Trader chose to kneel to make himself a smaller target for whatever might emerge, the Armalite braced at his right shoulder, finger on the trigger.

Abe was beside him, also crouching, the overhead lights glittering off the polished metal of the .357 Colt Python.

Jak Lauren had an almost identical weapon, but with a satin finish, held down at his side. He looked relaxed and almost disinterested, but Ryan knew that the albino teenager's reflexes would bring the blaster up ready for shooting at the first moment of need.

Dean, standing by Jak, legs apart, held his Browning Hi-Power in both hands, as the Armorer had shown him, his dark eyes fixed on the large sec door of the elevator.

Doc looked like an illustration out of a predark book on the history and etiquette of the duello. He stood sideways, squinting down the barrel of the Le Mat, tongue darting out to lick his lips.

J.B. had chosen the M-4000 Smith & Wesson scattergun, carrying its lethal load of 12-gauge fléchettes, the tiny inch-long darts that would star out and rip anyone within range to bloody tatters of skin and flesh.

Everyone was ready.

There was a hiss of hydraulics, and the heavy door began to slide back.

Ryan lifted the SIG-Sauer, taking up the first pressure on the trigger.

Chapter Six

"Empty," Abe breathed, the obvious relief in his voice setting off a round of slightly nervous laughter from the nine friends.

The door had hissed back to reveal a rectangular metal box. Its sides were completely smooth, unmarked by scratches or graffiti. It squatted at the bottom of its shaft, gently throbbing and humming. Ryan wasn't possessed of a particularly vivid imagination, but it crossed his mind that the elevator was strangely like a patient animal, waiting for someone to step innocently into its maw.

J.B. looked back at Ryan, waiting for him to give the word for them to get in.

"Sure. Let's go, people. Still on double red."

They crowded in. There was the faint smell of machine oil and warm metal. Trader was nearest to the controls, and he pressed the button to close the doors, following it with the single control that should take the car up to the higher level.

The door slid smoothly shut and, after a moment's pause, the elevator began to rise steadily.

"Hate this feeling," Dean said.

"Like your brain's falling through your asshole."
Abe cackled at his own joke.

"Near the top," warned J.B., who'd been watching the indicator.

Ryan had lost concentration, staring blankly at the steel wall in front of him. The Armorer's words jerked him back to reality and to the ever-present menace. With that came the awareness of just how exhausted he was.

Trader used to say that being tired was equal with triple danger.

The elevator came to a smooth halt.

"Hosiery, children's toys, saddlery, fine china and everything for the bride-to-be," Doc said in a singsong voice. "Let the ladies out first."

Ryan ignored him. "Here we go. Open the door, Trader."

It wasn't like the main sec doors where you could stop and start them in any position you wanted. Once the elevator door started to open, it would go all the way.

Ryan felt his skin crawl. It was difficult to imagine a more vulnerable situation. If there was an enemy outside, armed with blasters, then they could fill the car with lead and blood.

There was nobody there, only an open space, about thirty feet across, with a single corridor opening off it.

"Think we should put a guard on this elevator?" Trader asked, "in case we need it in a hurry?"

Before answering him, Ryan turned to Krysty. "You feel anything, lover?"

"No. Place is dead as granite."

Ryan looked at Trader. "There's the answer. No need. We'll just take a look around and see if anything got left behind when they pulled out of here."

Not that he expected anything.

Most redoubts were stripped clean either just before or just after skydark.

THIS ONE was different.

"Smallest redoubt I think we've come across," J.B. commented. "Must've been built just as cover for the gateway."

It had taken them only a half hour to explore the whole place. The main control section, which would house the comp nukes, was sealed off behind a coded sec door that they couldn't open. But a schematic plan of the whole complex showed how relatively small the place was.

Ryan looked at one of the maps. "Just the mattrans at the bottom of the elevator and the admin and living quarters up here. Not more than seventy or eighty men and women here. Probably less than that."

"If I may correct your hypothesis, my dear Cawdor, I would suggest that the greater likelihood was for there to be living quarters outside the redoubt. The dormitory we saw and the eating facility would hardly have served that many personnel. Probably just those actually involved on the six- or eight-hour work shift here."

J.B. nodded at Doc's words. "Could be right. When we get outside we can see. But look at what we already got here."

There were three dormitories, each with ten single beds; a dining room and kitchen; bathroom facilities, with hot and cold running water, and no sign of any sort of intrusive insect life; small armory, which was the only part of the redoubt that had been stripped clean; a larder with dried and frozen food supplies; a small number of separate study-bedrooms, and, to Dean's stunned amazement and delight, a room that held about a dozen sophisticated arcade-quality video games.

Ryan had to come real close to losing his temper with his son to stop the boy going straight there.

"No."

"Dad?"

"No!"

"Come on, Dad!"

"First things first, Dean. We make sure the perimeter's safe. Then all of us get a bath. You and me specially."

"I don't need a wash. I got wet during that second jump in Maine."

Doc patted Dean on the top of his curly head. "Getting wet in what smells like the contents of an abandoned septic tank isn't quite the same as having a good wash, my young prince among cherubim and seraphim."

"Then can I play the—"

"Then we eat."

"After that?" Dean's voice cracked in his desperation. "Please Dad!"

"Then I reckon it'll be about time for everyone to catch some shut-eye. Specially you and me, Dean."

The desolate look on his son's face made him smile.

"Give him a break, lover," Krysty urged.

"All right."

"Oh, thanks, Dad!"

Ryan lifted a hand. "But we do everything in the right order. Understand? And you do need some double-serious sleep. So, you stop playing when I tell you."

"I'd like to have a good look around this place, Ryan," J.B. said. "Quick glance at some of those small rooms turned up stuff left behind when they pulled out."

"Tomorrow morning?" Ryan suggested. "Rest of you can look tonight, if you want. Those jumps have really taken me apart and put me back together crooked."

The Armorer shook his head. "No. I wouldn't mind an early bed for a change. How about you, Mildred?"

"Ready when you are, John. Can we use one of the private rooms?"

"Only got single beds," Jak said, his pale lips tugged back off his strong teeth in a feral grin.

"All we need," Mildred replied.

THERE WAS THE SMUDGED residue of old pieces of soap in the metal dishes of the individual shower units and, by working hard with them, Ryan managed to produce a slightly scummy lather. He rubbed at the stinking slime that had crusted in his hair, washing down over his face and chest.

He got some of the yellow coal-tar soap in his eye, and he was blinking, blind, when he felt a warm soapy hand slide between his buttocks from behind and grip him by the cock.

Ryan's mouth opened in surprise, and he swallowed a mouthful of hot water.

"Cleanliness is being next to God, was what Uncle Tyas McCann used to say to me, back in Harmony ville," Krysty said, pressing her naked body against him, her nipples peaking against his streaming scarred skin.

"But he didn't have this in mind, did he?"

Ryan kissed her, the water flowing over both their heads like a divine benediction from the past. Her fingers still gripped his growing hardness, and he replaced the soap in the dish, putting both his hands to better use.

Krysty threw her head back, allowing the water to wash the grime and dust from her long, sentient hair. It hung loose across her shoulders, like liquid fire.

"Good to be able to relax, lover," she said, "and good to have you and the boy back safely."

"Close call," he admitted. "Have to watch out for that sort of accident in future."

"You believe that all experience is good experience, Ryan? You do, don't you?"

He nodded, nuzzling his chin against her neck. "Yeah. Even bad experiences, because you learn from them and that makes you a stronger and wiser and better person."

"I guess so. Hey, you need a shave. There's razors in sealed packs in the main part of the bathroom."

His hand was between her parted thighs, the middle finger probing into her moist depths, moving slowly in and out, making her moan in delight.

"Never done it in a shower before," she whispered in his ear, barely audible above the roaring hiss of the steaming water. "New experience. And... Bit harder, and use your thumb, as well. That's it."

Her fingers were tight, sliding back and forth over his swollen length, bringing him toward the brink faster than he'd have believed possible.

"Slower or..."

"Hold me," she said. "Under the back of my thighs, and brace yourself against the wall of the shower."

Her green eyes were smiling into his face, her fiery hair seeming almost to caress his skin, as he lifted her off the ground. Krysty spread herself wider, one arm around his neck, the other reaching down to guide him into her, then gently lowering, so that he impaled her.

"Oh, Gaia!" he moaned. "That's something else."

She nipped at the side of his throat with her teeth, very gently. "Fireblast!" she whispered, mocking him. "Now we both start to move like...this...."

EVERYONE IN THE GROUP took showers or baths, taking advantage of the rare chance to relish endless, temperature-controlled water, as well as the opportunity to feel safe while doing it.

Afterward, they all met in the dining area, Jak, Abe and Doc browsing through the packed shelves of the larder.

"Think it's safe, Mildred?" Trader asked.

"Should be—" she looked at the display and the expiry dates on some of the packaging "—although it's mostly a hundred years or so past its time."

DEAN FELL ASLEEP, facedown over his third helping of processed minced pork, with a mixed pepper sauce and frozen hash browns.

"Have to play those vid games tomorrow," Ryan said, picking the boy up and carrying him to the dormitory, where Krysty helped tuck him into one of the beds.

"Anyone want microwaved chocolate pie?" Jak asked.

"Yeah, me," Abe replied. "Still a few hollows stopping my belly and backbone from touching."

"Mildred?" the albino queried.

"Hell, why not? Shame it's not banana royale, with cream and a triple scoop and some pineapple chunks. Now that was something like a dessert! But this'll do."

RYAN AND KRYSTY TOOK one of the small study rooms, while Mildred and J.B. shut themselves into another. Everyone else was content to spend the night in the dormitory, along with the sleeping boy.

There was a small desk, its drawers emptied, in one corner of the room, the single bed along the wall opposite the door.

"Was it J.B. who said that there was still some junk in one or two of the other rooms?" Ryan asked, as he sat down to pull off his steel-tipped combat boots. "Fireblast, but I need this rest!"

"Meal was good." Krysty struggled to suppress a belch. "The sauce wasn't bad at all. That what they used to call convenience foods, I guess."

Not getting any response, she glanced behind her, seeing that Ryan, half-undressed, was lying flat on his back, mouth open, snoring slightly.

Chapter Seven

Ryan yawned and opened his eye, awakened by Krysty getting up from the narrow bed and switching on the overhead light. She was standing by the tiny washbasin in the corner of the room, splashing cold water in her face.

"What time is..." He answered his own question by checking his chron. "Seven o'clock. It's only seven. Why're we getting up this early?"

"We aren't. I am. You're the one made a triple jump, lover. Not me. I slept all right."

"I was out like a dead 'dillo."

She smiled. "I noticed. Tried to get some life out of you a couple of times. I reckon I'd have had a more positive response from a dead armadillo."

"Sorry. Make it up to you tonight."

"Depending on where we are, of course. Lie down and go back to sleep." She pulled on her white shirt, covering her superb breasts, which disappointed Ryan, as he was just beginning to discover that he wasn't quite as tired as he'd thought. "I'll go brew up some coffee and see if there's anything for breakfast that isn't too disgusting."

He held out his hand and she went to clasp it, bringing it to her lips. She took his index finger into her mouth and sucked it hard, running her tongue up and down it, and glanced down at the sudden movement beneath the layer of crumpled bedclothes across Ryan's loins.

"Mebbe we won't have to wait until tonight, after all," she said with a grin.

THE COFFEE SUB WAS HOT and black and even had a faint, residual taste of coffee, one of the great rarities in Deathlands, where the climate didn't favor it.

Ryan stirred three spoons of sugar sub into it, sipping at the brew as he lay back in the bed.

"Could get used to this," he said.

"Make the most of it."

"Where's my breakfast in bed?"

Krysty was sitting at the desk, drinking her own unsugared coffee. "Not much choice. Egg sub, so you can have an omelet. Some frozen meat, but Mildred recommended that we steer clear of that. Cans of tomatoes. Cans of luncheon meat that Mildred says should be all right if they're not blown."

"How's Dean?"

"Others are all still fast asleep. Don't know about J.B. and Mildred, though. Their door was firmly shut, so I just left it like that. Surprised they didn't have a Don't Disturb sign hung outside."

"Thought the boy might've been up and playing with those vid games. If they work, they'll probably be the first he's ever seen. Me too, for that matter."

"Omelet with canned luncheon meat and tomatoes?" She moved to the doorway. "And some more coffee?"

"Sure, why not?"

DEAN WAS STILL SLEEPING like a babe after all the others had risen, showered and eaten.

"Want me to wake him?" Jak asked.

Ryan shook his head. "No. Leave him be. Just Nature recharging his batteries for him. Lad needs it. And we aren't in any hurry to leave here."

"I'd vote for staying for another week, or more," Trader said. "Warmest crib I've come across in years. Surprised nobody's broken into it from outside."

J.B. wiped his mouth with his sleeve. "Shouldn't have put so much hot pepper sauce on that omelet. Double-stupe of me."

He turned to Trader. "Had a quick look around, but all of the main control areas and the ob section's locked tighter than a war wag's sec code. There's a way to the main entrance, but I figured better to wait until we're all together before opening that."

"Find anything else interesting?" Ryan asked.

"Smell of sulfur's strong close to the sec door to the outside. And salt, as well, like you figured."

"Yellowstone," Trader said.

"Western islands of California," Ryan stated, grinning at his former chief.

"We'll see about that."

"Yeah, Trader, we will."

ONLY TWO OF THE STUDIES hadn't been cleared out.

One of them contained a small pile of paperbacks. One without a cover was advertised as Stephen King's Big Fiftieth, and there were ancient Westerns that had been read so hard that they crumbled like the Dead Sea Scrolls when touched.

Doc had been browsing in the other room. "I say!" he called. "I believe I've found the remains of a diary or journal. It had become stuck between two of the drawers and overlooked when the redoubt was finally evacuated."

As Ryan came into the passage to examine Doc's find, he bumped into his son, walking blearily along, rubbing at his eyes and yawning.

"Yes," Ryan said quickly. "That's the answer to the question you were about to ask me. But first you have a shower and cook yourself something to eat. Then you can go play those games. I'll be along in a while."

"Wow, thanks. See you..." And he was gone.

JAK WAS ALSO sufficiently fascinated by the video games in the small side room off the refectory to want to remain behind with Dean. All the others had crowded into the little study where Doc had made his discovery.

"I believe that the young woman who wrote this had intended to take it with her," Doc said. "But she missed the last few pages, and here they are now."

The paper was flimsy and delicate, faded to the palest of greens. The woman, who was nameless, had written on the backs of some old military Stock-Indent forms, using a black pen and a small, neat hand.

Doc passed the sheets to Ryan, who held them to the light. "Can't make out the writing all that well. Mildred, can you read them to us?"

"Sure. Hand them over." She shuffled them, checking what she was actually holding. "They're dated, right through to January 20, the day the world ended."

The journal began five days earlier, opening up in the middle of a sentence.

"'...he think he is? Living in the dark ages with his ideas on what women can and can't do. Times like this with everything going to hell in a handbasket, it's everyone together. Only way we'll beat the Soviets. Luanne reckons they'll back off and stop their game-playing. I'm not so sure.'"

DEAN HAD GOBBLED DOWN some cereal with add-water milk sub, eager to get to grips with the half dozen games that he'd seen so briefly the night before.

"Reckon they'll work, Jak?"

"If do, will. If not, won't. If not, we can try make them work."

"Then let's go."

"'PRAYERS ANSWERED. Test came up neg, so at least no worries about maternity leave next summer. Won't tell the major for a couple of weeks. Make the bastard sweat like I did.'"

Mildred flipped over the next page. "Just some more personal stuff about her relationships. Then... Ah, then we get back to worrying about the possibility of a war.

"'Tracey whispered she'd seen a blue-code intercept from the *S* side of the fence. Their leaders have been in secret session for nearly two days now. Something big must be going down. Or going up? Shouldn't joke at a time like this. Hope Mom and Dad are all right back in Sioux Falls. They know about the buried control base there, but it never seems to worry them. Worries me.'"

"Wow! HOTTEST PIPE EVER."

The machines worked off quarters, but most of them had several spare coins lying in the reject slot, as well as another dozen or so pieces of silver glinting on the carpeted floor.

Dean and Jak walked around, touching the gleaming glass, peering at the garishly illustrated facades, one labeled Grand Prix.

"What're grand pricks?" Dean asked. "Looks like a fast wag-race game to me."

It was a capsule, shaped like an Indy car, in brilliant crimson plastic, flecked with gold and silver. The steering wheel was dark maroon. The large screen in front of it was blank.

"Try it," Jak said. "Get in. I'll put jack in."

Dean was suddenly shy. "Don't know how to work it," he muttered.

"Just go for it. Can't get chilled on vid game."

The boy adjusted the big blaster on his hip and clambered in, sliding comfortably into the cockpit. He grasped the wheel and glanced down to check the foot controls.

"Ready. I think."

Jak put a quarter into the slot and pressed the red Start button.

There was an instant howling sound and the screen came alive, showing a starting grid, other cars on either side. A pair of lights at the top of the screen were glowing red, and a man with a flag was waiting on a dais to the right.

The lights changed to green.

The other cars disappeared in a scream of burned rubber and roaring engines. Dean stamped on the foot control. The screen shuddered, and a patronizing voice came from the speakers.

"Bad luck, competitor. Too hard on the gas. Stalled on the line. Insert further money for a second attempt on the Grand Prix challenge."

And the screen went dark.

"Fuck that," Dean said, climbing quickly from the car. "Let's try another."

"'SEEMS LIKE SOMETHING big's happening. I've never seen such excitement. Nerves and tension and snapping voices. Word is that the Russkies are going to stage a preempt. Walter's been saying that we should fight to the last man and woman. Make it hot for the bastards. I don't see it coming to that. Crazy. Gateway's been busy with top guns from Washington and the Five-Sider. If they try and invade, then we'll likely be in the front line. Most went to bed early tonight. I watched "Dueling Dollars" and got nine out of the ten questions right. My best score ever. One wrong was stupid about some Chinese leader called Mow. Corey in filing said the shredders are overtiming it.'"

"WHAT'S VIRTUAL REALITY?" Dean asked. "Never heard of that before."

"Me neither. Mebbe best not put head in that helmet, Dean. Try another."

They stood and looked at the black headpiece with built-in goggles and headphones. The game was called Castle Douglas of Doom, and promised dark encounters in black dungeons and turreted towers with enemies from both sides of the grim divide. There were pictures of phosphorescent, leering skulls and sheeted ghosts with bloodied talons.

"Try next one," Jak said.

"You try it."

It was called Arnie the Armadillo, and the purpose of the game seemed to be a quest through a tropical forest to collect as many sacks of gold from the mines of the dreaded trolls before you ran out of lives.

Dean pushed in the quarter as the albino leaned against the front of the machine, readying his long white fingers over the controls.

An animated scuttling little figure began to buzz from left to right, along a narrow tunnel. As Jak struggled to understand the controls, it ran headlong into a wall of spikes. The genial voice cut in. "Ouch!

That sure hurt me. Be a bit more careful next time, will you?"

Less than four seconds later a lime-green batlike creature swooped from nowhere and picked Arnie up in its claws. Bit off its skull in a welter of crimson drops and spit it out.

"Ouch, that hurt worse. I won't get far ahead without my head. Only one life left."

That life was sacrificed when Jak pressed a button too hard and bold little Arnie went tumbling down a slide covered in slivers of razored steel that sliced him into a hundred animated fragments of bloody flesh.

"Ouch, I'm sure cut up about that. Three lives and out. Insert money for a replay. Better luck next time."

Jak spit on the floor, turning away. "Let's quit this triple-stupe shit," he said. "No fun."

"Still three games left. Mebbe we'll sort of get the hang of them in a bit."

"Right. Your turn, Dean."

"NOT MUCH MORE left," Mildred said.

"What is the date?" Doc asked.

"Only two days before the nukecaust," she replied. "Woman's starting to panic about what's going on. Writing's getting worse. Says there've been four deserters already in the last twenty-four hours."

"'Caught Sergeant Silvers from the motor pool before he got over the fence. Colonel Yossarian executed him with his own automatic in the softball yard. I didn't see it myself, but we all heard the sound of the shot. The pullout can't be far away. Why build this redoubt and then abandon it? Doesn't make sense to me. Worry about them at home.'"

THE FOURTH ARCADE GAME had malfunctioned and remained stubbornly dark and silent. It had been a combat game, pitting the finest American warplanes against those of the Communist Bloc.

"Shame," Dean said. "I'd really have liked the chance to gross-out in an airwag."

Fifth in line was called Urban Destroyer. Jak put in the coin while Dean readied himself at the controls. The screen offered him the chance to play any one of about eight different characters who had to make their way across Manhattan through the turf of dangerous street gangs.

Dean hesitated for a few seconds between taking on the role of Feuding Mick Norman or The Hooded Destroyer; finally picking the latter.

He turned out to be seven feet tall, carrying a long, hooked scimitar in one hand and a machine pistol in the other. He stalked narrow alleys, between towering skyscrapers like Dean had seen in old books and vids and mags.

Electronic music played, drumming out in a rising tempo, to heighten the feeling of menace.

"Yo, mother. You on Frag turf now and that means you is dead meat."

The aggressor was a powerfully built figure, with vaguely Afro-Asian features, swinging a fearsome rice flail that hissed through the air.

"Take him, Dean," Jak urged.

"Which button is for firing the blaster?"

A stream of silver lead shot from the Uzi, splattering the wall of the tenement building behind the menacing figure. But he had ducked under it, darting in and delivering a whirling, crushing blow to the head of the hooded terror, who staggered back and fell in animated slow-mo, finally landing in a crumpled heap against a hydrant.

"So perish all chicken-shit invaders of Frag turf," crowed the harsh, electronic voice of the victor, who stood there beating his chest.

The screen went dark.

"Let's go join the others," Dean suggested. "These aren't the fun I thought they'd be."

"One left." Jak walked and stared at the last machine in the room. "Sounds good."

"So you try it," Dean said, his face set in a sullen scowl. "Give me the jack."

It was called Shield of Freedom and showed a crewcut American GI flourishing an M-16, one foot on the throat of a brutish Russian soldier. There was a lot of blood around and more enemy soldiers in the background.

"THIS IS THE FINAL PAGE," Mildred said. "Funny, this is written by someone who was actually there, living through those last dark hours before the world ended. And writing about them. But, somehow, she can't convey what it must've been like."

"Could anyone?" Ryan asked.

"Did everyone expect that an outbreak of hostilities would mean the end of the world?" Trader asked. "I never quite saw how it worked. Like two men each with the muzzle of their blaster in the other's mouth, fingers white on the triggers, each of them knowing that if either fired, the other would also shoot. And they'd both inevitably get chilled."

"Called the balance of terror," Doc explained. "Only the balance finally tipped over."

"Carry on reading," J.B. said. "Like to hear the ending of it."

"'This is really it. We had a lecture about chemical and nerve agents and what to do. Walter said you pushed your head between your legs and kissed your ass goodbye. Seems we're too exposed here in western California, and as a matter-transfer redoubt we don't have proper defensive capabilities. So, we start withdrawing in about an hour from now. Take what we can. Command says to take all personal possessions and documents in case they helped an invading force. So, soon as I finish this I'll pack my clothes and stuff, and then take it with me.'"

TRYING NOT TO MAKE the same mistakes as they had on the other machines, Jak and Dean were painstakingly plowing through the instructions for Shield of Freedom before inserting a quarter and pressing the red Start button.

It was taking a long time.

Jak lost interest and sat by the vid game on the floor, leaning back against the wall.

" 'Makes me want to throw up, thinking those Red bastards might be walking in here one day. Maybe sleeping in my bed. Eating and drinking all our provisions that we don't take. Morag said we should open all the soft drinks and piss in them and put the tops back on. I believe that good old boy, Walter, has had the best idea yet to give them a shock.' "

"Wonder what this was?" Abe asked quietly. "If there's any booby traps, it'd be good to know where they are. We've been most places throughout the complex."

"Probably never did anything." Krysty smiled at Ryan. "Or they rotted with age. Certainly haven't seen anything that looked like a device."

" 'He says Ruskies are kids, and they'll head for the vid games section.' "

"What!" Ryan exclaimed.

" 'Linked a couple of grenades to his favorite, Shield of Freedom. The moment the Commie bastards press the . . .' "

Dean reached out to press the Start button on Shield of Freedom.

Chapter Eight

Ryan felt the force of the blast before he heard the familiar muffled crump. It ruffled its hot fingers through his hair, tightening the skin across his cheekbones, sucking some of the air from the corridor.

There hadn't even been time to shout a warning. Though the open area of the redoubt was relatively restricted, the games room was still some distance away from the small study-bedroom.

He had been the fastest to react to the passage in the diary of the long-dead woman. His mind seized instantly on the potential horror of the news of the planned booby trap, a potential that he guessed, in that heart-stopping moment, might well have been realized.

Two implode grens, in a confined space.

Ryan had seen the results of that kind of detonation, and he could already visualize what they would find in the remains of the room.

There would be a single pile of mangled flesh, stripped clear off shards of raw bone.

The muffled crump seemed to fill his ears, and he saw smoke and debris scattered across the corridor just in front of him. There were cries from behind him but he ignored them.

"Dean! Jak!"

"Over here, Dad!"

The boy's voice was strong, though shock and fear had given it a high, thin ragged edge. Ryan slowed from a powering run, peering through the haze, his boots crunching over splinters of broken glass.

"Here."

Now he saw them. Dean was on his hands and knees, one arm around Jak. The albino had blood smeared across his forehead, but he was obviously conscious, steadying himself against the wall of the corridor.

"Implodes," Jak said, coughing in the dust. "Wired up to one of the games machines."

"We know," Ryan replied.

Dean, deafened by the grenades, looked puzzled, shaking his head. Ryan noticed a trickle of blood was inching from the boy's left ear.

But Jak heard him. "How you know?"

Krysty and the others were grouped around Ryan. The air stank with chemical fumes from the explosion, and they could all hear the faint crackle of flames from one of the wrecked machines inside the games room.

"Just been reading a sort of diary left over from predark. Woman who worked here. Mildred was telling us all it said when she came on a reference to them sabotaging one of the games. Ready to catch Russkies if they invaded. That was the fear, just before skydark."

"It was called Shield of Freedom," J.B. said. "They wired up grens to it."

"I was just going to start playing a game called Shield of Freedom, Dad," Dean said, standing up unsteadily, accepting a hand from his father. His voice was unnaturally loud, showing that his hearing was still badly hit by the booby trap.

"How did you know, Jak?" Trader asked. "You never heard us shouting a warning. Bombs went off too quickly. How come they didn't hit you?"

Jak was also on his feet, shrugging off an offer of assistance from Abe. "Was sitting down while Dean played. Could see back of machine. Saw two scarlet-and-blue grens. Wired up. Knew were implodes. Grabbed boy and out in corridor, around corner. Just in time."

Dean was watching Jak's lips, fascinated. "I can't hear him," he announced to the group in general. "Is he saying he spotted the bombs while he was sitting down? Never saw anyone move so fast in all my life. If it hadn't been for Jak, I wouldn't have had any life left, would I?" Tears trembled in his dark brimming eyes as the effects of the shock started to get to him. "He dragged me around the corner, away from the worst of the blast."

Ryan clasped the hand of the albino. "Thanks, Jak. Owe you one."

Jak grinned. "Owe you plenty, Ryan."

Mildred looked concernedly at Dean, then spoke to his father. "I know someone who might just about fall down if he isn't got back to where he can rest and have something hot and sweet to drink."

"Yeah," Ryan agreed. "Fact is, Mildred, I reckon we could all follow that idea."

JAK WASHED THE CUT in his scalp, where a piece of flying glass had slashed him. Mildred checked the wound carefully to ensure that there were no splinters left in it.

Dean was unhurt, other than the temporary damage to his hearing, which started to gradually return.

The rest of the friends took the opportunity to replenish water supplies and ready some of the food to take with them.

Ryan found himself in the larder area with Trader. "I told you," he said.

"What? What did you tell me this time?"

"California. Western islands. I said that was probably where we landed up."

"So?"

"So, you said Yellowstone and the hot springs and stinking fountains up there."

Trader shook his head. "No, I didn't."

"You did."

The older man shook his head, pointing his finger at Ryan. "Times I wish that... What's his name? Abe? Yeah, Abe. Times I wish he'd never tracked me down like he did."

"It was 'cause he cared," Ryan said quietly.

Trader gave a strange, grunting laugh. "Cared. Think that means shit to me, Ryan? After all the long years we rode the blacktops together, you think that caring means anything? Caring means weakness."

Ryan shook his head. "I thought that, when I lived and fought with you. I believed it, because you said it. Like I believed most everything you told me. Since I've been away...away from your shadow, I realize that not everything in Deathlands is like you said."

"Like what?" Anger lay across the words.

Ryan shook his head. "I don't want this to turn to a falling out. I owe you too much for that. Just that your view of the world is your view. Now I see that a man has to have his own view, or he's not a man at all."

Trader bit his lip. "Yeah," he conceded. "I guess there's something in that all right. Thing I find hard is that you're in charge here. Not me."

"Wheel turns," Ryan said.

Trader grinned, patting him on the arm. "Now you'll tell me that what goes around comes around."

"I thought about it."

IT WAS TIME to move on.

Dean had most of his hearing back, but Krysty noticed that the boy was tending to keep a little closer to Ryan than usual.

They gathered together near the main entrance.

J.B. had been with Abe to check out the ruined remnants of the games room, making sure that the small fires started by the implode grens hadn't caused any damage. Now he stood with his hand poised over the control panel by the side of the big sec door that would open onto the outside world.

The stench of sulfur was much stronger, as was the salt smell of the sea.

"Ready?" he asked.

Ryan nodded. "Full red, everyone."

The Armorer pressed 352 on the coded set of buttons. After the usual momentary delay, there was the familiar rumbling of the powerful machinery behind the thick concrete walls, followed by the first movement of the dark green doors. Ryan waited until they had rolled a few inches apart, then he gestured for J.B. to stop them.

He peered out through the narrow gap, while the others waited silently.

"What?" Trader asked, breaking the stillness. "Anything out there?"

"Lot of sea. Looks like we might be on the remains of an island. I can see a blacktop that runs clear into the ocean. No sign of life. Open her all the way up."

J.B. pressed the triple-digit sequence again, and the sec doors finally rolled all the way open.

And everyone could see what Ryan had glimpsed.

THE INRUSH of the Cific Ocean along the coast of California had been devastating. In places it had rolled in for well over a hundred miles, right up to the foothills of the Sierras. In others, where the cliffs were higher, the effect had been less intense. But the quakes and volcanic action that had followed, both during and after the long winters, had changed the shape of the Golden State beyond all modern recognition.

A map of what remained of California now would bear little resemblance to what had been there before.

Ryan and his friends emerged, blinking, into bright sunshine. The blacktop, which must once have provided the route in and out of the secret redoubt, wound down the side of a broken cliff for about three hundred and fifty feet before disappearing beneath the rolling white breakers of the ocean.

It wasn't possible to see how big the island was, if indeed it really was an island. The crest of the rocks above them towered another two hundred feet high.

"Someone should go up there and take a look around," Trader suggested. "Find out the lie of the land all the way about us." He looked at Ryan. "I'll go do it."

"I'll come," Abe said eagerly.

"Rather go on my own." He paused. But thanks, Abe. No, a good stiff climb'll shake some of the jelly out of my old legs after sitting around."

Ryan nodded. "Sure. We'll wait here. No point in going down to the water if there's a better way."

Trader set off, Armalite slung over his shoulder, climbing nimbly among the sharp crags, watched by the others. He made good progress for the first hundred and fifty feet, then began to slow.

"Should've let me go," Abe muttered. "Old bastard won't face up to being older than he thinks he is."

Nobody else spoke.

Doc sat down, leaning his back against a guano-smeared rock, fanning himself with his hand. "Upon my soul, gentles all, but the odor of sulfur is devilish overwhelming. Would that I had me a pomander, studded with cloves, to remove the stench. It is worse than the jakes of Eastcheap in the midst of a visit to the court of good King Cholera."

"You talk some nonsense, Doc," Mildred protested. "I swear I can't tell how much of it's under your control and how much is plain gibbering madness."

He bowed to her, the wind tugging at his silvery locks. "If it is difficult for your perception from outside, madam, imagine how impossible it is for me from within."

TRADER REACHED THE CREST, waving both hands above his head. Dean responded to the old man, jumping up and down, waving energetically. "Made it, Dad," he said.

"Yeah. So I see. Now all we have to do is wait for him to get all the way back again and report what he's seen."

"Don't be bad-tempered, lover." Krysty sat next to him, her head on his shoulder. "I know the air smells like someone just cut the cheese, but we've landed somewhere fresh. We've pulled through some dangerous narrows, and we should try to relax and enjoy things. Come on."

He shrugged. "Yeah. Guess you're right. Too many close calls for my liking. Be good if we really could relax awhile." He looked up. "Trader's making better time downhill. We'll see what good news he brings."

"ISLAND." TRADER WAS out of breath. Mildred studied him, without letting him notice her attention. She noted that he was unnaturally pale, sweating profusely, his fingers trembling. He kept swallowing hard and coughing. Several times he rubbed hard at his left arm with his right hand. His respiration was too fast and too shallow. She guessed that he'd pushed himself a little too hard proving he was as capable as he used to be.

"Big?" Ryan asked.

"No. Mile across at the biggest. Can see what looks like the mainland, but it's—" He broke off as another coughing fit doubled him over. Jak passed across a water canteen, and Trader drank deeply before carrying on. "Thanks. Where was I?"

"Mainland," Dean prompted.

"Right. Can only just see it through a lot of smoke and fog and stuff. Must be around three quarters of a mile from the nearest point of this place."

"Any sign of life here or out there?" J.B. asked.

Trader shook his head. "No. Thought I saw seals to the north. Some pelicans. Nothing much else. No trees or nothing."

"Then how do we get over to the mainland?" Abe asked.

"We don't," Trader said. "No way to go, so here we fucking stay. Looks like it'll soon be jump time again, friends."

Chapter Nine

Ryan took a chance and split their force in two, taking Dean, Krysty and Jak with him, down to the bottom of the old blacktop, until they reached the point where it vanished under the waves. Then they headed around the small, craggy island in an easterly direction. J.B. went with Mildred, Doc, Trader and Abe, in a westerly direction.

The intention was to meet once again directly opposite the bottom of the old road.

The sun was hot—with a temperature up in the high eighties—and the atmosphere fetid and sticky. A light breeze was blowing, but it came from the far side, where Trader said the mainland lay, bringing the oppressively bitter smells.

The going was very hard.

Jagged rocks, some of them volcanic, were smothered in sickly orange-and-green lichens that were slippery to tread on.

"Like treading in dead man's guts," Jak commented.

"You do have a way with words, don't you." Krysty grinned, gritting her teeth as she nearly fell into a deep rock pool fringed with enormous anemones.

"Don't like the look of those," she said. "I reckon they've probably got strong enough poison to see off...even Trader."

Ryan didn't join the smiles from Jak and his son. He stopped and stood still on a flat-topped boulder. "Because Trader and I come close to fighting, it doesn't mean I don't have incredible respect for him and for everything he did. In his own way he brought a measure of order out of the chaos that was Deathlands, twenty or thirty years ago. Barons had to toe the line or he'd drive them under. Trader was truly a great power for good. Despite parts of him, like his cruelty and violence. If there was ever to be written a history of Deathlands, then Trader's name should lead all of the rest."

"What is Trader's name, Dad? I mean, his real name," Dean asked.

Ryan smiled. "Lot of people asked that, over the years, son. And not one of them ever got an answer."

"You know it?" Jak asked, staring up at a black-capped albatross sailing far above them.

"I don't even answer that question. Whether I do or not. It don't matter, Jak." He caught Krysty's glance at him. "I mean it doesn't matter," he amended.

"It doesn't look like there's ever been any kind of life on this place," Dean said. "Not a harbor or anything. Just dry, dead rock."

Ryan looked higher up, behind them. As he'd guessed, there was no sign at all of the concealed entrance to the redoubt. There wouldn't be any reason for anyone to come to the island and trudge up the old roadway.

And it *was* an island.

They could see that as soon as they clambered over a flat shelf, where a slice of rock weighing thousands of tons had sheared off and fallen from near the top of the peak.

The far side was a little less steep, making it easier to move along the shoreline, watching out for the occasional wave that came crashing in, larger than its fellows.

"Seals," Jak said, pointing out across the sun-dappled water. "About dozen."

They all stopped to watch the elegant creatures, cavorting and gamboling in the ocean. One of them had caught a glistening silver-scaled fish and kept tossing its limp body high in the air, in a rainbow of scattered spots of spray, like the sparks from a dying fire, then catching it again.

"Clever," Dean said, clapping his hands.

Now they could make out what Ryan assumed was probably the mainland, though it was difficult to see and it could easily have been another, larger island. J.B. hadn't bothered to use his minisextant, assuming that they probably knew more or less where they were.

"Good half mile," Jak stated, squinting toward the mist-shrouded horizon.

"Could swim that easy, Dad."

Ryan laid his hand on the boy's shoulder. "You always have to remember the people with you, son. Mebbe *you* could swim it. But you don't know what the currents are like. Might be a powerful undertow out there."

"An undertoad? What's that?"

Ryan answered him. "Undertow. Kind of whirlpool that you sometimes can't see but it can suck down the strongest swimmer, Dean."

The boy looked disappointed that the "undertoad" wasn't a real creature.

Ryan continued. "Even if you could swim it, then what about everyone else in the group? Think Abe could make it? Or Doc? Mildred?"

"Or me?" Ryan asked. "I reckon I'm a fair swimmer, but that's a long way."

"Guess so. Does that mean we have to go back to make another jump?"

"Let's carry on around the rest of the island and see what we can see. Might find something." Ryan grinned at the look of dismay on his young son's face. "Trader always said that a man who made his decision without having all the facts was setting one foot in his grave."

THEY COULD SEE the other five picking their way very slowly over the treacherous rocks, about three hundred yards ahead of them. Between them lay a small bay, about one hundred paces across, filled with banks of torn seaweed and a jumble of driftwood.

"Hey," Dean yelled, pointing at the timber. His shout scared away a pair of sea otters that had been exploring in the cove. "Make a raft, Dad?"

"Mebbe," Ryan said. "Mebbe."

THEY WERE REUNITED as they stood on the only patch of beach on the whole island, a strip of shingle barely twenty feet long, dotted with empty mussel shells.

"Nothing around this way," J.B. reported, staring out across the ocean. "Looks like our only chance of getting off to the mainland is to build some kind of raft."

"How about sharks?" Mildred asked.

Everyone considered that, looking in silence at the featureless expanse of water.

"Don't see any sign of anything." Trader spit into the pebbles. "Nothing to be scared about, lady."

"Point about being scared of a great white, Trader, is that you don't see it until it comes up from underneath and bites you in two."

"Yeah, all right. But if we can make a good raft, it should be safe enough."

"Plenty of wood." Abe shaded his eyes against the sun. "What do we tie it together with?"

"Can see ropes and stuff," Jak said, pointing to a straggling coil of orange hemp.

Ryan looked around at the rest of the group. "We going to try for this?"

Doc raised his cane. "I have to register a still, small voice of calm. I mean, of dissent. My memories of occasions when we have taken to the water is that they have almost always been tainted with the proximity to disaster."

It was true.

"Just walking through a quiet wood on a summer day can get you chilled," Trader said. "Try and avoid a risk, and you run smack into another one."

Doc nodded. "I can't refute the veracity of that, my old companion. Indeed, it puts me in mind of the legend of the fabled ruler of classical times. A soothsayer told him—"

"A what?" Abe asked.

"Soothsayer. Shaman. Wise man. Prophet. A doomie. A seer on the future."

"Oh, sure. Sorry."

Doc carried on. "This—wise man warned the king that he had dreamed and had received a warning that the king's only son, a merry little chap of some eight winters, would meet his ending at the hands...the claws, of a lion. Well, the father was horrified. Such omens often came true. He built a wondrous palace, with barred windows and stout doors, filling it with armed men. So that no lion could possibly reach his son, who was forbidden ever to leave the palace."

"So, there was no way that a lion could chill him, Doc?" Dean asked.

"Right, dear boy. But his son was curious, having heard the rumors from the servants. He asked his father what a lion looked like. So the king purchased a huge painting of a fearsome lion, crouched over its prey. The picture was in a massive, ornate golden frame and was hung in the boy's bedroom where he often stood and admired it.

"I know this," Krysty said. "I'm sure Uncle Tyas McCann told me the fable when I was a little girl back in Harmony ville.'' She saw the look on Doc's face. ''Sorry to interrupt. Go on.''

''Very well. One day the lad was staring raptly at the painting when there was a mighty thrumming sound, like a bowstring being drawn back. A sharp crack, and the cord supporting the picture snapped through. The painting fell on the poor little prince and crushed his skull like a Kerry pippin.''

''So, the father didn't manage to save him and the omen was true,'' Dean said. ''Hey, hot piping story, Doc. You got any more like that?''

Ryan interrupted. ''Yeah, Dean, it was a real good story. And I know for a fact that Doc's got himself several hundred more adventures.''

''All of 'em the same,'' Mildred muttered.

Ryan carried on. ''But we'll hear some more of them at a better time. Right now we have to go in and get some timber out of the sea, along with that rope. And get started on building ourselves a good raft.''

''THAT SMELL REALLY SEEPS into your heart,'' Krysty said. ''Gets so you don't want to draw in a full breath.''

''Yeah.'' They were all soaked to the skin from the battle to retrieve their raft-building materials from the stubborn, weed-bound bay.

The dark green coils were up to a hundred feet long, and they had suckers that attached themselves to the lengths of driftwood that were needed to construct their ramshackle craft. It was impossible to tear them loose, and every bit had to be cut away by hand, using knives, hacking through the coarse lengths of weed, some of them thicker than a man's wrist.

"Mebbe a jump would be easier," Abe panted.

"Like wrestling with a shack full of drunk stickies," Trader said, sitting down in the shingle to take a breather.

"I reckon we could have used this creeper stuff instead of ropes to tie the raft together." J.B. took off his fedora to wipe sweat from his forehead.

"Soon be dark." Jak was trying to restore an edge to one of the short throwing knives, rubbing the steel against the flat side of a smooth stone.

Ryan glanced up at the sun, seeing to his surprise that it had already started its final plunge out over the western border of the ocean. The shadows had lengthened, and the air had become noticeably colder.

The raft was taking shape, but there was no possible way that it would be finished before night came swooping in.

"We could go back up to the redoubt," he suggested, "or build a fire down here. Not much danger. We haven't seen any kind of life that can threaten us."

"Steep climb," Trader said. "Have to say that this is harder work than I'd figured it would be."

"Stay here with a fire?" Nobody raised an objection. He turned to Dean and Abe. "We'll carry on until the light goes. You two start collecting some of the drier wood from higher up among the rocks. Get it piled ready for a fire."

J.B. BROUGHT OUT ONE of the self-lights that he always carried to get the flames started. Dean had found a vast bundle of dried seaweed that he'd hauled across the rocks, using that as the base. Abe piled some of the smaller pieces of dry driftwood that he'd picked out from the higher rocks, placing them carefully among the crackling, yellowed weed. Then both of them had hauled some larger hunks of wood and stacked them on top.

With the sun well down and the light almost gone, Ryan called a halt to the raft-building, ordering everyone in the party to scavenge for more wood to try to keep the fire going during the chill of the night ahead.

Trader queried the need. "Island isn't inhabited, Ryan, and I don't think seals are going to give us much trouble. Unless you figure there's some sort of marine stickies swimming around out yonder, just waiting their chance to creepy-crawl in and haul one of us off to their undersea caverns?"

Ryan ignored the heavy-handed attempt at sarcasm. "You and me've seen stranger things than that in our life, Trader. And it wouldn't be impossible for someone on the mainland, on the coast, to see the light of the fire and come out in their boats to investigate."

"If they did, we could steal their boats," Dean said.

"Raft's nearly finished," J.B. protested. "Not having all that work for nothing."

"Post a watch?" Jak asked. "There's fog coming offshore. Doubt they'd see fire."

"Better not to take a chance," Trader insisted, unexpectedly changing tack. "With nine of us, it'll only be a short while each on lookout."

THE FLAMES BURNED BRIGHT, the golden smoke circling on the thermals, mingling with the thick mist that had descended over the California coast, bringing with it the strongest smell yet of rotting eggs.

Everyone was tired from working waist-deep in the icy water, battling with the ropes of weed and the sodden wood that lay tangled together in the bay. After a snack from the supplies they'd brought from the redoubt, everyone lay in a rough circle around the fire, readying themselves for sleep.

Dean was first on watch.

RYAN WAS AWAKENED by a shake of the shoulder from Krysty. He sat up immediately, the SIG-Sauer miraculously cocked and ready in his fist.

"What?"

She kissed him on the mouth, sliding her warm tongue between his teeth. She kneeled, smiling at him, hair seeming to be ablaze in the glow of the fire, which everyone had kept burning brightly during their turns on watch.

"Nothing, lover. Just that it's three in the morning. You're on guard." She lay down as he stood, tugging the collar of his coat around him against the chill night air. "Oh, and we're nearly out of wood."

"Doesn't matter much." He looked up at the great vault above them, trying to pierce the blanket of mist.

"Dawn can't be too far away. Not worth hunting around for more wood. It'll mostly be wet anyway." He yawned. "See or hear anything?"

"Seals. Heard great whales moving a couple of times. Far off, but you know how sound carries at night. They were heading south. A pod of them, I think. Most amazingly mournful, moving sound. Thought I heard something moving in among that Sargasso Sea of weed in the cove, but I think it was probably just the waves, or a fish. Or something."

"Something?" he whispered. "I'll keep a triple careful lookout for that 'something,' lover."

"Do that. Kiss before leaving."

Ryan stooped down, brushing his lips against her cold cheek, straightening and walking past the glowing embers of the fire. He picked up some half-burned pieces of wood and lobbed them into the heart of the flames.

RYAN WALKED SLOWLY up and down for a few minutes, right at the limit of the water. The mass of weed jammed into the bay stopped the big ocean breakers, and the waves barely rippled onto the shingle. The mist had dropped visibility to less than a hundred yards. He peered out to where the mainland, if their guesses were correct, was waiting.

The raft, almost complete, lay like a tumbled cabin, odd-shaped spars and lengths of timber all bound together with the uncoiled orange rope.

Ryan looked at it, silhouetted against the dying fire, where a large balk of timber finally collapsed in on itself, sending a cascade of tiny sparks soaring skyward into the fog, like brilliant rubies.

In the stillness, he turned from the island and looked back across the cove. What had Krysty called it? A Sargasso Sea? Ryan had a vague feeling he'd heard the name before, perhaps in some old predark mag, a vast bed of weed that floated somewhere in the center of the Lantic Ocean, trapping even big, powerful ships in its clammy grasp and sentencing their helpless crews to a miserable death by starvation.

There was just enough light from a waning moon, filtering through the bank of swirling mist, for him to make out the strange writhing movement of the various chunks of flotsam and jetsam amid the clinging weeds, the sea beneath pushing and pulling below the surface.

Ryan stared more carefully into the gloom, trying to decide whether he'd possibly seen the "something" that Krysty thought she might have spotted. But the odd motion that had caught his eye wasn't repeated.

He walked away, trying to move quietly to avoid disturbing his sleeping companions. He sat by the fire, his right hand resting on the butt of the SIG-Sauer in its holster. Somewhere above him was the redoubt, with the mat-trans unit, which set him to wondering about the strange rumors of Orientals suddenly appearing here and there in Deathlands.

His attention was suddenly distracted.

Chapter Ten

Part of the true horror of the moment was that Ryan realized he'd been sitting and looking at it for several seconds, perhaps for half a minute, before his brain finally accepted that the thing was real—not just a rippling in the water beneath the matted, tangled lengths of seaweed, not some freakish combination of the broken driftwood that was caught up in the carpet of weed.

It was a pair of eyes.

Eyes on stalks.

Stalks that were over two feet in length, as thick as a human femur.

The eyes seemed to hang suspended in space, swiveling from side to side, out to the ocean behind it, back again to the short expanse of beach, the single, wakeful human, the eight sleeping figures.

Ryan swallowed hard, making a conscious effort to tear himself away from the hypnotic glare of the twin eyeballs. As he started to stand, the thing made its own move. Beginning to emerge from the slime that had kept it concealed.

"Fuckin' fireblast!"

He was sickeningly aware that he and six of the others had been working out there, amid the green layer of weed, waist-deep, soaked and cold, possibly moving within a few feet of the hideous monstrosity.

There was a faint rustling sound, like pieces of old leather rubbing against each other, a creaking noise, overlaid with water dripping off the armored carapace.

And a distinct clicking sound from the giant claws.

It was by far the largest crab that Ryan had ever seen, larger than anything that a fevered imagination could dream in the deeps of the worst nightmare.

As it slowly emerged from the weed, green fronds draped all across it like the rotting robes of a long-dead monarch, Ryan realized that it was at least fifteen feet across and stood taller than a full-grown man. The main claws, opening and closing very gently, were six feet in length and looked as though they had the power to slice through the center of a human body like a power press crushing a peach.

The eyes had stopped moving on their long stalks. They had centered on Ryan, seeming to lean toward him, trying to entrap his mind.

Now that he knew what he was up against, Ryan's combat reflexes finally came to his aid and he snapped himself clear of the murderous spell.

A shout might bring the crab rushing at him, giving no chance for anyone to wake properly. At the moment, it seemed to be apprising itself of the situation, moving with an exaggerated, almost delicate air through the weed, gradually drawing closer to the strip of shingle.

Ryan was sitting by the smoldering fire, the SIG-Sauer now in his hand, though he doubted that it would do much to stop the huge mutie crustacean.

He shuffled very slowly backward through the tiny damp pebbles, toward the others, keeping his eye fixed on the creature. But it didn't seem concerned by the small movement of the puny little animal in front of it.

J.B. and Krysty were the two nearest to him and Ryan woke them both, using the old and tried technique of the hand laid firmly over the mouth. Krysty first. He whispered into her ear, seeing the bright startled eyes looking up at him.

"Mutie crab. Triple huge. Lie real still but get ready to move fast."

He gave the same message to J.B., the Armorer doing nothing except cautiously placing his glasses on the bridge of his narrow nose, reaching for the Uzi.

Ryan woke Mildred and Trader.

The woman nodded her understanding, keeping still, her right hand moving toward the butt of her 6-shot revolver.

Trader was more difficult.

His first gut reaction was to fight against the dark shadow that had gagged him. Ryan had expected it and lay his whole body weight on top of the struggling man, keeping his arms pinned to his sides.

"Quiet, Trader, quiet. Me, Ryan. Quiet. Get ready to move. Big mutie crab in the bay. Don't move yet. Might bring it in at the charge."

Trader finally relaxed, his right hand on the butt of the battered Armalite.

"Yeah," he breathed.

Abe didn't even wake up at first, snoring gently, only opening his eyes when Ryan squeezed harder across his mouth and nose, the moist hairs of the drooping mustache against his palm, pinching off the air. When Abe heard the message he nodded once, already holding the big Colt Python.

Surprisingly Doc came easily out of sleep, the deepset, intelligent eyes taking in what Ryan whispered in his ear. His leonine head nodded to show that he understood. But the old man was unable to resist the temptation to raise himself a little and peer at the leviathan, now much closer to the edge of the beach. "By the Three Kennedys!"

Jak was the next around the circle, his tumbling white hair making him stand out in the semidarkness. As Ryan reached him, the dark eyes of the skinny albino were already open. "Seen it," he said quietly.

Dean was the last.

Ryan eased himself toward his son, glancing back to see if the crab was showing any signs of surging into an attack. But it was still moving slowly, the great claws held clear of the water, opening and closing with a menacing, velvet softness.

Just as he was about to wake the boy, Ryan spotted a change in the crab's movements. It had stopped, about twenty paces from the shingle, claws lifted higher, its long legs dancing up and down in the scummy water. It seemed to be gathering itself, bracing for an attack.

"Now," Ryan said in a voice urgent enough to be heard by everyone around him.

Simultaneously the gigantic mutie crustacean at last made its move.

Claws waving, eyes revolving on their stalks, it began to rush toward its prey. It added a perspective of horror that the thing made almost no sound, apart from the lethal noise of its serrated claws closing and opening.

Everyone opened fire at once.

Right at Ryan's side, Dean woke up at the sudden bedlam of gunfire, scrabbling for his own automatic, his eyes catching a sight of their gigantic adversary. "Oh, shit."

In the ragged mist, and with the poor light, it was impossible to see precisely what sort of damage the hail of bullets was doing. Ryan could hear some of them ricocheting away, howling into the darkness, while others were actually striking sparks from the barnacle-crusted armored shell.

The crab didn't exactly stagger away, but it did stop its advance, crouching, belly in the ocean, its claws waving faster as though it were trying to deflect the flying full-metal jackets from itself.

"Pick your target!" Ryan yelled. "Mildred, can you take out its eyes?"

"I'm already trying, for Christ's sake!" she shouted back. "But the bastard's moving too much."

She was standing up, feet planted firmly apart in the pebbles, shooting as though she were in the butts at the Olympic finals, picking her shots.

Ryan was also trying for the eyes, until he decided that it was too difficult and he was wasting bullets, shifting his aim to what he imagined was the creature's face.

Doc was struggling to shift the movable hammer on his commemoration Le Mat, so that he could begin to shoot the nine rounds of .36-caliber ammo.

"Coming at us!" yelled Trader, who was firing the Armalite from a kneeling position.

The crab had started to move again, edging sideways toward them. But it was clearly hurt. One of the legs, with spikes of thick hair at the joints, was dangling uselessly behind it, and a sort of dark, phosphorescent ichor was leaking over its shell in a number of places. Mildred had succeeded in picking off one of the questing eyes, and it seemed to have affected its sense of direction, so that it now crept parallel to the beach, rather than directly toward the blasters.

"Hold fire!" Ryan stood watching the mutie nightmare as it lurched, splashed and staggered, nearly falling over. One of the giant front claws had almost been severed by a burst of 9 mm bullets from the Uzi.

In a few seconds, the fearful specter from the ocean's unplumbed deeps had become something tragic.

Dean was up on his feet at his father's side. "Looks like it's done for," he said.

"I could probably take out the other eye, now it's slowed down," Mildred called.

Ryan shook his head. "No. Let's wait and see whether it still wants to fight."

"Chickenshit's had enough," Trader crowed, his exultant cry sounding oddly flat and hollow.

The crab was standing still, at the edge of the cove, its one eye glowering balefully at its intended prey, its single huge claw clicking open and shut.

"Had enough," Abe said, echoing Trader.

"Looks like it," Ryan agreed, reaching around to start reloading the SIG-Sauer, noticing that J.B. was doing the same with the Uzi.

"Yeah," Dean breathed.

The monster finally decided that the meal wasn't worth the suffering and turned clumsily, starting to make its way back through the sea of weed and driftwood toward the safety of deeper waters.

Above the constant smell of sulfur seeping across from the mainland, Ryan could taste a fresh, incredibly bitter scent in the night air, like a mixture of cold iron and hot blood. Then the crab finally vanished from sight under the dark ocean, and the smell also stopped.

There was the instant burst of nervous chatter among the nine companions that always broke out after such a close brush with death.

"Think it'll die, Dad?"

"Upon my soul, but that was a creation worthy of the talent of Hieronymus Bosch."

"I think I could've put out the other glim if Ryan had given me the word."

"Shit-eating bastard! Wish it'd gotten closer so we could have chilled it. Always liked crabmeat. Mebbe we can take the raft and go after it."

"I thought I was going to shit myself, Trader. I never saw anything like that."

"Might be others. Crossing to mainland on raft could be dangerous."

"Used up a lot of ammo on that. How're you fixed for 9 mm, Ryan?"

"Got enough. You all right, lover?"

"Once I stop shaking I'll be fine. That what the Bible means by the works of the Lord and his wonders in the deep? If it does, then the Lord can keep them."

THEY ALL SCOUTED among the jagged rocks above the strip of beach for more dry wood for the fire, bringing it back to flaming life. Though none of them actually came right out and said it, the idea of having a good blaze helped to dispel the demons of the night.

J.B. went over to sit by Ryan, taking off the Uzi and starting to fieldstrip it, wiping the moisture of the night away from the metal, cleaning the action with a piece of oily cotton, removing any fouling from the blaster.

"How about the raft, Ryan?"

"Seems solid enough. We've got some pieces of wood about the right size and weight for paddles."

"More worried about that crab. Dark night, but it was a true monster!"

Ryan nodded. "If something like that came at us out in the strait between this island and the mainland..." He allowed the thought to hang between them.

"Be somewhere between a triple-small chance and no chance at all."

"Agreed. Then again, it won't be coming after anybody for a while."

The Armorer dropped his voice, making sure nobody could overhear them. "If we don't try the raft, we have to jump again. How do you feel about that? And the boy?"

"Rather face that mutie crab's mother and father. No, seriously, I think we have to try for the mainland. Despite the stink of farts."

J.B. looked around. "Fog's lifting. Be dawn in an hour or so. When do we go?"

Ryan stood and stretched, grunting at the tightness in his shoulders. "What I remember about the western islands, word was that they weren't heavily occupied. Rad hot spots as well as the boiling mud and stuff."

"I checked the rad counter."

"Yeah, me too. Been veering between the low yellow and a sort of mid-orange. Bad, but not too bad."

The Armorer stared into the mist that still obscured the other side of the channel. "Best we try and get landed soon after first light."

"In case anyone's on lookout?"

"Sure. Be dead meat, floundering around on that raft, if anyone's got hostile intentions toward us. And if they got a good long gun."

"Can't argue with that. Best tell everyone to get themselves ready. We'll push off in fifteen minutes."

THE OCEAN WAS AS FLAT and as still as a sheltered millpond, with only the slightest suggestion of a swell.

They launched the raft as near to the end of the beach as they could, to minimize the struggle through the thick, clogging weed, finding themselves in clear water within a few yards. The wooden craft settled lower than they'd expected, with only a couple of inches freeboard, and some of the makeshift timbers shifted as everyone clambered carefully on board.

But it floated.

The mist was almost totally cleared, and the unknown mainland beckoned them.

They were on their way.

Chapter Eleven

"'Row, row, row the boat, gently down the stream,'" Doc sang, digging the crude paddle into the limpid waters of the strait, watching the tiny whirlpool as it drifted away behind every stroke.

"Keep your voice down," Ryan warned. "You know how sound carries across water. This part of the day, just before the dawn, is a quiet time."

"My sincere apologies, my dear fellow. Just brought back the merry days of punting down the Cherwell when I was at Oxford. I had a small rented room in the suburb called Jericho, just south of Summertown. Ah, me, such happy days were those. The dreaming spires of honey-colored Cotswold stone and the warm, green-muffled Cumnor Hills."

"Don't you ever shut your fucking mouth?" snapped Trader, who had been in a foul mood since driving a splinter of wood deep into his palm in the first minutes of their journey.

"Only when I have nothing to say," the old man replied. "And when I do open my mouth I endeavor to avoid foul and obscene language whilst in the presence of ladies."

"Well said, Doc." Mildred paused in paddling to clap her hands.

Trader sucked at the jagged wound, spitting crimson over the side of the raft into the sea.

"Might attract the sharks, blood like that," Abe said worriedly.

Krysty smiled. "I think it might take more than that to bring in the great whites."

"You never know." Abe was kneeling on a triangular slab of timber, leaning out to paddle, and he kept glancing around through the vanishing veil of mist.

There was a swirling ripple in the dark water, about fifty yards from the raft, on the starboard side. Dean saw it and called out to his father, finger pointing.

"Seal," Jak said calmly.

"Sure?" the boy asked.

"Sure."

A moment later the albino was proved right when a sleek whiskered head popped out of the sea in a welter of silver bubbles, grinning directly into Dean's face, making him jump so much that he nearly lost his balance and fell over the side.

"Told you," said Jak.

RYAN WAS AWARE that the sulfurous smell was becoming stronger as they made their way over the placid water. But, by now, he had to admit that he hardly seemed to notice it anymore.

Dawn was rushing across the land, bringing a lightening of the sky from the east. It was becoming possible, now that they were better than halfway over from the island, to make out some of the features of the mainland.

"Something behind us," J.B. said, holding his dripping paddle clear of the water, looking at the ocean a hundred yards or so astern. The first sliver of sun was peering over the distant mountains, glancing off his glasses.

"What?" Ryan asked. "Everyone stop paddling for a minute. All quiet."

"Don't know what, but I'm sure I saw the surface kind of change. Like something big had moved by, deep down."

Ryan stood, steadying himself with a hand on the shoulders of Krysty and Doc Tanner, trying to see beneath the glittering water. At first there was nothing.

"Hope it's not another of those mutie crabs," Dean said, shuddering.

There was a flicker under the sea, about twenty yards off, slightly behind and off to the port side. Ryan shaded his eye and stopped a little to see more clearly.

Then he saw it.

"Hang on. No sudden movements. It's several big whales."

Everyone promptly turned to see for themselves, tipping the raft sharply to the left, coming close to toppling it. There was some splashing and shouting, but it eventually settled down again on an even keel.

Now the whales were very close, one on either side and two more off a little distance to starboard.

Mildred stared at them, a fascinated smile on her face. "They won't hurt us. Not deliberately."

"How do you know?" Trader had pulled out the Armalite, holding it across his lap.

"Use that and you could easily get us all chilled," the woman warned. "All the guns we got together wouldn't do more than irritate one of these fellows."

One surfaced, whooshing a great jet of spray from its paired blowholes. Its side was scarred and marked, slick and shining. Dean put out a wondering hand and stroked it. The tiny eye seemed to revolve in its socket and look solemnly at the boy.

"What kind is it?" Doc asked. "Right whale?"

Mildred shook her head. "No. Saw them from a small boat, more fragile than this, down in Baja, the summer before skydark. Gray whales. *Eschrichtius robustus*. Grow up to fifty or sixty feet. They were endangered once from the bloody harpoons. Became protected and were flourishing when the world ended. Probably there's more of them now than ever."

"Will they eat us?" Dean asked.

"No, honey. They're mainly bottom feeders. Scooping up thousands of the tiny crabs and the like. What the scientists call gammarid amphipods. Sailors named them devilfish because they would fight hard to protect their young."

Everyone sat still.

One of the whales rubbed its back along the rough timbers of the raft, making it rock from side to side. Trader cursed softly under his breath, hanging on tight with one hand, blaster in the other.

"They are the true wonders of the Lord in the deep," Doc whispered, sounding as reverential as if he were sitting in a cathedral.

"There's a young calf over there," Ryan said to his son, pointing to the left toward the mainland. "See how its mother keeps between it and us."

The whales moved on southward with a wonderful, ponderous grace. As they came closer together, a couple of hundred yards in front of the raft, they all dived in perfect unison. The last of them showed its flukes as it rolled, its enormous tail hanging in the dawn light for a few magical moments before it finally disappeared.

"Wow," Dean said on a sigh. "Now that was something."

Ryan picked up his paddle. "Time to get moving again."

"LOOK AT THE SMOKE, or the steam, from those hot springs and geysers," Krysty said. "Seems like the whole of the land's boiling or on fire."

"They dangerous?" Abe asked.

"Only if you get too close." Ryan was steering them carefully toward what looked like a natural inlet.

Jak and Dean had stopped paddling, both standing near the front of the raft, keeping watch for any signs of danger from the shore.

"Small hut," Jak said, "right by water. Could be boathouse."

"Any smoke from a fire?" Ryan asked.

The albino hesitated. "Can't be sure. So much steam and shit. Don't think so."

They were about a hundred yards away, moving through shallow water with rocks protruding above the water and many more lying in wait below the surface.

Dean was kneeling, calling out warnings. "Bit to the right, now left." The clumsy craft was moving so slowly it was hardly likely to be damaged by any collision.

"I just saw a gigantic conger eel," Doc reported. "Long and thick as a telegraph pole. I don't think that I would relish swimming in these waters."

It was full dawn, enabling them all to see the extent of the blighted land ahead of them.

There was a beach and some rocks, with the building that Jak had mentioned. It seemed like there was a track leading away from it, vanishing inland. Then there came a belt of mist, smoke and steam, with the tops of distant mountains, snow-capped, visible far behind it.

Rad count's getting higher," J.B. stated. "Into the orange."

If they landed and found that the region of orange radiation extended very far, they would have no choice but to return to their raft and either try a little farther up or down the coast, or cut their losses and return to the hidden redoubt to make yet another jump.

"See the bottom," Dean called.

"Rocks, shingle or sand?"

"Sort of shingle and sand, Dad. I can see a crab, as well."

"What?"

Everyone dropped their paddles and snatched for their blasters.

"Only about half as big as my hand." Dean sniggered. "Sorry if I scared anyone."

"You little bastard," Abe moaned. "I nearly shit myself all over again."

THEY MADE a perfect soft touchdown.

There was still only the lightest breeze, bringing in tiny breakers that hissed on the gleaming pebbles. With a little effort they managed to heave the raft up the beach, hauling it above the high-water mark.

Immersion in the ocean had tightened some of the knots in the rope, but the whole structure was much looser, and it was clumsy and difficult to handle.

"Might have to do some work on it before we go back to the island," Trader said, kicking at the timbers.

Ryan nodded. "Unless we can find us some alternative transport."

Mildred looked at the raft. "Think it's safe there? How about if the tide comes in?"

"Should be up far enough," Abe said. "The piles of weed there show high water." He looked up at the deep blue bowl of the sky, unsullied by a single cloud. "And there's no sign of any sort of storm."

Dean coughed, hawking and spitting. "The smell gets on your chest," he said, pulling a face. "And it makes your eyes sting, as well."

J.B. was busily wiping salt spray off his spectacles. "It looks clear farther inland," he said. "Depends on how far we have to go to get clear of the fumes."

"And the rad hot spot," Ryan reminded.

"Yeah, and the hot spots."

THEIR FIRST STROKE of luck came when they reached the building. As they drew nearer they could see that there was a rough concrete slipway running from it, toward the sea. The double doors were badly weathered, bleached by the onshore wind. A plain bolt and hasp held them shut.

Inside the dark hut were a clinker-built boat, about fifteen feet long, with an unstepped mast and a set of oars in each. A hole marred the hull.

"Sails," Jak said, pointing to some shrouded bundles on a shelf running along one wall of the windowless shack.

"Lover?"

"Yeah, Krysty?"

"Is this God telling us that we should fix that hole, cast off this ruined place and go north or south?"

Doc laughed, a harsh, booming sound in the muffled stillness of the boathouse. "I confess that I have always been puzzled by that aspect of the omnipotence of the Almighty."

"How, Doc?" Mildred asked.

"When people say that God is trying to give them a sign or a warning. If our Divine Creator is truly all-powerful and all-knowing and all-seeing, then why does he have to resort to such clumsy methodology to pass on his messages? Why not a neat little card pressed into your hand by invisible fingers?'' He put on an even deeper voice. '' 'To Krysty Wroth and friends—It is my wish that you sail north of here and I have provided a craft for your journey, though it needs a slight repair.' Why not be up front about it?''

Most of the party laughed. But Krysty wasn't to be deterred. ''Doesn't answer my question, Doc. If there's bad nuke radiation here, mebbe we should simply take the boat and move away from it.''

Ryan bit his lip, balancing the options. ''Orange isn't too serious, providing we don't stay for days. I don't like the idea of moving away without exploring at all. I've never been here to this part of the western islands. None of us has.''

''Do we need to see some stinking hot springs when we can smell them?''

''You got a bad feeling about it?'' Ryan asked her. ''That why you want to move on?''

Krysty stepped into the early-morning sunshine, the brightness accentuating the living flames of her brilliant hair. She looked out to sea before replying. ''No. Can't say that there's a bad feeling. Not like danger from anyone. But this seems such a foul place.''

Ryan joined her, laying his hand on her arm. ''Tell you what. We know about this boat if we need it. We'll see what it's like for a mile or so inland. If we can't get through, then we'll come back and fix it up. All right?''

She nodded, giving him a quick kiss on the cheek. ''All right.''

Chapter Twelve

Doc tried to lift flagging spirits by recounting an anecdote of the time that he and his wife had visited Yellowstone in March of 1892, when it had been open as a national park for precisely twenty years.

But the oppressive nature of the region through which they were walking lay heavy on the old man. He started to become confused, repeating himself, frequently losing the point of the tale, which seemed to center on an extremely plump mother and unmarried daughter, a hungry brown bear cub, two tubs of pecan ice cream and Old Faithful.

Finally he fell silent.

Ryan was relieved when the old man eventually gave up on his pointless and muddled tale.

He had never seen such a depressing and alien terrain. Not anywhere through all his thirty-odd years in Deathlands. Here was only a bleak, crazed despair, as though the malevolent and psychotic Lords of Chaos had given vent to all of their most profoundly horrid imaginings.

The path from the coast snaked through a region where not a living thing existed. No birds flew through the tainted, misty sky. No animals walked between the twisted columns of flowering sulfur. No fish could hope to survive in the steaming, bad-water pools that fringed the trail.

Not a flower bloomed there—not even the ubiquitous Deathlands daisy. A few fossilized stumps of ancient trees stood stark, here and there, among the bubbling lakes of yellow mud, blasted by the impossible climate and the stinking fumes that drove away any hint of clean air.

There weren't even any flies humming through the fetid, humid air, or iridescent beetles to crawl around in the soft, sticky mud that seemed to lie everywhere.

The group of friends trudged along in single file, Ryan out at point, J.B. bringing up the rear. The path snaked in a generally easterly direction, inland, gently upward. Despite that, all of them were finding it arduous going, panting and sweating.

The rad counters were still showing orange, though it seemed that they were sliding a little way down the scale, closer to the yellow section.

"Can we stop for a sip or two of water?" Doc asked. "I still have a drop left in my canteen."

"Best keep," Jak said, rubbing his fingers through his long white hair, staring in disgust at the bright yellow stains on them.

"You kept yours?" Trader asked.

"See."

The teenager took his canteen from his belt and tossed it hard at Trader, who caught it easily, shaking it in disbelief. "Fucking full!"

"Not quite. Taken some small drinks. Most left."

"Not all of us are supermen, my dear magnesium-maned chum," Doc said.

Ryan interrupted the conversation. "Best we hold what water we've got. This is all undrinkable. Probably poisonous. Just keep going."

"LIKE GOLDEN FLOWERS of stone, aren't they?" Krysty had paused to look at a strange rock formation just to the left of the pathway. The rounded boulders were covered in crystalline sulfur, in delicate stalactites, with water dripping from them into a large steaming pool.

Somewhere out of the wreathing fog ahead of them there was a great roaring sound that stopped everyone in their tracks. It was a venomous noise, hissing, gurgling and bubbling, like the biggest mutie snake in the world.

"What the..." Trader said, automatically bringing the Armalite to his shoulder.

Doc laughed. "Need more than bullets to try to stop that, my friend. Perhaps a particularly enormous cork driven into the vent of the geyser might do the trick."

"Geyser! You mean one of those pissing jets of hot water? That all it was?"

Ryan licked his lips. "Yeah. You can actually taste the warm spray."

THERE WAS A BRIEF PASSAGE, when they were walking along the rim of what looked like a missile crater, that the rad counters went soaring into the high orange, verging on the lethally dangerous crimson.

But a hundred yards farther they had eased back down again into the low orange, and another quarter mile saw them showing yellow.

"Thought it was clearing up a bit," Krysty said, as they followed the narrow, winding trail down into a patch of much thicker fog.

Ryan stopped before answering, not wanting to take the risk of carrying on walking while looking behind him. The path was less than a yard wide in places, sometimes covered in scattered stones and sometimes slippery with thick ocher mud. To his right was a layer of crystallized rock salts that he suspected might only be a couple of inches thick and covered over a lake of water that was close to boiling point.

On the left was a steaming swamp of foul-smelling mud that bubbled and plopped. It ran as far as the eye could see, into the mist.

To stumble and fall on either side would mean, at the best, horrific scalding. At the worst it would mean a hideous way to buy the farm.

Everyone had stopped.

There was no wind at all in the sheltered region, and the fog seemed to be a permanent feature, settled down over them like a large and noisome animal.

"When we passed across that higher part, by the old tree stumps, I thought I spotted clearer ground a half mile ahead," Trader said.

"Can't go on forever," J.B. agreed, taking off his glasses for the fiftieth time since the raft had landed, trying to clean away the sticky condensation.

"My chest hurts," Dean complained, squatting on his heels and coughing, retching as if he were trying to remove phlegm from his throat.

"Sooner we move on, sooner we find some clean air and green grass," Ryan said, helping his son to his feet. He echoed the Armorer. "Can't go on much longer."

MILDRED SAT BESIDE DOC at a point where the track was wider. They'd stopped in a natural amphitheater, with a small pool of water at its center. The fog had diminished until it was only a light mist.

Dean had walked down from the others and was sitting on a smooth rock, picking up pebbles and lobbing them into the steaming water. The boy seemed vastly better, once they were away from the choking fumes of the fog.

"Amazing to think that all of this was once California," she said.

"The judgment of God on a truly biblical scale," he replied. "Even in my day the place was too wealthy. Too smug and sure of itself. By the time that the Armageddon plunged from the skies, it can only have been a thousand times worse. It considered itself the chosen land, did it not?"

"Guess it did."

"More like Sodom and Gomorrah. And it received the scourge of the Almighty."

"It *is* like some sort of dreadful apocalyptic wilderness, isn't it? Something out of the Book of Revelations." Mildred looked around her, wonderingly. "They sure must've opened up the seventh seal here."

Doc seemed to have lost interest in their conversation, staring intently down at the surface of the water where Dean was playing.

Krysty caught his attention. "What is it, Doc?"

"I just suffered from a strange visual distortion. It seems to me that the level of that pool keeps on rising a little, then subsiding. Then rising a little farther again. I cannot for the life of me imagine why that should—" He stopped, his jaw dropping, suddenly leaping to his feet. "By the—"

He started to rush down toward the boy. "Dean, come away from there!" Doc's ancient knee boots slipped on the damp yellow-stained rocks, threatening to send him cascading all the way to the bottom of the large hollow. "Away for your very life!"

Dean stood, his dark curly hair matted to his head by the moisture in the air, looking up at the bizarre sight of the respectable Dr. Tanner leaping toward him like a deranged gazelle, waving his arms, face red, yelling some kind of warning at him.

"What?" he shouted, moving a couple of paces away from the small pool.

Everyone was up on their feet, Ryan and Krysty both taking a few steps in pursuit of Doc, who had nearly reached the boy, hands outstretched toward him, still shouting incoherently.

"Away! Before it blows!"

"Before what blows?" Trader asked, standing on the rim of the basin.

Mildred was quickest. "It's a geyser," she shouted. "Doc figures it's about to blow. If it does..."

Doc had Dean by the hand, tugging him up the slope, the boy still bewildered, resisting the old man.

"Run, son!" Ryan yelled. "Boiling fountain about to blow up behind you!"

Abe started toward the couple to try to help, but his feet skidded away from under him and he fell, yelping in alarm. Arms spread to try to save himself, he was rolling directly toward Doc and Dean, but he managed to grab hold of a spur of rock and pulled himself upright just before crashing into them.

Ryan looked at the pool, cursing his own lack of attention in such a hostile land. The level was much higher, and it was bubbling and steaming. The surface of the liquid surged and roiled with the unbelievable pressures beneath the earth.

"Keep back, friends!" Doc panted, now over halfway toward the crest.

Now they could all hear.

A sullen roar that they could feel vibrated through their feet, like a long-caged beast thrusting up toward the murky sunlight.

The water in the dark pool was becoming violently agitated, swelling higher, then sinking back for a few heartbeats, then rising to twice its original height. Ryan had checked quickly where the prevailing wind was, knowing that even a light breeze could carry the boiling droplets for fifty yards or more.

Now Doc and the boy were close enough for helping hands to tug them up and over the top, pausing for a moment to gather breath. "Farther!" the old man panted.

They were less than a dozen yards away from the highest point of the rocky bowl when the geyser finally blew.

Everyone dived flat, covering heads, ears and faces, J.B. making certain that the Uzi and the Smith & Wesson M-4000 were both safely beneath his body.

Ryan risked a glance over his shoulder, seeing the great column of boiling water and superheated steam surge upward, at least a hundred and fifty feet in the air, its top drifting away from them on the small wind.

The noise was deafening, and the ground trembled beneath them, hot water splashing all around.

But Doc's reflexes had been just fast enough to save all of them from what could have been very unpleasant injuries from the geyser.

And fast enough, beyond any doubt, to save the life of Dean Cawdor.

Ryan clasped Doc's hand, feeling the way that the old man was shaking, from the shock and from the exertion. "Well done," he said. "And thanks."

Dean, soaking wet, was wiping water from his eyes. "You saved my life, Doc."

"What friends are for, dear boy." He blushed slightly. "Just what friends are for."

"LOOKS LIKE WE'RE GETTING toward the end of this hot-springs part," Ryan said.

They'd stopped again, a quarter mile of winding trail farther on. The rad counter was now showing only the palest of yellow, shading toward the green of safety, indicating that the worst of the missiles had fallen very near the coast of California, triggering the quakes and letting in the ocean. Here, much closer to the Sierras, it was cleaner and safer.

There was still that deceptive alkaline crust on one side of the trail, and bubbling mud on the other. But it really did look as though the rising ground just ahead of them was going to be the end of the bad times.

They were strung out in the usual single skirmish line, Ryan taking a turn at the rear, with J.B. in the lead. The path doglegged sharply to the right, in front of them, round a sulfur-stained bluff with hot water streaming down it.

J.B. suddenly held up a hand, seeing a number of figures running toward him, through the mist-wraiths, waving spears and daggers.

Simultaneously Ryan glanced behind, seeing if their line of retreat was open and safe.

It wasn't.

At least a dozen more men were charging silently, the nearest less than a dozen yards away.

It was a perfect ambush.

Chapter Thirteen

There was the brief moment of recognition.

Ryan didn't even have time to breathe the word "scabbies" before the first of the muties was on top of him. But his eye had sent that message through to his memory and brain.

Scabbies were a particularly repulsive type of mutie, often considered to be some kind of offshoot of the more common stickies. But they were found more often near regions where there were many nuke hot spots, combined with some kind of local climate or conditions that had bred the disgustingly hideous skin diseases that gave them their name.

They were generally believed to be a little more intelligent than stickies—which wasn't saying much—without the latter's profoundly perverse love of enormous bright fires and thundering explosions.

Like most of the mutated peoples, scabbies weren't keen on blasters, finding them too difficult to keep clean and much too hard to shoot accurately. They preferred to attack with old-fashioned edged and pointed weapons.

It hadn't seemed a potentially dangerous situation, with absolutely no sign of any sort of life, and Ryan had been walking along with the SIG-Sauer in its holster, the powerful Steyr rifle slung across his shoulders.

Now a scabbie was on top of him, its mouth opening in a screeching yell of hatred and triumph as it leapt at the defenseless man.

But Ryan Cawdor was never without a defense.

His reflexes took over. There was no time at all to try to draw any of his armory of weapons, with the scabbie already in the air, jumping at him, a broad-bladed notched knife clutched in its right hand.

Ryan stooped a little, reaching with his left hand for the mutie's right wrist. He locked his fingers and stooped further, pulling the helpless mutie onto his shoulders, then straightening at the perfect moment, heaving the scabbie high in the air, off to the left of the trail.

The battle cry of rage and hatred changed in midair to a scream of shock and despair, seeing his own inexorable doom rising up toward him.

He crashed down on his right arm, the blade of the knife snapping on impact. But the thin layer of crystallized salts wasn't thick enough to take his weight and he plunged through it, vanishing in an eruption of stone splinters and boiling, hissing water.

Ryan didn't have time to look to see what happened to the mutie, but the agonized yell and the frantic thrashing told its own terrible story.

A second scabbie attacked Ryan, lunging at him with a long-shafted spear, its point tied in place with thin strips of rawhide. There was a moment when they were face-to-face, and Ryan recognized the ghastly deformities that characterized the breed of mutie.

Every inch of exposed skin seemed to be a single festering sore. Flaps of whitened skin were peeling off across the forehead, dangling over the deep-set eyes. The mouth was lipless and toothless, surrounded by a nest of dried craters and fresh, yellow boils. One ear was missing, the other hanging loosely from the side of the skull, tethered by a strip of gangrenous gristle.

The hands holding the long spear were covered in a scaly golden rash of spots, spreading up the forearms, high above the elbows.

What hair there was on the head was limp and colorless, pasted flat by the steam in the air around them.

Ryan batted the clumsy weapon aside with his left hand, jabbing a vicious punch into the scabbie's solar plexus. The air whooshed out of the mutie's lungs and he started to double up, dropping the spear. He stumbled past Ryan, who chopped down a vicious rabbit punch on the back of his neck with the hardened edge of his right hand as he went by.

The mutie went off the opposite side of the trail to his colleague, tumbling headfirst into the deep, golden mud. He was swallowed completely, without even a scream, his feet sliding below the bubbling, boiling surface.

Ryan was aware of yelling behind him, then the tearing sound of the Uzi, fired on full-auto.

Two more scabbies charged him, undeterred by the awful fate of their two comrades. One of them suddenly stopped, staggered a couple of paces, then fell on his disfigured face. Ryan saw the taped hilt of one of Jak's throwing knives protruding from his throat.

In close combat, there was sometimes the temptation to go for the handblaster. But, as Ryan had learned over the years, that wasn't always the best option to take. You might get the chance only for a single shot, and if it didn't put your man down, then a blaster was a useless weapon for hand-to-hand.

He drew the eighteen-inch panga from its sheath in a single smooth, rehearsed action, feeling its familiar weight and balance.

Cutting from left to right, backhanded, he stopped the nearer of the scabbies, who was armed with a short-hafted ax. The mutie moved back from the intended blow, ducking and trying to slice at Ryan's legs.

But the one-eyed man had been expecting it, swaying away like a dancer, pivoting to his right and using the panga like a long dagger. He stabbed directly at the scabbie's neck, but the man was quick, hunching his shoulder, so that he only took a shallow flesh wound at the top of the left arm.

He whirled, his ragged clothes fluttering about his scrawny body, feinting toward Ryan's face, then changing the direction of the blow to his hand and wrist.

The ax rang on the honed steel of the big cleaver as Ryan parried it, feeling the shudder of the blow run clear up to his shoulder.

He heard a handblaster boom close behind him and saw another of the attackers throw up his arms and topple over onto the crust across the scalding lake, which opened to receive the body in a mass of steaming bubbles.

But all of Ryan's attention was concentrated on his own opponent, who was grinning at him from the leathery mass of corruption that masked his brutish features. He was panting from the grim exertion of the fight, whispering to Ryan in a harsh, croaking voice.

"Come, outie, come on... Cut your outie heart and fuck'n eat it up."

Ryan didn't waste his breath.

Around him, he could hear all the sounds of a pitched battle. Several blasters were in operation, which made him think the firefight should be going their way. J.B. and the others at the front had been lucky enough to have a couple of seconds more warning, giving them the precious moment to draw and start shooting at the attacking scabbies.

The handblaster opened up again, close behind him, and another of the muties rolled backward, most of its face vanishing in a fountain of blood, bone and brains.

"Got the bastard!" It was Abe's voice, sent soaring up the scale by the adrenaline rush.

The ambush had failed.

Beyond his own opponent, Ryan could see that the rest of the scabbies had turned to flee, calling out in their broken, guttural voices as they ran back along the pathway, to disappear into the swirling bank of mist.

But the man facing Ryan wasn't about to give up. He was still swearing and muttering to himself as he tried to find a gap through the norm's impenetrable guard, lunging and swinging with the deadly ax.

"Let me take him, Ryan," Trader called. "Other shitters broke and ran. Those that still could."

"No!" The word was shouted angrily over his shoulder, his good eye not moving for a moment from the scabbie's distorted, suppurating face.

The man was becoming tired. Ryan could sense it, almost taste the fatigue.

The hacking blows were slower, less skillfully aimed. It was nearly time.

Ryan realized that it had become silent, after the racketing of the blasters and the yells and screams. Now there was only the bursting of bubbles of the scalding gas and the faint hissing of steam.

And the ragged breathing of the mutie who was trying to kill him.

Ryan hefted the eighteen inches of sharpened steel, as if he were about to cut at the scabbie's throat, dropping his aim to the groin. As the ax was lowered to counter it, Ryan swung back toward the neck.

Sixty seconds ago the mutie would have been fit enough and fast enough to dodge or parry.

Now he wasn't.

There was enough residual combat skill in him to thwart Ryan's purpose of hacking the head off his shoulders. He flinched, half lifting his left arm, protecting his throat, paying the price for his slowness.

The razored edge bit deep into his arm, a couple of inches above the wrist. It cut open skin and flesh, splintering through both the ulna and the radius, coming within a quarter inch of severing the hand, which dangled loose by a length of torn muscle. Blood gouted bright crimson, pattering on the path, into the boiling mud, staining the yellow dirt a deep orange.

The scabbie staggered back, looking in disbelief at the flapping, useless hand.

Ryan readied himself for the final, mortal blow, swinging the panga back to his shoulder.

His enemy saw death coming and tried to avoid it, whimpering in agony. But the lethal wound had made him clumsy, and he tripped over his own feet.

He started to fall, the ax tossed high in the misty air, spinning over and over as he toppled backward. His scream of mortal terror was loud and shrill enough to shatter crystal at fifty paces.

"Enjoy the bath," Trader called.

The mutie landed on the left of the narrow trail, breaking through the thin layer of scale across the lake.

He went clean through, hurling up a wave of spray that obscured him for a few moments.

Unbelievably he surfaced, still alive, kicking in the boiling water, head strained back, the cords in his throat standing out like drawn wire.

"God help him," Mildred whispered. "Take him, Lord, take him."

The scabbie fought in silence, mouth wide open, pulling at the water with his right arm, legs thrashing, reaching out for the edge of the path.

But he was being cooked alive.

The searing heat of the lake was broiling him. The disfigured skin across his face and neck was blistered away, hanging in empty, ballooning sacks. His fingers had vanished as the flesh became grotesquely swollen. The eyes were gone, sealed behind a bloody pink puffiness.

It was impossible to imagine the unthinkable horror of the mutie's suffering.

The nine companions watched him, silent, until Krysty broke the spell that held them motionless.

Drawing her Smith & Wesson double-action pistol, she put a .38 round into the middle of the suffering man's skull, blowing him into eternity.

As his body floated, the only sound was Doc kneeling down and being sick. "My apologies," he mumbled, wiping his mouth on the sleeve of his stained frock coat. "But it was the smell of boiled meat that—" He promptly threw up again.

"Best we go," Ryan said. "Sound of shooting could have been heard. Might be others."

The three scabbie corpses lying on the winding path were quickly manhandled over the edge into the seething yellow mud.

"DEFINITELY BETTER AIR," Krysty stated, sharing the lead with Ryan on a wider, straighter path.

The battle with the muties was close on an hour behind them, lost in the lower ground of hot springs, geysers and poisonously yellow mists.

Now they could see the mountains more clearly, with a stretch of wooded valleys lying directly ahead.

A high, thin waterfall glittered over a shelf of rock; Ryan's guestimate put it at around twenty miles east.

The sun was just past the halfway mark, starting its long, slow descent toward the west, over the distant ocean.

Ryan whistled between his teeth. "More like it, lover."

She nodded. "It is. Look at the height of some of those trees ahead."

They were giant redwoods, towering well over two hundred feet. Ryan stopped at the top of some rising ground, shading his eye. "Looks to me like some sort of camp down there among the trees," he said.

Krysty probably had the best day sight of anyone in the party. "Think you're right. Tents. Might be Native Americans."

"Don't reckon there's many of them in these parts," Trader said. "Never were."

"Well, best way to find out is to go take a look." Ryan eased the strap of the Steyr on his shoulder. "Slow and careful."

Chapter Fourteen

"Something odd."

They were lying in a straggling line along a ridge that hid them from the encampment, a quarter mile below them. There were groves of piñon pines scattered among the redwoods, filling the afternoon air with their scent.

"What, Trader?" Ryan asked.

"Counted the tents. Not too good with numbering, as you know. I make it up to forty."

"Thirty-eight," Dean said quickly.

"Remember that nobody in Deathlands admires a smart-ass, sonny," Trader growled. "Specially them that tries to dump their olders and betters into the shadows with how bright they think they are."

There was real venom in the words, and Dean wriggled a little farther from the older man, closer to the protection of his father.

But Ryan did nothing. "So what, Trader? What's your point about this?"

"I sort of counted at the women and children and men running around down there. But Mr. Button Bright here probably done that, too."

Dean glanced at his father, who nodded. "I made it eleven what I'd call children. Younger than me. Twenty-six women. And only about eight or nine men. Can't be sure as they moved around a lot, going in and out the tents."

"Close enough, Dean," J.B. confirmed. "See your point, Trader. Too many women."

"And not enough men. More to the issue, J.B., there's not enough fighting men." Trader shuffled to a more comfortable position. "Where the fuck are all their men? They ain't muties, by what I can see."

Ryan had already realized that. But it gave Trader some self-respect if he announced that kind of news. Like he was still real sharp, despite his age.

Which he undeniably was, despite a slight blurring around the fighting edge.

"Don't look in-laws," Jak said. "Wolf's-heads in brushwood. Step careful if go in. Don't trust far as spitting."

Ryan nodded at that, too. "No argument with that. How about weapons?"

Predictably it was the Armorer who'd been paying particular attention to that.

"Children nothing, unless you count three or four little short-bladed hunting knives. Most of the women down there are wearing knives." He took off his hat and scratched his head. "Kind of strange that, when you think about it. Virtually everyone's got a blade of some kind. Three or four of them are also wearing tomahawks at their belts."

"Men all got knives," Jak interrupted. "Some got two. Working blades and fighting blades."

"Not many blasters. One's wearing an AK-47. He's..." J.B. paused. "No. Sorry. Couldn't see it properly. It's the AK-74 not the 47. Folding stock."

"Never could work out what the difference was," Trader said.

"One of the main differences is in the ammo," the Armorer replied, locked into his favorite topic of conversation. "The newer 5.45 mm has a flatter trajectory than the 7.62 mm. Means you got better aim around the four-hundred-paces mark. Very tight rifling, so it spins quicker."

"Makes it more stable?" Ryan asked.

"Right. But it has a relatively low muzzle velocity. Below three thousand fps. The M-16 goes around three two-fifty. But here's where the Russkies got clever. Cunning Old Mikhail Timofeyevich Kalashnikov. Basic cartridge has a mild steel jacket. That covers a lead sheath. Then a core of mild steel about fifteen millimeters long. The base of that's at the base of the jacket. Then comes a three millimeter plug of lead. Right in the nose is simply five millimeters of air. So, it's a bottom heavy round, with the center of gravity tilted much closer to the rear of the bullet than usual.

"Because it's unbalanced, it starts to tumble immediately after it hits anything more solid than air. Dumps all of its kinetic energy and rips apart flesh. Big high-velocity round goes in and straight out the other side and doesn't do much damage. I saw some pix in an old mag of test-firing into jelly blocks. Tore them apart, the 74 did.''

"Anything else interesting?" Abe asked. "I haven't see one of them Russkie blasters in a 'coon's age. Seen lots of the old 47s.''

J.B. nodded. "Yeah. The muzzle brake's a lot better. Cuts down on noise and flash. And it also counters some of the recoil with a movement that's slightly down and forward. Brilliant piece of blaster design.''

"I saw three muzzle-loading muskets, just inside one of the tents," Dean said. "And three of the men have got handblasters holstered.''

"Still doesn't explain where all of the men from the camp have gone." Krysty looked around, almost as though she were tasting the air.

Trader leaned toward Ryan. "Men are out hunting or raiding," he guessed.

"Unless they work for a local baron." Another thought occurred to him. "Could they have been chilled in some way?''

Trader considered the two possibilities, slowly nodding. "Could be either of them.''

"We going down, lover?" Krysty asked. "I can smell baking bread.''

Ryan had also noticed, a fresh, delicious odor that was already doing something to scrape away at the harsh layers of sulfur from his taste buds.

"I'll go on down there, just with Dean and Abe. Talk some. Let them know we got some armed forces watching. Kind of test the water.''

"Careful, lover. I can't catch the feeling properly, but it's not all friendly."

DESPITE KRYSTY'S reservations, the greeting was largely hospitable.

The first warning came in a cry of "Strangers!" from one of the smallest children, which brought the men together, some with blasters cocked and ready, while the women gathered all the little ones, shepherding them into the hide tents.

Ryan introduced himself and the others, saying that they were from a group of traders who'd been sailing up the coast. A freak storm had turned over their boat, and several of the party had been lost.

It was a useful story to account for their arrival in a place without knowing much of the vicinity, and one that Ryan had used before.

The leader was a man called Ditchdown. He was in his fifties, with dark hair that carried a slash of white. When he noticed that Dean was fascinated by it, he explained that it had been the result of a bad cut with a knife and the hair had grown back white.

He invited Ryan to call down the rest of the group, saying that they didn't have much food to spare as most of the men were out hunting. He hesitated a fraction of a second before the word "hunting," and Ryan noticed the pause.

"But you're all welcome to what we got. There's some bread just out of the ovens."

Ryan thanked him and gave the signal for the others to come down from the surrounding trees.

The people of the tented community didn't pay much attention to the outlanders, until Jak and Krysty appeared, walking and talking together.

There was a burst of excited chattering, and Ryan heard the name of someone called Straub repeated several times among the women and children.

"Looks like you're a hot pipe here, Jak," Dean said, laughing nervously.

"Same everywhere," the albino replied, brushing his hand through the tumbling snow-white hair, getting an even stronger reaction from the watchers.

They were offered seats around a long table, and hunks of fresh bread were placed in front of all of them, with crocks of salted butter and earthenware dishes of jellies and preserves, and beakers of good, sweet water.

The children pressed in closer, one or two of the bolder spirits reaching out to try to touch Krysty's mane of fiery hair, which coiled itself protectively around her nape. One of the older women saw what was happening and scooted the little ones away.

Ditchdown sat himself at the head of the table, looking at each of the outlanders, as if he were trying to get their measure.

"Fine blasters," he said finally.

Ryan looked up, wiping crumbs off his chin. "Fine bread," he replied.

The camp leader nodded. "Good baking's important to us. We like the best when we can get it."

Krysty glanced around her at the ramshackle tents and the ragged children. "Seems like you haven't had the best for a while."

"Right, lady. Times haven't... By all the gods that ever were, but your pelt is like burning magic. I swear I never saw the like of it."

A woman, gray-haired and scrawny, had been leaning against the side of the bench beside Ditchdown, absently running her fingers back and forth along the patch of white in his scalp. "We got better times coming, don't we?" she said. "Once Schickel and the rest come back."

Ditchdown reached up a large hand and squeezed her arm, smiling up at her. "Don't flap your tongue in front of strangers, Annie, or I'll nail you to a tree by it." Her face had gone as pale as scoured ivory, and Ryan could see the way the man's knuckles had whitened with the strain.

"Sorry," she muttered. He let her go and she walked stiffly away, rubbing at her bruised arm.

"Who's Schickel?" Trader asked. "Your fight leader?"

Ditchdown sniffed, picking up a piece of bread and starting to break it apart. He rolled the crumbs into tiny pellets, flicking them in the air and catching them in his open mouth. "Fight leader?" he repeated. "Suppose so."

"There a baron in these parts?" J.B. asked. "Not many parts of Deathlands don't have a baron."

"Name's Weyman. Got a ville about fifteen miles inland from here."

"That where the rest of your men are?" Trader asked, speaking with his mouth so full of bread and cherry preserve that gobbets of it slithered back onto the table.

"You got a lot of questions for an old man," Ditchdown said, standing. "You pack are guests here, and it's best you remember it."

Trader stood slowly, laying the Armalite on the scarred wood in front of him. "You want to try and see what an old man can do with you, woodlander?"

Ditchdown hesitated, then forced a laugh. "We're simple people here, Trader. I know a horse and a dog and a woman. Plain and straightforward."

"Then tell us straightforward what the rest of your men are doing." Trader stared at Ditchdown until the larger man lowered his eyes.

"We have to live," he muttered. "They said when we were on the road that Weyman's a blown fruit, ready for the plucking." He recovered a little of his aggression. "What's it to you? You baron's men?"

"We're our own men," Ryan replied. "The way you live is the way you live. Not our business. We thank you for the bread, and we'll be on our way."

"Day's wore on," Ditchdown said. "Welcome to stay the night with us. We lost three in the last couple days to the fucking pigs in the forest, so there's spare room. Give you two tents to yourselves for a night, if you wanted them."

"Pigs?" Mildred said. "Is that slang for sec men?"

The man looked at her in bewilderment. "Don't take your meaning, lady."

"What are pigs?"

"Pigs is pigs," he replied.

"Oh, you mean *real* pigs? Like fat and snorting with lots of little piglets, waddling around ready for bacon time?" Mildred laughed, then saw that the man's face was set like stone. "That what you mean?"

"I mean mutie beasts that come in close to a thousand pounds and can rip a man from throat to groin with one hook of their bloody tusks."

The woman looked away from him. "I didn't know," she said quietly.

"Not uncommon." J.B. was sitting next to her, and he patted her on the arm. "You weren't to know."

"I guess I've seen a fair range of mutated flora and fauna since arriving in Deathlands," she said. "So murderous porkers shouldn't surprise me."

Ryan looked at Ditchdown. "Can you give us a few minutes to talk in private? Whether to take you up on your offer and stay the night or not?"

"'Course. Like I said. Woods are dark and deep around here. Baron's men might not take to strangers. Safer to stay here with us. When Schickel gets back he'd like to talk. Be impressed with your blasters. Mebbe ask you to come join us."

He stood and walked away.

Ryan looked around the table. "Anyone got anything to say on this?"

Trader spoke first. "Raggedy load of bare-assed bastards like this won't cause much trouble to any well-armed baron. Nor to us. If they want us to stay the night and eat their food, no questions asked and no debts owed, then I don't see why not."

"Fair enough. Krysty?"

She was busily licking plum preserve off her fingers. "There's a lot of tension and excitement here. Part of it's waiting for this man Schickel and the rest of the hunting party. But there's something about me and Jak that I don't get. Somehow linked to Straub, whoever he is."

J.B. lifted a hand. "They aren't just out hunting. Obvious. Seems no doubt they plan to try and take this Baron Weyman for what they can. I agree with Trader. From what we've seen they won't be too much of a threat."

"Unless baron isn't strong," Jak interrupted. "Straw house blows down easy."

Ryan rapped on the table with his fist. "Main point is whether we are likely to be in any danger. Be good to have somewhere to sleep. Long as we post a watch."

"Few smoothbores and a Kalashnikov or two won't present much of a threat," J.B. said.

"I see no real threat."

Doc coughed. "If I may interject? I understand that they are inviting us to share both their beds and their board. It would be churlish to reject such kind hospitality. Particularly if the supper is in the same league as their bread and confitures."

"All right then." Ryan looked around once more. "We reckon that it's worth the small risk to stay a night. Then move on in the morning. And we all keep a good watch."

Chapter Fifteen

Ryan and the rest of the group had been shown to their tents. Both were made from a mixture of crudely woven wool and animal hides, which, from their acrid smell, had never been properly cured. There were piles of furs and old blankets in each tent. Ryan and Krysty took the smaller of them with Mildred and J.B., leaving the other, larger one to be shared between Doc, Trader, Abe, Dean and Jak.

Ditchdown had come around to see if they were settling in. "Good to have outlanders with us," he said. "Schickel's sure goin' to be impressed with those blasters." Then he'd nodded to himself and moved on.

THE FIRST WARNING of the hunters returning was when all the dogs in the camp started to bark. The children and women came out of their primitive huts and tents, setting up an ululating cry that rang around the forest.

Krysty had tied back the front flap, trying to let in some fresher air to take away the mustiness. "Coming," she said quietly.

The light was poised between day and night, with a ghostly mist creeping around the tops of the taller redwoods. There was no wind, the smoke from the cooking fires rising vertically into the still air, vanishing among the topmost branches of the trees. Ryan could see shadowy figures, a few on horseback, most walking toward the camp, some with muskets slung across shoulders. Several of the party had animal carcasses tied to poles. The light wasn't all that good, but Ryan thought that all of them were deer. There was no sign of the mutie pigs.

"How many?" J.B. had joined him in the opening to their tent.

"Close to thirty. Looks like only two or three with serious blasters."

"See an M-16, like Trader. And another of the AKs. Which one's their chief?"

"Schickel?"

"Yeah. Probably the one on that big stallion. Fur coat, cross-belted."

"Carrying a scattergun. Sawed-down. Just the sort of blaster you'd take on a hunting trip."

The Armorer smiled at Ryan. "You and me never believed that story, did we?"

Mildred and Krysty were also watching, the entrance to the adjacent tent crowded with Trader and the others.

"Plenty of fresh meat, Dad," Dean called.

"That boy certainly takes after his father, doesn't he, Krysty?" Mildred said.

"You mean only thinking of his stomach?"

"Yeah."

Krysty nodded. "You couldn't be more right."

THE MAIN MEAL DIDN'T quite measure up to the delicious bread they'd eaten earlier. But what it lacked in quality it more than made up in quantity.

The nine companions were seated at a low table, cross-legged on rush matting, with wooden dishes in front of each of them and small pitchers of beer standing at intervals. Ditchdown had gone to their tents to ask them to come and be seated, telling them that the hunt had been successful and that Schickel and some of the older men would join them once they'd washed.

Women of the tribe carried in the food, haunches of venison, slightly blackened on the outside, bloody when the knives penetrated them, and whole salmon, the skin glinting silver. The vegetables were overcooked—potatoes and carrots and black-eyed peas with a mess of refried beans.

"Do we start?" Dean asked, his mouth watering as the supper dishes stood steaming in front of him.

The scene was lighted by smoky torches tied to long staffs of wood jammed into the dirt.

"Wait for their leader," Ryan ordered.

"Food getting cold," the boy protested.

"You want to get to eat supper?"

"'Course I do, Dad."

"Then sit still and keep quiet."

J.B. nudged Ryan. "Here they come."

It was a tense and potentially dangerous moment. The nine companions had brought all of their weapons, including the Steyr and the Uzi, ready for any card to be turned up.

But the twenty or more men who came striding through the camp, past the line of night fires, didn't seem any great threat. A couple had handblasters at their waists, but the rest were armed only with knives.

Schickel was at their head, still wearing the thick fur coat that made him look even bigger than he was. Ryan put him at six-three, weighing around three-fifty pounds. He wore crossed ammo belts over the coat. His knee-length boots were splattered with mud. The sawed-down 16-gauge Ithaca, the Model 37, was tucked into a long greased holster, strapped onto the right side of a broad leather belt.

He looked to be a few years shy of forty, with sparse graying hair, a sharply hooked nose and a ruddy, outdoors complexion. The eyes that scanned the nine outlanders were deep blue, set unusually wide apart.

His gaze finally settled on Ryan. "You'll be the one called Cawdor, leader of this shipwrecked band," he said. "And you're Trader. I used to hear my father tell me stories of a man called Trader. Rode with war wags and his own private army. Heard he got chilled fighting against some rebel Commanche, out along Death Canyon Road. You the same man?"

"Not if I got myself chilled by a band of Commanche," Trader replied easily. "Plenty of men in Deathlands call themselves traders."

"That's true. And the boy with eyes bigger than his belly. Be your son, Cawdor?"

"Yeah. Dean. He's eleven."

"Baron Weyman has an eleven-year-old," Ditchdown said, standing next to the war chief. "Called

Jamie. Bright, they say. Being trained to take over from his father."

Schickel laughed. "Not if we can all get there first, eh, brothers?"

"You're aiming to try and take this baron, are you?" Ryan asked.

"Why? You have a problem with that, Mr. One-Eyed Cawdor? Mebbe you don't see things too clearly."

His witticisms drew bellows of laughter from the rest of the hunters.

"I heard most barons had sec men. I heard most sec men had better weapons than a couple of Kalashnikovs, a sawed-down Ithaca and a few smoothbores," Ryan observed.

"You heard right. Yes, indeed you heard right. So, your ears work well."

"So, I guess you know things we don't," Ryan concluded, sustaining a pleasant smile, suppressing the temptation to cut the throat of the grinning oaf.

"Sure. We been around Deathlands." He slapped himself on the chest. "I seen barons whose piss would blight the land for a thousand years. Seen barons only had to look angry at you and the bullets melted in the chamber. Then again—" he paused for dramatic effect "—I seen barons like Weyman whose idea of giving you a hard time is to stop you having an extra smear of butter on your bread. Know what I mean?"

"You mean he's a weak baron?" J.B. asked.

"Sure." He stared hard at the Armorer. "You got four eyes there, friend. That to make up for Cawdor only having one?" Schickel turned around to bathe in the wave of raucous laughter.

"So I can see properly when I have to put a full-metal jacket through the hearts of bragging stupes," J.B. said quietly.

"Whoa back, buck! Hold on to them hosses, little Dix. Don't get your drawers in a tangle, eh? Guess it's true what they say about small men. They all got them ferocious tempers." He pretended to shiver with fear. "Have to step light when this pint-size fury's around us, brothers."

Ditchdown glanced back over his shoulder and whispered something to the bulky figure of the leader.

"How's that, Ditchdown? Who's on... Oh, yeah. I noticed for myself. Can't hardly miss them, can you? Like having one eye froze with snow and the other burned with fire." He smiled broadly at Jak and Krysty.

"So merry and so fat can ne'er live long, they say," Doc whispered to Mildred.

She whispered back. "A man can smile and smile and still be a bastard villain, Doc."

"True, madam, true."

Schickel saw the exchange and hesitated, as though he were working on another wisecrack, changing his mind. "Food's getting colder than a snow bear's dick. Let's all sit down and eat and drink. Get to know each other better."

Dean didn't need a second invitation, grabbing at several slices of venison from the nearest plate, then helping himself to a pile of potatoes and carrots. He ladled himself a generous portion of gravy, so rich and thick that you could've sliced it with a good knife.

Ryan was about to tell the boy off for his greediness and poor table manners, then he realized how hungry he was himself and set to with a will, generally eating left-handed, as J.B., Jak, Trader and Abe all did, so that his right hand was free to sit snugly on the butt of the SIG-Sauer.

But there hadn't seemed any direct threat.

As far as this Baron Weyman was concerned, Ryan couldn't have cared less. Any baron in Deathlands was fair game. That was up at the head of the list of unwritten rules.

Tough barons held their villes.

Weak barons lost everything.

If this gang of brushwood heroes wanted to chance their arms, Ryan wouldn't bother to take sides—though his emotions lay with the poor, not with the powerful.

"Jak wants to know what's happened to the man called Straub." Krysty whispered, passing on the message from the albino teenager. "One we heard about when we arrived and everyone seemed so interested in me and Jak."

"Ask Schickel."

"Right. I will." Krysty raised her voice above the hubbub of conversation. "I heard the name of someone called Straub in this camp. Where is he?"

It was as though she'd uttered some dreadful blasphemy in an old predark cathedral.

Everyone around the tables stopped eating, spoons and forks frozen halfway to gaping mouths. All eyes turned to look at the redhead.

A young woman next to Schickel answered Krysty. "Straub comes and goes when he wants, outie. He's not one of us. Not with us, so to speak."

"But not against us, Madge," Schickel said. "Straub's not against us, is he?"

"Oh, no. No, he's triple-not against us. Then again, Schickel, you can't sort of say he's with us."

"Well, you know how it is. Straub comes and goes when he wants."

"I said that."

Schickel nodded. "Know you did, Madge, know you did. I was agreeing with you."

He turned to Krysty. "Straub's his own man. Trades in a special way. I reckon that you and the white-headed boy, Jak, will interest him a lot."

"Why? Why me and Jak in particular?"

"He can tell you that for himself. Likes to speak his own words, does Straub."

"Look forward to hear him," Krysty said tersely, tearing at a sinewy hunk of roasted deer. "Hope he isn't going to keep us waiting too long."

"The waiting is over, lady. I'm Straub and I'm here."

Chapter Sixteen

The voice was soft and gentle, with a strange caressing quality to it.

It reminded Krysty of her mother trying to persuade her to do something she wasn't keen to do.

It reminded Ryan of a high-class gaudy slut he'd once known near Aurora in the Carolinas. She'd been the mistress of an elderly baron and wanted some tender young meat to carve, and picked on the dark-haired, brown-eyed youth with the scarred face and the missing eye. She'd had a voice that could've charmed birds down out of the tallest trees in the forest.

Dean remembered his mother Sharona's voice during the rare times that they weren't running and hiding. There'd been a small vacation cottage from predark, amazingly well preserved, in the Black Hills. The local Lakota had been friendly to the woman and her little boy. And at night, by the side of the crackling fire, Rona would tell her child tales of heroes and villains, while he gnawed on a crust smeared with wild honey.

Straub's voice didn't remind Abe of anything in particular, though he found himself turning around with a sudden and unanticipated smile on his face.

Trader remembered a golden girl in a cornfield on a golden Kansas afternoon when he was young and supple.

Mildred also found herself smiling at the friendly voice. Her father had a younger brother, Josh Wyeth, who'd been a Baptist minister in Alabama. He used to sit the skinny little girl with the ribboned plaits—who he called Millie—on his knee and tell her stories of the Bible.

Jak heard the voice of Straub and, for some wholly unaccountable reason, thought of Mama Jeanne, the wise voodoo woman in the bayous, and her tale of the gator that changed himself into a smooth-talking man to try to charm little children down to the muddy deeps, among the gnarled roots of the ancient mangroves. There he would change back to a reptile again and devour them.

J.B. listened to the smooth, gentle voice, and he had a vision of an old breed gunsmith he'd once met, close to Norleans, a tiny, halt figure in a cane-backed wheelchair, his spine twisted sideways from a birthing accident. His eyes were as bright as chips of Sierra ice, and his delicate hands could turn a rusted, moldering relic into a fine piece of crafted weaponry. He had talked while he worked, and young John Dix had sat at his bench, sometimes handing him a chisel or an auger. But most of the time he would just sit and listen.

Doc had turned around at Straub's voice, blinking his rheumy old eyes.

Why did it remind him of Las Cruces, New Mexico?

There had been a pueblo, forty miles or so north, and a kiva. Doc had been made welcome, and the shaman had taken him through a healing way that had eased all the tension and all the worries from his mind and body.

The voice of Straub reminded him of that ceremony.

But there was something different about it.

Dark steps led down into the circular kiva, and the smell of the smoke and the voice of the elderly Navaho calmed him. But now it seemed as if the man wore a shape-changer mask that hid his face and altered his words, rendering evil for good.

Doc blinked again, puzzled.

Straub walked into the circle of light from the nearest of the fires, bowing slightly to the visitors.

He was slimly built, a little over six feet, around fifty, with a shaved head that glistened and reflected the orange flames. There was a large opal in his right ear, and a gold tooth glittered at the front of his mouth as he spoke.

Ryan noticed that the man had unusual eyes. They were so dark a brown they seemed to be almost black, with tiny flecks of silver whirling in them.

Straub wore a black shirt and black jeans with silver rivets. A silver snake was embroidered around his black Western boots, and a necklace of raw turquoise hung around his neck. He didn't appear to be armed.

He walked slowly around the main table, pausing to shake hands with each of the outlanders, muttering their names as if to fix them in his memory.

His clasp was surprisingly strong, his eyes staring intently into Ryan's face. "Good to have such a large and well-armed party along with us," he said.

For an odd moment, Ryan felt slightly sick. The food in his mouth tasted of bitter ashes, and he nearly spit it out in the trampled dirt beneath the table.

Then Straub laughed quietly, and it felt like a spell had been broken.

Krysty was next along.

"Ah, the woman with the most wonderful hair of fire in all Deathlands. It is truly an honor to meet with you." He stooped and kissed her hand.

He paused and paid particular attention to Jak.

"A pure albino. Forgive my using the word, won't you, young man?"

"Why not? What I am."

Straub touched the great mane of stark white hair, running his fingers through it and holding the silken strands so that they caught the reflected light from the fire.

He breathed out in a languorous sigh. "Magical. Truly magical. So fine and so long."

"I bet you say that to all the boys," said Mildred, next around the table.

Straub crouched and looked into her eyes. "You know about medicine," he said in an oddly accusatory manner. "Now, how can that be? I see knowledge that..." He straightened, his brow furrowed. "That I don't understand."

Mildred saw sudden danger from this strange man, and she quickly changed the subject. "But you don't think very much of my hair?"

"I like the beading, Mildred Wyeth. But the hair itself is, forgive me, common."

"Oh, I forgive you. 'Course I do."

"Whereas both Krysty and Jak have absolutely wonderful hair. Among the most rare I have seen. And I do know what I'm talking about."

"You don't spend all your time with these people?" Trader asked.

Straub looked at him. He ignored the question and asked one of his own. "The suffering has become less over the last two or three years, hasn't it?"

"That comes under the roof of my fucking business, not yours," Trader retorted.

"You a seer?" Dean asked. "You can see things about people? Can you?"

"Sometimes, young man. Both Mildred and the venerable Doc have shades to their auras like none I've known. And Krysty also." He shook his head. "But time is wasting and the food is getting cold."

Ryan felt as though a load had been removed from his shoulders. There had been the bizarre sensation of countless ghostly fingers probing inside his skull, as though they were searching through a cobwebbed attic in an ancient mansion for something valuable long hidden.

Straub went and sat at the head of the table, beside Schickel, the two men immediately becoming deeply involved in conversation.

Krysty leaned toward Ryan, her mouth almost touching his ear. "One to watch, lover," she whispered.

"Yeah. Felt like he was looking inside me."

"He was. Dean was right. Man's a seer. And I think he was also trying us all out as subjects for hypnotism."

"Hypnotism! Never!"

Ryan hadn't realized that he'd raised his voice until he looked up from his plate to see those dark silvery eyes staring intently at him, the pale lips breaking into a smile.

He lowered his tone. "I know there's something double weird about Straub."

"You felt it, lover. I did. We all must've done. It's dangerous not to accept the threat. That way he might be able to gain control over one or more of our minds."

Ryan helped himself to a pair of ribs from the nearest dish. "All right," he said softly. "I *did* feel something happening. You reckon he has that power?"

Krysty nodded, still half turning, her hand over her mouth to conceal what she was saying. "I know it. Straub's one of the most lethal men I ever met."

But there was no more threat. The reverse was true, with everyone showing friendliness to the strangers.

The food, despite the poor cooking, put down a layer between backbone and belly, and the nine companions did justice to the meal.

Three of the women stood during the supper and sang together, unaccompanied. It was a song that none of the nine outlanders had heard before, about a sister wishing to visit a ville called Hammond and what happened to her there. The voices blended perfectly, striking pure, crystal harmonies.

When it was over they all applauded.

"A little something I wrote myself," Straub said, bowing. "Long ago."

Mildred leaned over to J.B. "I don't know, John," she breathed. "Thought at first that I never heard it, but I'm sure now there was something a tad familiar about it. Bet you a peanut to a candy bar that creepy bastard never wrote it."

Straub was looking at her, and Mildred felt herself flushing. Almost as if he could hear her words. Or read them out of the center of her mind.

Schickel banged on the table with the hilt of his hunting knife. "Friends, friends. Straub here has been telling me the results of your successful hunting. Some of which has delighted us all tonight."

Ryan leaned back on the bench, feeling the chill of dusk on his skin, and gazed up into the sable sky. The evening star had been glowing brightly for some time, now accompanied by the first pinpricks of light from countless other stars.

The makeshift camp was like hundreds of others he'd seen over the years. He knew that in the predark days the people who chose to live this way had been called travelers. It was a term that was still used, but now the word had a darker connotation.

Camps like this were often used as hideouts by wolf's-heads, men and women who lived outside the law, often running with a blood price on their heads.

It had been no surprise to learn that Schickel and his people were planning to usurp power from Baron Weyman. It was a common enough tale, told around a thousand campfires.

"The baron's weak."

"His ville's vulnerable to a few brave men."

"We can sit where he sits. Rule where he rules. Become powerful as he was powerful."

The number of times that Ryan had heard of gangs of brushwood people succeeding in toppling a baron in the past twenty years could be counted on the fingers of both hands.

But it did happened.

Could happen.

It depended on what kind of man Weyman was and how he'd organized his sec force. Trader had a saying about a baron being as good as his sec boss, and it was true.

Ryan recalled the infamous ville of Mocsin, the baron, Jordan Teague, who'd once held Doc Tanner prisoner, and his notorious sec boss, Cort Strasser.

There was something about the man Straub that reminded Ryan of Cort Strasser, a chilling coldness and more than a hint of a bitterly ruthless streak, lying buried in a shallow grave beneath the quiet self-possessed exterior.

Schickel had been talking about the deer that had been caught and killed, within the bounds of the domain of Baron Weyman. "'Baron Half-a-man' is what I call him."

The words were greeted by general laughter and applause.

"And our good comrade Straub. He has also done a little more work toward our big plan. We'll talk more about that tomorrow. Meeting of all fighting men an hour after first food."

It was obvious that the evening was breaking up. Ryan welcomed the chance to get an early night in their own tent and stood. "Thanks for your hospitality," he said.

Schickel looked surprised, leaning down as Straub tugged at his sleeve. He listened to a few hasty, whispered words, then straightened again.

"Not quite yet, Ryan Cawdor."

"No?"

Schickel shook his head. "We would like a few more minutes of your time. Just Straub and myself. Just you, and perhaps one of your friends."

It was a barely veiled command.

There were times when Ryan would have felt it necessary to make a point by ignoring the "request" and doing the opposite. But there seemed no danger here in the camp, so he was content to go along with what Schickel wanted—though it seemed likely that it was rather more what Straub wanted.

"Sure. J.B., hang around. Rest of you go to the tents. Be careful."

Krysty squeezed his arm as she stood and eased herself past him, whispering in his ear, "Don't turn your back on Straub, lover. Not for a second."

The shaved head was tilted toward Krysty as she walked out of the circle of firelight, Jak close behind her, the two heads of miraculous hair in stark contrast, the fire ruby and the moonstone.

"Wonderful." Straub sighed, his gold tooth gleaming in the dark cavern of his smiling mouth.

"What?" the Armorer asked.

"The hair, my friend. The hair."

"Just what's your interest in hair?" Ryan asked. "Keeps coming up."

Straub's long pale fingers—of what Trader might well have called "strangler's hands"—were toying with the chunky necklace of turquoise.

"I have many 'interests,' outlander Cawdor. I travel here and there and do not stay overlong in any place. That is my way. But there are things I do to keep myself in eating jack. Oh, so many different things do I do."

"Yeah?" Ryan waited for the answer to his question.

"I trade in hair," Straub said eventually, after a long, overlong pause.

"Human hair?" J.B. probed.

"Ace on the line, Dix. The hair of humans."

"What do you do with it?"

Straub smiled and stared at Ryan, who found himself consciously avoiding the dark silver eyes. "It is one of the immutable truths in this blighted world of Deathlands, outlander Cawdor, that there is always a market for everything."

"Sure. That's what our friend, Trader, always says. All you need to do is bring buyer and seller together. The result is happiness and mutual profit."

Straub laughed out loud, nudging Schickel in the ribs. "I *like* these outlanders and their sayings."

"And their blasters," the chief muttered, rubbing the spot where Straub had poked him. "Don't forget you also like their blasters!"

"You got another name, Straub?" J.B. asked curiously.

"No. I came grinning, with a fine full set of sharp teeth, from my mother's womb, damn the foul-living slut! Called Straub. No first name. Or should that be no second name? Who knows? What's first is last and sometimes the last shall be first. So it says in the Good Book."

"Who do you sell all of this hair to, Straub?" Ryan was insistent, sensing that the man's interest in Krysty and Jak could mean menace.

"Not all that much hair. I sell only the finest and rarest to the old wives of rich barons who have it spun into wigs that chase away the years for them. It is costly." He sighed, rubbing his hands together like a preacher bemoaning a poor collection. "But these people can well afford the cost."

"There is a market for hair? Then who sells it to you, Straub?" This time it was J.B. who was unable to hide his disbelief and revulsion.

"The poor, of course. Oh, don't misunderstand. I pay a fair price to them. But I only want, as I said, the best. Most poor folk have dull, lifeless *ordinary* hair."

"And that's why you're fascinated with Krysty's and Jak's hair?" Ryan laid both hands flat on the table, exercising careful control. "Just what do you want with them? You want to buy their hair?"

Straub licked his lips, showing the first real emotion that Ryan had detected. "I would pay any price for their tresses. I am jack-wealthy, and I know that I could obtain anything I wanted for a wig of fire or a wig of snow."

Ryan stood up from the table, followed instantly by J.B. "Waste of both our times. There's no way this would ever happen. Never."

"Never say 'never,' outlander Cawdor," Straub said, remaining seated.

"You try to take hair from anyone, and you'll find yourself knee-deep in your own blood."

Now Schickel was also on his feet, pointing angrily at the two outlanders. "You threaten me, here in my own camp, with three dozen armed men just a shout away?" He was hissing the words, like an enraged cottonmouth.

Ryan shook his head, fighting for his own self-control, feeling the crimson mist clouding his vision and his mind. He struggled against it, knowing that anger was weakness.

"No, Schickel. The threat comes from you. From Straub."

"What threat?" The pale hands spread, the picture of injured innocence. "I said that I would pay a fair price in jack or trade if I could purchase the hair of two of your company. You have made it clear this can't happen. How can there be any threat from us, Cawdor?"

J.B. was about to speak when Ryan placed a hand on his forearm, quieting him.

"No," he said, almost to himself. "No, this is pointless. Nobody wants blood." He looked across the table at Schickel. "We are grateful for your hospitality and the food and the beds for the night."

"All right." The war chief made no attempt to brighten his surly scowl. "All right."

Straub finally got to his feet, brushing some imaginary specks of dust from his black shirt. "One more small thing."

"What?"

"Baron Weyman. Schickel here's told you about our plans to take over the ville."

"Yeah, he told us."

"You've eaten our food and taken our hospitality. In return we'd like you to help us. You're well armed, and it's kind of obvious you all know how to use your blasters. Use them for us, and you'll not be sorry."

"Meaning we'll be sorry if we don't help?" J.B. asked, easing the sling on the big Smith & Wesson scattergun across his shoulders.

"For us or against us?" Schickle queried. "No road runs down the middle."

Ryan glanced at J.B., but it was impossible to judge the Armorer's reaction. His eyes were invisible behind the dark lenses of his spectacles.

"Well?" Straub prompted, tapping one finger gently on the scarred wood of the table. "Our plans are not quite ready for us to move against Weyman. But it won't be long."

"You got to be with us," Schickel said, now so angry that a thread of spittle sprayed from his open mouth. "Now you know what we intend."

Straub turned and looked at him, staring for a long time, until the purple faded from the chief's temples and cheeks. "That's better, friend. Rage makes enemies of friends, doesn't it? And none of us want that."

"They could go tell the baron," Schickel mumbled, but his words seemed to have been dragged from a long way off, barely audible to the outlanders.

"They won't do that, will you, Cawdor?" Ryan didn't answer. "Because they're honorable men, Schickel. I understand that, even if you don't." Straub lifted his eyes toward the two outlanders. "Sit, Schickel," he said, without looking around.

The war chief sat heavily, like a dumped sack of grain. He looked to be in a stupor, and Ryan recalled Krysty's suspicion that Straub might be some kind of hypnotist.

"We're going to bed now," he said, turning away, followed by J.B.

Straub's voice followed them into the darkness. "Sleep well and safe. You have my word of honor that not a hair of your heads will be harmed."

When they were a safe distance away, J.B. spit in the dirt. "Honor," he said. "Knows where he can put his honor. Where the sun don't shine."

Chapter Seventeen

Mildred and Krysty were already under the piles of fur and rags that passed for blankets. Neither had got undressed at all.

"The others sleeping clothed?" Ryan asked as soon as he and J.B. were safely inside the tent.

Krysty nodded. There was a small tallow lamp guttering in a holder, suspended from the low roof, giving only a dim yellow light. "Yes. Jak insisted. Doc wanted to at least pull off his boots, but Jak said we might need to get out fast."

"Straub gave us his word of honor that nobody would harm us during the night," J.B. said.

"He tell you why he's so interested in me and Jak?"

"He's a trader in human hair," Ryan replied. "Sells it to rich bitches for fancy wigs. He said he'd pay high jack for your hair and for Jak's."

"Smooth, bald shit," Mildred said. "Son of a bastard probably sold his own hair."

Krysty didn't smile. "I tell you, friends, that there's something specially wrong about Straub. I can't read him at all. We'd do well to leave now."

The Armorer was sitting on the makeshift bed beside Mildred. "They're scared of our blasters, Krysty. I don't think they'd dare try anything."

"The two women who showed us to these tents and pointed out the water and relief facilities—both of which are the stream about fifty yards east—were telling us about this baron, Weyman." Mildred was unselfconsciously holding hands with J.B. "Told us that he's a swift and evil man. That it would be better if he was to be overthrown."

"Well, they would say that, wouldn't they?" Ryan said. "Of course, they could be telling the truth. Could be we'd do well to support them and pick up some free jack for ourselves. Yeah, could be."

"Then again, lover," Krysty said with a smile, "these mutie pigs might fly."

"We'll move on after dawn tomorrow. Freeload first food off them." Ryan yawned. "Fireblast! Listen to that drum. Hope that doesn't keep up all night."

The sound was steady and regular, coming from somewhere on the far side of the camp, almost like the muffled beating of a huge heart. They all listened for a few moments, but the drumming didn't seem to be getting any louder.

"How about putting a guard on?" J.B. suggested. "Might be safer."

Ryan yawned again. "I don't know. Enough of us here. Enough blasters."

"I think you're wrong." Krysty slapped him on the arm. "Wake up, Ryan. You're dropping off to sleep."

"Mildred's already gone," said J.B., also starting to yawn. "Feel more tired than I'd have thought. Was going to check the Uzi and the scattergun but, but I guess I'll just leave them this once."

The drumming was echoing around the forest clearing, seeming to come from all sides at once. Krysty crawled across the trampled dirt floor and stuck her head out of the flap, seeing no sign of life. It looked like everyone in the settlement had packed it in and gone to bed early. It had become much colder, and she could see her breath misting the darkness in front of her.

The rhythmic beat was a little softer and a little slower.

Krysty found herself yawning.

The smoke from the campfires was drifting around, carried on a light, eddying breeze. The woman sniffed at it, tasting piñon. There was also something different, a sharp and sweet scent of herbs. It reminded her of the incense that they'd burned in an ornate golden container at a Catholic church she'd once visited when she was a little girl.

She yawned again, blinking her eyes, feeling them growing heavy.

From the tent next door, Krysty caught the sonorous sound of Doc snoring. He'd been complaining that he had a badly blocked nose and hadn't really been able to savor much of the venison at supper. The old man had insisted that Trader snored far worse than he did and had even gone to the extreme lengths of shoving bits of shredded rag into his ears to try to sleep better and cut out the noise.

"Doc's well away," she said, pulling the flap across the front of their tent.

But nobody answered her.

All three of them were fast asleep.

Krysty lay down beside Ryan, feeling his body move a little as she eased herself close to him for comfort.

The last thing she saw as she drifted into the warm, waiting blackness was the strange dark-and-silver eyes of the man who called himself Straub.

AS HE GOT OLDER, Doc had become increasingly aware of niggling problems stemming from what his mother would have called "the waterworks."

When he took a leak it no longer gushed out in a proud, forceful stream. Nowadays it tended to be more of a forked dribble, and he would find himself standing there, behind a tree, for what seemed like hours on end, waiting to finish.

The other aspect of the problem came to Doc in the still of the night.

In his youth it generally happened that he was able to go all the way through the night without needing to take a single piss. Now it wasn't that unusual for him to have to get up three or even four times.

He opened his eyes, rubbing at them, aware of the now familiar pressure on his bladder.

"By the Three Kennedys!" he muttered softly. "Is there no respite from this?"

For a few beats of the heart he lay still, wondering whether the gods might be kind to him and allow him to slip back into sleep.

But it was a waste of time.

His body wouldn't be denied.

Sighing, Doc kicked off the sheepskin robe that had been keeping him warm, taking great care not to disturb the others. Even though he knew from previous experience that it was almost impossible to stir a limb without waking Jak, probably jerking Trader from sleep, as well.

But this time he was lucky.

He sniffed, aware that his cold had eased, which was one small blessing to be grateful for. His knees creaked as he stood, stooping under the ridge of the tent. The night seemed oddly silent, until Doc remembered that he'd stuffed some small pieces of cotton rag into his ears to shut out the endless rasping of Trader's snoring.

He took them out and placed them carefully in a pocket of his ancient frock coat.

"What?" he whispered.

There was the sound of a drum, coming from somewhere within the camp, very soft, its rhythm like a much-slowed heart.

Doc opened the flap of his tent and peered out. He saw a quarter moon, riding high behind slivers of thin cloud, but there was no sign of life.

There was a ghostly frost dusting the ruts and furrows of the track through the camp. Doc remembered something about a stream a little way to the east, and he picked his way in that direction, guided by the faint sound of tumbling water, a sound that began to work on his "problem," making it more urgent.

The banks of the narrow river were steep in places, but the trail led to a shallow ford. Doc stood at its edge and unbuttoned, taking the habitual precaution of looking all around him to make sure he wasn't being observed.

A large owl sat on the low branch of the nearest redwood, staring intently at Doc, who discreetly turned his back on the bird.

When he finally finished, Doc was vaguely aware that the drumming had been getting even slower, each muffled beat now seven or eight seconds apart.

He buttoned up his breeches and started to pick his careful way back toward the tent. A sheet of thin ice glazed over some of the puddles, and Doc stopped for a moment, just within the fringe of trees, to work out the best route across the frozen mud.

The tent where Ryan was sleeping with Krysty, J.B. and Mildred was a little closer to him, barely twenty yards off, his own tent just beyond it.

Standing quite still in his black clothes, Doc was almost invisible.

The slowly beating drum was closer and louder, as though it were being carried through the sleeping camp.

"Devilish thoughtless," he whispered to himself. "Wake everyone up with their noise."

He put his head to one side, thinking about what he'd just said, sniffing at the air and catching the faint scent of burning herbs, something he hadn't really noticed before on account of his cold.

"Something is afoot, Watson," he said. "Think of the strange affair of the light-sleeping albino and what happened when the drum was pounding near him. But Holmes, nothing happened. The lad did not wake. Precisely, my dear Watson. Jak has not awakened. Nor did he stir as I blundered out of the tent. Now, why can that be?" Doc crouched behind a young aspen. "But soft, who comes hither?"

A dozen or more men approached him from the center of the camp. They were moving quietly, and Doc could make out the glint of moonlight off edged steel. One of them carried the drum at his waist, beating on it with a padded hammer.

At the front of the group were Schickel and Straub, the latter easily identifiable by his shaved head.

Doc drew his Le Mat and eased back on the hammer, cocking it over the .65-caliber shotgun round. He held the revolver low, so that the silvery wash of light wouldn't catch on the blaster's gold decoration.

Straub held up his right fist and the drummer stopped. The light was very poor, and Doc strained to see just what it was that the bald man held in his uplifted hand. It was either a short-hafted scythe or a long pair of shearing scissors.

"Doesn't much matter which," Doc breathed, talking to himself to steady his nerves and boost his courage.

For several seconds the menacing gang of brushwood men stood still and silent. Doc watched the tableau, his brain working overtime, making connections: the scent of strange herbs; the rhythmic beating of the drum; the deep sleep of his friends; friends whose reflexes would normally stand comparison with a mountain cougar.

"Mesmerism," he whispered. "Straub has laid some deep hypnotic dream upon them all."

One of the men with Straub and Schickel had gently pulled back the flaps of both tents, peering cautiously in with a hooded lantern, returning and giving a thumbs-up sign.

"For earth and water and air," Straub said, again lifting what Doc could now see was a pair of long scissors.

Why earth and water and air? Doc wondered. It was probably some sort of mock-mystical incantation.

"Ready?" Straub said to the others, moving a little to one side.

Doc bit his lip. Now he didn't have a clear shot at the leader of the group, who was hidden behind several of the other men. In that case, Schickel would have to do, as the putative head of the ragged community.

That decided "who."

And it was clear that "when" was now.

"Now," Doc said, steadying his right wrist with his left hand, looking straight down the gold-chased barrel.

His finger tightened on the trigger.

RYAN HAD BEEN in an uneasy slumber, tossing and turning, aware of physical discomfort, yet not quite able to drag himself clear of the trap of sleep to do anything about it. It was as though he lay beneath a log jam that had crushed his brain, making it impossible for him to act at all.

All of his instincts were yelping at him, trying to warn him that something was grievously wrong. But it was as if his mind were shrouded in several layers of clinging plastic film.

The boom of thunder ripped away that muffling veil and jerked him fully awake, his hand grabbing automatically for the butt of his SIG-Sauer, aware now of screams and shouts from just outside the thin fabric of their tent, aware of J.B., Krysty and Mildred also suddenly coming awake around him.

"Le Mat," the Armorer said, as terse as ever.

THE SHORT UNDERBARREL of the Le Mat carried the 18-gauge scattergun charge. It was hopelessly inaccurate at any range much above twenty paces, where the shot would star out so far that it was only likely to cause relatively minor flesh wounds. But, as a light cavalry handgun, it wasn't likely to be used at anything other than point-blank range.

Schickel was standing about sixteen yards from the dark shadows where Doc was crouched. His face was half-turned away, toward the entrance to the nearer tent, where he was about to order his men to take the helpless outlanders prisoner. Or chill them. It didn't much matter which. Just as long as it gave Straub the chance he needed to get his lusting fingers on the two superbly unique heads of hair sleeping within.

As Straub had rightly said, "If the fucks aren't with us, then that has to mean that they're against us. Nobody argue with that?"

Nobody had argued.

Schickel's mouth was open when, out of the corner of his eye, he caught the tiny red flash of fire from among the bushes to his left.

Before his mind had even begun to attempt the problem of what could have caused the crimson spark, Schickel was hit in the face with unimaginable power.

The pellets had spread out sufficiently to strike the war chief between throat and forehead. His left ear vanished, as did his left eye, pulped by the lead. His left cheek opened up under the impact, and his teeth in both upper and lower jaw were shattered, the jagged splinters of bone driven through by the slugs to rip apart the right cheek, bursting it outward like an exploding melon.

Doc couldn't resist a whoop of delight before concentrating on the fiddling task of shifting the hammer of the massive Le Mat so that it would strike on nine rounds of .44-caliber ammunition.

The attackers were thrown into total confusion by the murderous attack from the blackness. Schickel was down, dying, felled like a stricken oak tree, before they even heard the thunderous boom from the blaster. None of them saw the muzzle-flash, but the billowing cloud of powder smoke among the trees was impossible to miss.

As well as being soaked in arterial blood and peppered with shards of bone, three or four of the men had also been hit by stray pellets from the 18-gauge, one of which had ripped through the big drum.

Schickel was still rolling in the dirt, the fountain of blood already slowed to a trickle as the heart ceased pumping, when panic started.

Straub had reacted quickest among the milling, yelling crowd, turning toward where Doc was crouching, gesturing with the shears. "In there. One of them has escaped us. Take him before the others awaken!"

Ryan heard the words with an unnatural clarity, as if each syllable had been hewn from a mountain of glass.

The moon was strong enough to penetrate the thin fabric of the tent, showing him the silhouettes of a number of people moving around outside. In that first waking moment he had no way of knowing whether they were friend or foe, though all of his combat instincts told him they were hostile.

He fired three quick rounds, aiming high, the bullets ripping up into the night sky, the noise of the shots deafeningly loud inside the tent.

"Outside!" he shouted, hoping that the rest of the group, in the other tent, were all awake and alert. A small part of his mind wondered what Doc was doing out in the trees, firing the Le Mat and causing chaos.

As he dived out, Ryan was immediately aware that there was some serious shit going down.

There was a dozen or more men, most of them with either knives or blasters drawn. Straub stared straight at him, with what looked like a big pair of scissors glittering in his right hand, an automatic pistol in his left. And there was a dying man, half his head blown away, thrashing bloodily in the dirt like a gaffed salmon. There was no sign at all of Doc, whose Le Mat had to have done the chilling.

It was immediately obvious that Ryan didn't have to worry about whether he hit friends or enemies out there.

There were only enemies.

Chapter Eighteen

The greatest threat to Ryan and his companions came from their own blasters.

Just as Ryan came out from his tent, Jak slithered from the other shelter. Within less than five seconds they were all out in the open night, with blasters ready.

The planned attack on them had turned into a hopeless bloody shambles. The shocking death of Schickel had thrown everyone into utter confusion, wondering where the next death would strike. Despite all of Straub's efforts to regain discipline, nobody wanted to stay around.

Ryan put down two more of the brushwood men, picking kill shots in the good light of the sailing moon. Jak's excellent night vision came to his aid, enabling him to take out another two with the booming .357 Magnum.

In those few moments, the raiders broke and ran.

Seeing that the field was theirs, Ryan shouted for everyone to calm down and stop firing.

"Get your stuff and we'll move out," he yelled.

Doc emerged from the undergrowth, still muttering under his breath, struggling with the Le Mat. "I fear that I was of scant use after my first preemptive strike," he said. "Now I'm ready to wreak some more bloody and savage vengeance and the rogues are fled."

"Should go after them and spill some more blood," Trader said, looking longingly toward the main body of the camp, where the fleeing men had vanished. "Could take out the whole lot of the bastards."

"Five dead's enough price." J.B. took off his glasses and polished them on his sleeve. "Agree with Ryan. This is the time to move out."

Krysty stood with one arm around Dean's shoulders. The boy kept looking from side to side, barely awake, visibly frightened.

"What happened, lover?" she asked.

"Don't know." Ryan shook his head. "Some sort of drug in the food. Something like that, I guess."

"Then how come Doc escaped?" Mildred asked. "He ate what all of us did."

"Ah, I believe that I have the solution to that enigma," Doc said, smiling broadly.

"Not now, Doc." Ryan was watching the camp for any sign of life, particularly for a sight of Straub's bald head. But the stillness was absolute. It was likely that they might regain their mislaid courage and stage a counterattack at any moment, and next time they might be more careful and successful.

It took only a few moments for everyone to retrieve their scant belongings from the two tents, those who needed to reload their blasters taking the opportunity.

"Ready?" Ryan looked around the circle of faces. "Then let's move it."

THERE WAS NO ATTEMPT at pursuit from the raggedy camp. Not a dog barked and not a shot was fired.

The moon continued its gentle progress across the star-scattered sky, and the temperature dropped further as dawn came closer.

The nine friends followed a trail toward the east. There had been a brief argument about whether they should return to the sea again and make another jump from the redoubt, but only Abe was strongly in favor of that plan.

Trader spoke out against the idea. "I reckon we should seek out this baron. What's his name?"

"Weyman," Jak said.

"Right. Find him and tell him that the brushwood people are planning to try and topple him."

"Should we tell him about the scabbies, as well, Dad?" Dean asked.

"Figure if he's been in charge of a ville in this region, he must know about the muties. But the threat from Straub's something else. Something seriously dangerous about that man. Still, we can play that one as it lays. If we can find his ville." Ryan looked around to Doc. "While we've stopped for a breath, you might tell us what you figure was happening back there. How did Straub trick us?"

"John Barrymore?"

"What, Doc?"

"I am having a little difficulty in changing the hammer back so that it strikes on the shotgun round. Could you possibly do it for me?"

"Sure. Give us the Le Mat."

"I am most obliged. Now, my good friend, the Lord of Cawdor, who shall be king hereafter."

"What?" Ryan peered in the moonlight at the old man's grinning face.

"A quote from the Bard of Avon, my friend. You ask me what happened back there?"

"It was the drum, wasn't it?" Krysty said. "Kind of doped us all up."

Doc Tanner nodded. "Partly, in part, *inter tres partes,* like all of Gaul. Oh, my aching head! Stress and pressure always addles my poor pate even more than usual."

"Good convenient excuse," Mildred muttered, but Doc didn't hear her.

"I believe that the villain had also used some sort of sleeping drug in the campfires. The wind blew the scent directly to our tents."

"And the drum?"

"Indeed, Krysty. I believe that it was operated at an almost subconscious level, probing at the alpha rhythm of the brain, synchronizing with the heartbeats and then going slower and slower, bringing a deeper level of darkness to our minds. Most devilishly cunning."

Mildred poked a forefinger at his chest. "So, how come you're up there playing Sir Galahad? Riding in to the rescue of us all? Why wasn't your mind sucked down to a dark level?" She answered her own question. "Maybe because it was already too damned dark inside your skull."

"No. I would love to tell you—" He broke off as J.B. handed back the gold-decorated Le Mat. "My thanks, my dear fellow. Now, where was I?"

"In the tent with everyone else," Mildred snapped.

"I had a cold, which happened to close my nose off from the soporific effects of their herbs. And I had blocked my ears to try to shield myself from the rumbling snores of Trader. So, to cut a long story short, I was strolling among the trees, admiring the beauty of the night—"

"Taking a leak," Mildred interrupted.

"Possibly. Very possibly. You may say that, my dear madam, but you can hardly expect me to comment on it. I returned from taking a...from admiring the beauty of the nocturnal forest, when I witnessed the arrival of friend Straub, Schickel and their choice chums."

"They planning to chill us and take all the blasters?" Trader asked.

"More than that, I do believe. Straub is, as we know, a trader in human hair. He aspired to obtain the scalps of both Miss Wroth and young Master Lauren. He was holding a large pair of shearing scissors as they approached the tents.

"Fucking bastard," Jak said calmly and quietly.

"Kill me for my hair!" Krysty shuddered, hunching her shoulders protectively.

"Shame you didn't get the bald bastard on the last train to the coast, instead of Schickel," Trader commented. "Guess you never thought of that."

"Of course I thought of it, you oafish lout!" Doc was suddenly furious, pointing his sword stick at Trader's chest. "Straub was shielded by other men. Time had fully run out, so I did what was best. I had to warn you poor refugees from Sleeping Beauty's castle, did I not?"

Trader flapped his hand at the ebony cane, knocking it away. "Don't threaten me, you dumb old bastard! Makes a change that you do something almost right. Most of the time I tell you that all I see is Ryan and the others carrying you like a worn-out suit of clothes."

There was a whisper of steel as Doc drew the rapier from its sheath. "By God, Trader, but you try my patience too far! Until you arrived back, with the half-remembered relics of your pomp draped about you like the ragged banners of a forgotten army, we all got on well."

"You going to make me leave?" Trader lifted the Armalite and aimed it squarely at Doc's chest. "Because it looks like one of us is leaving, Doc." His lips were peeled back off his teeth, like the snarl of a hunting wolf.

Ryan stepped between them, without drawing his own blaster. "I reckon that's enough," he said quietly. "Enough from both of you."

Nobody moved.

The only sound in the clearing among the towering redwoods was Trader's harsh breathing.

"Doc saved all our lives back there, Trader. You think what you like, but Doc pulls his weight like everyone else. Like you do. Like I do."

"Hah!" Trader snorted in disbelief.

"And you have no right, Doc, to insult Trader the way you did. For most of my days, he was the most powerful figure in Deathlands. And in my life. Now, we've been through a close call. Come out safe the other side. It's the middle of the night. Things get said now and then. Best unsaid. Put down the Armalite, Trader. Doc, sheathe up that sword."

For a time, neither of the old men moved.

Finally, slowly, Doc took a half pace back, picked up the cane and sheathed the slender blade, nodding to Trader. "I concede that I was less than fair to your reputation."

But the Armalite hadn't moved.

Ryan looked at his former leader. "Put the blaster down, Trader."

"You telling me or asking, Ryan? Best you answer me that right here and now."

"I'm asking you this time around. Next time is when I tell you."

"You'd push this to a killing over a triple-stupe old prick like Doc?"

"I'd push this whoever was concerned. Including you, Trader. Put the rifle down."

Ryan's skin crawled, aware that it could go either way. Doc had backed down, but he wasn't a man like Trader. For Trader to back down was something else.

"I could finish you, Ryan."

"Mebbe."

Trader shook his head vigorously. "No. Not mebbe, Ryan. Right here and now I could put a cluster of 9 mm rounds into your guts."

"You wouldn't live to take the next breath if you did that," Krysty said, her own double-action Smith & Wesson 640 rock steady on Trader's chest.

"She's right." Jak held his own Colt python on Trader.

"Goes for all of us, Trader." J.B.'s face was invisible in the shadow under the fedora's brim, but the threat of the Uzi was all too visible.

"All of you?" Trader turned toward Abe. "Don't see your Magnum speaking out on my side."

The little man shuffled his feet nervously. "Have to say that I go along with what Ryan says. Not that Doc should've said what he did," he added hastily.

"I have already acknowledged that to Trader, Abraham," Doc said solemnly. "I now await his apology in return."

Trader laughed, a sudden snorting, barking laugh. "What the fuck!" He switched the Armalite to his left hand, offering the right to Doc and shaking firmly. "Words don't mean shit after a firefight, Doc. Nothing to worry about. You saved us all and I thank you for that."

Ryan surreptitiously wiped his sweating hands down the thighs of his pants.

"WHAT HAPPENED to their leader, Ditchdown?" J.B. asked. "He kind of disappeared once Straub came on the scene."

Ryan nodded. "I read that he's a sort of senior man. Schickel was really their war chief, and Straub was someone who'd come along and was using them all to his own advantage. That how you see it?"

"Sure. It means that they might still try to go ahead with that plan they had to go after the baron."

"Could be. He say how far off the ville was, J.B.? Was it fifteen miles?"

It was the Armorer's turn to nod. "We've been going around four hours. Dawn can't be far off. Should be within about three miles or so of the ville."

"Yeah. So far so good."

THE FIRST PALLOR of the false dawn was creeping over the land, and the snow on the mountaintops ahead of them was already touched with pink.

They had crossed a couple of old blacktops, the surface of the pavement rippled like taffy from quakes.

The tall trees were behind them, and they were moving through a mixed forest, on a broad trail.

When they heard the pigs.

Chapter Nineteen

The companions were moving in a loose skirmish line, with Jak stalking along at point, his white hair like a glowing beacon for the others to follow.

Ryan and Krysty, with Dean just ahead of them, brought up the rear of the group.

"Lovely morning," the woman said, her hand resting gently on Ryan's arm. She breathed deeply. "Just smell that freshness. Think the air was as good as this back in predark days?"

"Don't know. Supposed to have had all sorts of pollutants and chemicals and lead and stuff that destroyed the atmosphere. As well as the nuke leaks."

She nodded. "I read some old mag once that said the planet would have become sterile and dead within twenty years if skydark and the long winters hadn't come along first and both destroyed and saved."

"Skin cancers increased by fifty percent in the last few years. That breathing sickness in kids was massively worse. What's it called?"

"You mean asthma, lover?"

"Right. They reckon— What's up?"

Jak held his right hand raised, the warning signal for silence.

They gathered around him, everyone with a blaster drawn and ready.

"What?" Ryan whispered.

"Real quiet and listen. Caught it twice."

Everyone stood still.

The dawn chorus of birds was only just beginning. A bright-breasted jay sat on a branch only yards away, head thrown back, noisily greeting the new day. Jak stopped and picked up a fallen pine cone, lobbing it at the bird, missing by inches, sending it fluttering away.

"Can't hear what heard," he explained.

Suddenly they could all hear it, a snuffling, grunting sound, a rutting, scratching sort of a noise.

"Pigs," Trader said. "The mutie pigs those brushwood bastards told us about."

"How far off?" Ryan asked.

J.B. lay down, pressing his ear to the packed earth of the forest floor. "Can't tell," he said. "Moving this way, I think."

"How many?" Dean was looking nervously around him, sizing up the trees to see if any of them looked possible to climb. But most were full-grown pines, with their lower branches only starting thirty or forty feet from the ground.

"Can't tell," the Armorer replied. "But if we can hear them, then there must be a herd. That the right word for pigs? A herd of pigs?"

Doc nodded. "A herd of swine sounds right, does it not? There was a time when I could have rattled off dozens of such collective nouns for the creatures of the

earth and water and sky. A host of sparrows, a pity-
ing of turtledoves, a skulk of foxes, a—''

Ryan tapped him on the arm. ''All right, Doc. I
think we get the idea. Doesn't much matter what
they're called. Just so we know there's a lot of pigs
coming this way, and they could be mutie killers.''

''Run, hide or fight?'' Trader asked.

''If we run, we might run into the middle of more of
them.'' Ryan considered the other two options. ''Fight
and we can certainly chill more or less any number of
them. But we'd spend a lot of ammo doing it.''

''And make a shit-load of noise,'' Abe added.

''Right.'' Ryan nodded. ''And we think we might be
close to the ville of this Baron Weyman. Don't want to
greet his morning with an alarm. Sounds like one of
your fancy names, Doc. An alarm of sec men?''

''Upon my soul, Master Cawdor, but that's a most
excellent jest. Perhaps we can think of other droll and
amusing examples. Let me see—''

''Leave it, Doc,'' Mildred snapped. ''Got more important things to think about. Like becoming a mess
of piggy chowder if we don't get our asses into gear.
That noise is definitely getting louder and closer.''

''Hide,'' Ryan decided. ''Best place is up trees.''

''Not many good ones to climb, Dad. I've been
looking around. There's a big oak over there.'' Dean
pointed toward a large-boled tree about fifty yards to
the left, just visible among the pines.

''Good boy. Anyone got a better idea?''

''Mebbe we could take them out with knives,''
Trader suggested. ''No ammo and no noise.''

"We don't know how many." Ryan shook his head. "If they're really mutie killers, then we could find ourselves deep in big muddy."

They all heard a strange sound, an unearthly shriek that echoed all around them, making it hard to tell the direction.

"Let's climb," Trader said.

AT FIVE FEET FOUR INCHES and stockily built, Mildred had the most difficulty making it into the lower branches of the live oak.

In the end, J.B. dropped to hands and knees so that she could stand on his back, while Jak and Abe, already in the tree, reached down and hauled her up.

"I recall seeing one of the great whales being heaved up to the masthead of a schooner, by a team of merry chantymen," Doc stated. "The image is strangely familiar at this moment."

Panting with the effort, Mildred looked down at him, shaking her head angrily so that the myriad tiny beads rattled softly. "I wouldn't piss on you if you were on fire, Dr. Theophilus Tanner," she grated.

The noise of the pigs was becoming closer.

Only Ryan and Doc were now standing on the ground. "Come on, Doc, up you go."

"After you, dear friend."

"Not that easy a scramble."

The old man smiled condescendingly. "I was scrumping for apples before you were even a gleam in your father's eyes, Ryan, old friend. In fact, I was doing it about one hundred and seventy years before your father impregnated your mother.''

"Well, do it now, Doc.''

Ryan glanced around the tree toward the northeast, where the sound seemed to originate. He realized, to his dismay, that he could now see the dim shapes, moving in the morning shadows, like great gray ghosts, sliding between the pines.

"Very well,'' Doc said, oblivious to the closeness of the danger.

He reached up for an ancient burr on the side of the live oak, grasping it firmly and kicking himself into the air, legs scrabbling for a purchase, failing to find it and dropping, panting, to the ground again.

"Like us to drop a rope for you?'' Mildred called.

The last thing Ryan wanted was to instigate a panic in the old man, but the animals were moving ever nearer, stopping to dig with their hooked tusks among the roots of the trees, seeking mushrooms or grubs.

The ones that Ryan could see looked to be appreciably larger than normal pigs, but distance was deceptive and he couldn't be sure. At least the light breeze was blowing from the north, so that they wouldn't yet have scented the humans.

"Move it, Doc.''

Despite his efforts to stay cool, the old man picked up on the frayed note in Ryan's voice. "Are we about to enjoy some company?'' he asked.

"Looks that way.''

"Perhaps you should climb up yourself, first, my dear fellow. You have a great deal more to lose than I do."

Ryan responded by holstering the SIG-Sauer, cupping his hands together like a stirrup. "Up," he said.

Doc shoved the sword stick into his belt and placed his right foot in Ryan's hands, glancing up to see that Jak and J.B. were hanging on to the lower branches of the big oak tree, waiting to help him.

Dean's voice came from much higher up the tree, from among the luxuriant foliage. "Dad!"

"I know," Ryan replied. "I know. Up you go, Doc, quick as you can."

The old man knew better than to argue when that cold steel tone entered Ryan's voice. He pushed down while Ryan lifted, reaching up for assistance. There was a grunt of effort, then Doc was gone, only the familiar cracked knee boots waving for a few moments.

Ryan risked a last glance around the side of the tree, seeing that the pigs had somehow detected their presence. They were running toward the oak at a fair speed, muzzles low to the earth like hunting dogs. Now that they were near, less than fifty yards away, Ryan could appreciate how enormously big and powerful the mutie animals were.

The nearest was a boar, one tusk broken off short, leaving a jagged point, the other tusk curving wickedly, its tip stained with clotted mud. The creature had to have stood nearly five feet tall at the shoulder, better than ten feet from snout to the tip of its curling tail.

"I'll shoot it," Trader yelled.

"No, don't!" Ryan jumped for the same rounded burr that Doc had tried for unsuccessfully.

Though Doc had an extra inch in height, Ryan had vastly more strength and agility. He reached and held, swinging his legs up over a protruding branch in a single easy motion.

What he hadn't realized was how close the nearest pig was and how fast it was moving. Something caught the heel of his combat boot as he pulled himself safely into the tree, and he was aware of stinking breath and a snorting grunt of rage immediately below him.

"Gaia!" Krysty's emerald eyes were wide with shock. She held out her hand to steady him, helping him to climb a little higher into the tree. "Close, lover."

"Too close."

Suddenly there were pigs everywhere, crowding around the tree, banging into it, jostling one another, their tusks clashing like sabers. Ryan looked about him, seeing that everyone was perched higher up, all of them finding a nook or cranny to hang on to. Everyone stared down at the maelstrom of murderous animal flesh below them.

The whole tree was now vibrating under their weight and pressure.

Ryan peered down, seeing that the monstrous pack leader, with the broken tusk, had struggled to rear itself up onto its hind legs, muzzle questing toward the man. Its slobbering lips were pulled back off the drool-smeared fangs, wheezing in its desire to reach Ryan.

"Fuck off." Trader was just above Ryan, straddling a thick branch, plucking acorns and hurling them at the pigs. "Why not chill them."

"Reason I told you. They'll get tired and move off. They know they can't reach us."

The huge boar seemed to have heard Ryan as it dropped back to its four feet, head turned at an angle, tiny furious eyes glowering at the nine people in the tree.

But the herd of pigs still showed no immediate interest in moving away.

Altogether Ryan counted thirty-eight or -nine of the brutes. It was difficult to be totally accurate because they kept milling around among the trees. There were only a few piglets, the rest of them being mainly young sows and boars, with a scattering of older animals.

The sun was now up, behind the jagged peaks of the Sierras, with the promise of a fine day to come.

"When they goin' to give up, Dad?" Dean asked plaintively from among the leaves.

At the sound, nearly all of the pigs stopped their rooting around and looked up into the tree.

"Soon, Dean. Real soon."

Ryan wished he felt more certain of that.

Chapter Twenty

Another hour had drifted by. The pleasant morning was being ruined by the presence—and the stench—of the mutie pigs. They were still all gathered around the oak tree where Ryan and the other eight friends were clustered. Every time anyone in the branches made any sort of noise, the pigs would stop and stare hungrily upward.

The leader of the herd had started pushing against the scarred trunk of the tree, snorting and snuffling to the others, seeming as though it were trying to organize some of the larger young boars to help him.

Mildred guessed first what the creatures were trying to do. "For the Lord's sake! I never thought that I'd be threatened by ten tons of bacon on the hoof. They're going to try to rock the tree clean out of the ground. Look! Some of them're burrowing away around the roots."

There was the harsh metallic click of Trader readying the Armalite.

Ryan hesitated a moment. "Not yet," he decided.

"You mean to wait until the tree falls down and drops us among those fucking pigs?"

"No. I mean to wait a little longer. Most animals don't have the patience to hang around for too long."

"Most animals don't have nine ready-made meals sitting up a tree just waiting to be eaten."

"I said we'd wait. If there's a real danger of them felling the tree, then we can take them out easily enough. But it'll take a mess of ammo and make too much noise."

For twenty minutes or so, nobody spoke.

Ryan watched the pigs, fascinated by their grim dedication. A number of the younger boars were digging away at the base of the live oak, tunneling into the moist earth and gnawing or snapping through any roots that they encountered.

The old boar was organizing the sows to keep pushing at the trunk, rocking it back and forth, the upper branches and leaves swishing with the jerking movement.

The animals were enormously, freakishly powerful. Their skin was coarse and thick, covered in long bristles, scarred with the wounds from old injuries and dappled with a leprous scaly condition. Hooves were sharp, suited for digging or trampling, and they all had vicious teeth and tusks.

From where he was perched, Ryan could see a little way across the forest, toward the east, where they believed the ville of Baron Weyman lay. He could just make out a thin column of white smoke rising into the morning sky, about two miles off that he guessed might be the cooking fires for first food.

While he stared toward the mountains, Ryan was picking off bits of dry, dead twigs, flicking them down onto the backs of the pigs.

One piece hit the huge boar with the broken tusk on the ear, making it give a roar of rage. It charged the tree square-on with its shoulder, making the whole thing shudder.

There was no warning of the disaster, just a sharp cracking sound from above Ryan and a cry of shock and despair from Abe.

The little gunner rode the snapped branch down, clinging to it as it bounced off other, lower branches, slowing its progress. Jak tried to grab Abe as he plummeted by, but he couldn't quite reach him.

The shriek of dismay from Abe, and the loud noise of the breaking branch, saved his life.

It scattered the pigs, who suspected a trap from the skies, sending them lumbering clumsily in all directions, so that Abe and a chunk of the live oak hit the ground at a place free from any of the animals.

The fall completely knocked all the wind out of the gunner, leaving him sprawled flat on his back, wearing a leafy crown and a long, shallow cut across the forehead that was already seeping dark blood.

Any hesitation was likely to be fatal.

Ryan was fastest out of the tree, swinging down onto the ground, landing with perfect balance, the SIG-Sauer in his hand. Jak was second and Trader a close third, followed a half second later by J.B.

"Now?" Trader asked.

Ryan was watching the herd of pigs. They'd stopped their panicked run at the edge of the clearing, all of them looking back at the bunch of humans, seeming as if they were gathering themselves for a charge.

"I guess as soon as they start running."

"Might be too late."

Ryan glanced quickly upward into the tall tree, attracted by the noise of movement. He saw that both Dean and Doc were readying themselves to pick their way down again, Krysty and Mildred at their heels.

"Stay there! We might need to climb back in a hurry. Just get ready to shoot."

The gigantic boar was scraping at the ground with its hooves, like a bull about to launch itself into a pounding attack. Drool, tinted with blood, hung from his open jaws, his eyes shining like firestones.

"Take him out first," Ryan said quietly, unslinging the Steyr from his shoulder.

He called up into the live oak. "You hear that, Mildred?"

"What?"

"Take out the big one first. Only a brain shot'll do the job on it."

"You got it."

Out of the corner of his eyes, Ryan could see that the woman was standing in the main vee of the oak, between the two large forked branches, steadying herself while she drew a bead with the Czech target pistol.

"Take them out early. Pack of bastards like that'll come fast and hard." Trader had the blaster at his shoulder, squinting along the barrel.

Ryan wasn't about to argue with his old war chief over that one.

There was a tension in the still morning air that was almost visible. It seemed as if the giant boar were stirring up his herd, turning his massive head from side to side, snuffling and raging at them.

Suddenly the animal stood stock-still, little fat-buried eyes turning away from the huddled group of humans, toward the east, as though it were listening to a secret message.

"Horses," Jak said.

Ryan looked at the albino. "How can you hear that above the noise of the trees?"

The teenager looked blankly back at him. "Can hear horses." He shrugged. "That's all."

"Pigs are listening to something," J.B. said, pointing with the Uzi. "Got them worried."

"Dozen or more." Jak had narrowed his red eyes, concentrating on the distant sound. "Coming this way."

. "I can hear horses," Krysty called from the branches above them.

"Jak already heard it," Ryan replied. "Send Dean high up, see if he can make anything."

Then he caught the noise himself, a faint thundering, definitely moving toward them. It was coming from where they believed the ville lay, which could mean they were simply going to exchange one kind of menace for another.

The pigs were ready to run, though the leading boar was reluctant to let their prey go. It took a few hesitant, menacing steps toward the oak tree, and everyone raised their blasters. Then discretion overruled its lust for blood, and it turned ponderously about and trotted off into the deep shadows of the forest, followed by the rest of the herd, vanishing within seconds.

"We could hide in the trees," J.B. suggested, "until we see what's coming."

Trader banged the butt of the Armalite angrily in the dirt. "Come on, John Dix! All those years you rode with me and you learned nothing!"

The Armorer sniffed, pushing back the fedora. "Yeah. Guess that's right. Once we get up there and they spot us, we're dead meat. Nowhere to run."

"Right." The old man patted him on the shoulder. "Leave the women, Doc and the kid up there. They can cover us if we need it." He glanced at Ryan. "Right?"

"Yeah, Trader. Makes sense." Ryan called up to Krysty to pass on the command.

Dean's thin excited voice floated down to them. "Can see dust. Quarter mile or so. Twelve riders. No, fourteen mounted men."

"Coming along this trail?" his father shouted.

"Straight toward us, Dad."

THE HORSEMEN WORE uniforms of dark green, drab and patched. Their animals were a motley mix of elderly mares and geldings, with a couple of rangy mules. The men were armed with nothing more menacing than crossbows, though the leader had a long-barreled musket across his shoulder.

When he saw the five men standing in a loose circle beneath the big live oak, he held up his hand and halted the party. Ryan's keen eye noticed immediately that their discipline was casual to the point of sloppiness.

He held up his own hand to greet the men. "Saved us from some mutie pigs," he called. "Thank you for that."

"Herd with a giant boar? Got a broken tusk?"

"Yeah."

The man pursed his lips. "Then you were lucky, stranger. Not many folks survive a meeting with the General and his posse. Been in these woods for longer than anyone knows. Some of the brushwood folks says he can't be killed. Certainly taken a toll of life in the last years."

"Name's Ryan Cawdor. These are some of my friends."

"Only 'some' of them?" The sec man was quick. He stood in the stirrups and stared around at the trees. "So, where's the rest of them?"

Ryan grinned. "They're close by. Heard there was a ville not far off."

"You heard right."

"Baron Weyman?"

The sharp, foxy face was becoming suspicious. "What you been hearing, outlander?"

"Nothing."

"Which way do you come in?"

"North along the coast."

"Through the yellow hot pools? I can still smell it on you. You see any brushwood people on your way inland?"

"Just the pigs."

The sec man laughed, a harsh, barking sound. "Not much difference between the pigs and the brushwooders. Both of them vicious. Both smell of shit. Looking for food and shelter for a night or two?"

"Could be."

The man stared at them in silence for several long seconds. "Something about you I can't... I never saw a group of outlanders as well-weaponed as you are. Nor a group who looked more like they knew how to use the blasters."

"That against the law?" Trader snapped. "If it is, then you best tell us right here and now."

The man held up a protesting hand. "Whoa back, old-timer. Keep the hammer lifted. I'm not a stupe. I know our bows wouldn't last us a dozen heartbeats against what you're carrying. Though, I could bet one or two of you wouldn't see another sunset if it came down to it."

"You got a name, sec man?" J.B. asked.

"Sure. Rainey. Bill Rainey." He leaned forward in the saddle, hands clasped together. "You sure you haven't seen the brushwood dogs? Man called Ditchdown with a white lightning burn in his hair? Schickel? Bald man by the name of Straub?''

"Told you we hadn't seen anyone," Ryan repeated.

Rainey nodded slowly. "Sure. Reason I ask you so particular is that we heard a whisper here and there, carried on the wind, you might say, that this Straub and Schickel and the rest are planning to try and topple the baron from his ville. We wouldn't much go with that."

"Would they succeed?"

Rainey's face hardened, and he straightened. "There's your business and there's our business, Cawdor. You just crossed over the line between them."

"Sorry. Just curious."

Rainey relaxed a little at the apology. "Sure, but you know what curiosity did to the cat? How many of you are there? And where are they?"

Ryan didn't answer for a moment. He glanced at Trader and J.B., both of whom nodded slightly. He saw that the sec man hadn't missed the exchange.

"Up the tree. There's nine of us in all. Ville able to cater for that many?"

"We can cater for anything and anyone. Baron Weyman always says to welcome outlanders unless we figure they might present a threat to him and the ville."

"Then what?" Trader asked.

Rainey grinned. "You got the look of a man who knows the answer to that question before he asks it." He waved a hand to drive away a cloud of small gnats from near his face. "Time's passing. We have to keep on patrol."

"Looking for the brushwooders?" J.B. asked.

"For trouble. Any size and shape."

One by one, Krysty and the others climbed down from the lower branches of the leafy tree. The appearance of the women attracted the predictable leering interest from the mounted sec men, until Rainey turned and hissed something under his breath that wiped away the smiles and gestures.

But it was Dean who got the most response when he dropped to the ground.

"What are you doing here, Jamie?" Rainey shouted. "Your father'll skin us all if he—" He stopped as the boy spun to face him. "You aren't... Be damned! Now I see the darker hair and the eyes. But there is one hell of a resemblance between that boy and the baron's son, Jamie. You're Cawdor's son?"

Dean nodded, blushing at finding himself the sudden center of attention.

"Not many lads of his age in this part of the country. If Baron Weyman agrees, you could meet Jamie. I know he gets a mite lonely. What's your name?"

"Dean. Dean Cawdor."

Rainey smiled approvingly. "Could be that your son, outlander Cawdor, might be the best ville pass you could want to give you a fine welcome." He slapped his horse on the neck. "Now, I'll ride back and warn them of strangers. Rest of my boys can finish the patrol. And you nine can walk a couple more miles due east, following this trail, and you can't miss the ville. You'll be expected."

He set spurs to his horse and rode off at a fast trot. The sec patrol, without another glance at the outlanders, moved westward in a ragged line.

Ryan looked around at his friends. "So far so good."

Chapter Twenty-One

"Rad count's eased up into the yellow, again," J.B. observed. "Still nothing too much for us to worry about, but it looks like there might have been some hot spots around here in the long winters."

The companions were in sight of the ville, having just breasted a rise in the snake-back trail. They spotted the drifting gray smoke from among the trees, finally seeing the building itself.

"It resembles a Victorian boarding school," Doc stated. "Look at those Gothic chimneys and the proliferation of gables. By the Three Kennedys, but I swear that it's the most elegant ville that I have yet seen."

The house was built from gray stone, weathered over the years, stained with creepers and lichen on the second and third floors. The mullioned windows with leaded lights contributed to the impression of age and style.

"Handsome," Mildred agreed. "If it was privately owned, then he must've been a fat cat."

"Fat cat?" Dean repeated. "What's that mean?"

"Jack rich," she replied.

The boy nodded. "Like a gold rat. I get it."

Trader spit in the leaf mold that lay all around them. "We goin' to visit this baron, or do we stay here and chatter the day away?"

"We go visit the baron," Ryan said.

RYAN CHECKED OUT the defenses of the ville as they trudged wearily toward the main gates. It had been one of his special tasks when he rode with the Trader. Most of the war wags' crews, when entering a strange ville or frontier pesthole, would appear uninterested and would wave and shout to the inhabitants, greeting sec men in the same way, making it appear like they didn't care about the way a place looked.

But Ryan and, sometimes, J.B., would be hidden away, using the ob slits, carefully taking note of every detail of the defenses and the layout of the buildings, reporting to Trader within the hour and giving him a sketch plan that showed the relevant points of strength.

And weakness.

The ville of Baron Weyman was solidly built, looking as though it probably dated from around the latter half of the nineteenth century.

The outer wall was a dozen feet high, granite, tipped with iron points, some of which had corroded and rusted. Threads of razored barbed wire still hung here and there, plaited around the remaining spikes. In its day it had to have been a formidable barrier, but now it wouldn't have stopped a determined ten-year-old.

There was a set of double gates, made from wrought-iron, in a complicated pattern of leaves and vines. Two sec men stood by the gates, each holding a crossbow. Beyond them there was a cobbled courtyard, with the house closing in on three of its sides. The first-floor windows were barred, with ironbound sec shutters. A wide path lead around the side of the building to what Ryan guessed was probably the stable area of the ville and the sec force's living quarters.

"What a fine building," Doc said admiringly. "Such a truly superb setting at the foot of the mountains."

Trader looked at him as though he had serious doubts about the older man's sanity. "What you are looking at, Doc, is a pretty peach with a rotten center that is just sitting here waiting to be plucked."

"You the outlanders that Rainey warned us to expect?" one of the guards called.

"Yeah."

"Go straight on through. Main door to the ville's ahead of you. Rainey's inside someplace. Likely he'll take you to meet Baron Weyman."

They filed through the gates. Ryan turned and looked back along the trail, J.B. stopping at his shoulder.

"Thinking what I'm thinking?" the Armorer asked.

"I'm thinking that the trees and bushes should be cut right back for a good hundred paces. Way they stand now, any stupe mutie could crawl in close enough to rush the gates."

J.B. adjusted his glasses. "Crossbow can be deadly in the right hands. But it's one of the slowest weapons in Deathlands. Can take fifteen or twenty seconds to crank it up and loose a second bolt."

"And in twenty seconds a charge could be through the gates and into the house."

"Right. I've seen a crossbow quarrel go clean through an inch of planed oak. For a man on watch, assuming that there's a serious shortage of decent blasters, give me a good yew longbow every time."

Ryan agreed. "Seen Apache and Oglala have six arrows in the air at once from a longbow."

"You two coming in?" Krysty stood by the heavy front door to the ville.

Bill Rainey had appeared behind her, with a young boy at his side. Ryan immediately saw the passing resemblance between his own son and Baron Weyman's boy. But Dean was stronger built, broader across the shoulders and his hair was longer.

And he carried a Browning Hi-power 9 mm blaster at his hip.

"Come ahead, outlanders," the sec boss called. "Baron's waiting to greet you."

He pointed at Dean. "Come and meet Jamie Weyman, young Cawdor."

Dean took a couple of steps, giving a casual half wave to the other boy, who came directly down the short flight of stairs, hand extended toward him.

"Welcome, Dean Cawdor," Jamie Weyman said in a confident, clear voice. "Welcome to my father's ville."

"Thanks. Yeah, thanks." He hesitantly shook the other boy's hand.

"Think they'll hit it off, lover?" Krysty whispered in Ryan's ear.

"Mebbe."

A LARGE ENTRANCE HALL led toward a wide staircase of stone. The carpet had obviously once been rich and ornate but now looked dusty and threadbare.

The walls were wood-paneled, with rectangular spaces where paintings had probably once hung. There was a notable absence of any kind of decoration—no decent draperies, no china, no furniture of note. Just the barest essentials.

Rainey led the way up the stairs toward a shadowed landing with a number of doors. Ryan followed, with the rest of the group trailing along behind him. Dean and Jamie Weyman brought up the rear. The baron's son was keeping up a flow of bright chatter, while Dean was limiting his replies to monosyllables.

"I heard that you and your companions had a confrontation with the mutated pigs."

"Yeah. We did."

"Was the legendary wild boar, called the General, among them?"

"Mebbe."

"It has a damaged tusk on one side. That enables one to recognize it."

"Yeah, it did."

"What does your father do for his living?"

Ryan half turned, wondering what his son would reply to that one.

"Helps people."

Jamie was intrigued. "Helps them, Dean. That's really most interesting. How does he do that? Is he a teacher of some sort, or perhaps he is a doctor?"

"Mildred's a doctor."

"Ah, I must admit that your father didn't appear to be the sort of a man who would have medical skills. I hope you don't mind my saying that."

"No."

They reached the top of the stairs, and the conversation briefly halted.

Krysty was right at Ryan's shoulder, and she whispered in his ear. "Never heard a more grown-up little man than that Jamie Weyman. He talks better than I do, and he can't be more than eleven years old. Can't see him and Dean really becoming the closest of friends, can you?"

Before Ryan could answer, Rainey was beckoning for them to follow him along the corridor, past shuttered casements, pausing before a closed door.

"Baron's in there," he said. "When you've finished, come on down to the eating room, left at the bottom of the stairs, and I'll get some food rustled up for you."

The sec boss knocked on the door, waiting to hear a muffled voice call for them to enter. Then he turned and strode away along the passage, ruffling his fingers through the hair of the two boys as he did so.

Ryan turned the handle and opened the heavy door.

The room was so dimly lit, with heavy shutters drawn across the windows and only a single oil lamp for illumination, that he thought for a moment that there was nobody there. Then he saw a gray figure, wearing a gray coat, sitting in a deep, gray armchair to one side of an empty fireplace.

"Come in, outlanders. I hear from Bill Rainey, excellent fellow, incidentally, that you were on your way. As far as Bill is concerned, ask him if there's anything you want or need. Food, beds, that sort of thing." The man waved a languid hand. "But do come in where I can see you properly. Oh, is that my son and heir I spy bringing up the rear as usual?"

"Good day, Father. This is my friend, Dean. He's the same age as I am, aren't you, Dean?"

"Yeah."

"I'm delighted to meet you all. You're Ryan Cawdor, aren't you? Fellow who's a little deficient in the optical area?"

"What?"

Doc was at his heels. "Baron means you've only got one eye."

"Oh, right. Yeah. Shall I introduce you to the others?"

"No, no. Not here and not now. There is some sort of poor meal prepared for you. I shall join you there in a short while. Do go on down and enjoy whatever humble repast there is on offer."

He paused. "Jamie, perhaps you would remain with me for a few moments longer?"

"Of course, Father. Can Dean stay, too?"

"I think not. He should go with his friends. You will have plenty of time to see him later."

He waved his hand. "Now, outlanders, off you go to eat."

Like young children being dismissed by their wise and elderly principal, they all filed out, J.B. quietly closing the door behind them.

"That man needs his balls pushed into his throat," Trader said, his face flushed with anger. "Who the fuck does he think he is, treating us like that? If we had the war wags here, we could blow his penny-ante ville into the mountains."

"I didn't think he was that bad," Abe commented.

"Shows what a piss-poor judge you are, Cohn," Trader snarled. "Always were and always will be."

"I'm Abe," the gunner said. "I wish you'd try to get my name right."

Trader turned on him, looking for a moment like he might smash him to the floor of the corridor with the butt of the Armalite. He restrained himself with a visible effort, his voice surprisingly gentle. "I'm trying, for Christ's sake, Abe! You think I'm not trying?"

Ryan cleared his throat. "Break it up, friends. Last thing we want in a strange ville is to get ourselves locked at one another's throats."

They moved toward the head of the stairs. J.B. eased the Smith & Wesson on his shoulder. "Weyman didn't seem that bad. Talks like he's swallowed a word book. But he's kindly to us."

He turned to Trader. "Not many barons in Deathlands greet outlanders as friendly as that, do they?"

"Mebbe and mebbe not. Just that I never liked a man thought himself so clever."

"Right," Dean said loudly, making everyone turn to look at him. "His kid's the same. All smart ways of saying things to put you down and make you feel small."

"What did I tell you, lover?" Krysty whispered.

Ryan didn't answer her. "Let's go eat."

RAINEY WAS WAITING, leaning against the frame of a door. "In here." He gestured with his thumb. "Baron said he was going to come down and join you, didn't he?"

"Yeah," Ryan said. "Mean he won't?"

The sec man rubbed a finger along the side of his narrow hooked nose. "Baron has a funny way of talking. You probably heard that. But he's straight as a crossbow quarrel. Steadfast, loyal and true, that's Baron Weyman." He grinned. "But he sometimes loses track of time. He's got a collection of predark coins up in his rooms. Takes them out and stares at them through a bigger-glass. Hours on end. Anyway, come and sit down, and I'll tell the kitchen staff to get their asses into gear."

THE REFECTORY TABLE WAS a good thirty feet long, carved from a single length of wood, and easily the finest article of furniture that they'd so far seen in the ville.

The dishes were brought out by a gaggle of giggling young women, most of them unable to stop staring at Jak, while the albino teenager completely ignored them.

The food was of much better quality than they'd eaten in the brushwood gypsy camp. The soup, so thick you could almost have sliced into it with a knife and fork, was flavored with delicate herbs and pulses. Salmon in a pastry shell was smoked over oak chips and served with leeks in a cream-and-wine sauce.

"If the main course is going to be pork, then I'll take a rain check on it," Mildred said, getting a laugh from the others.

Rainey leaned forward. "Better to eat those mutie porkers than be eaten by them, Dr. Wyeth."

Jamie had appeared and joined them, explaining that his father would be down shortly. He was sitting next to Dean. "Pigs are one of the most omnivorous of creatures on the planet, you know?" he said.

Dean looked across the long table to his father for help, but Ryan shrugged his shoulders. Doc quickly came to the boy's assistance.

"Do you know the roots of that word, Master Weyman?" he asked, a kindly twinkle in his pale blue eyes.

"You mean the derivation?" The lad looked down at his plate and blushed. "I think it's probably Latin. Is it?"

"*Omnis,* meaning 'all.' *Vorare,* meaning 'to eat.' Our word 'devour' comes from it. *Omnivorus.* The Latin is almost exactly the same word. Means that pigs eat everything."

"Including people," Mildred added.

"We hunt them when we can. But it's dangerous for the horses," Rainey said. "Pigs get in close and rake them along the belly with their tusks. And out fall the guts. Messy death.''

''We would also hunt other prey.''

Rainey stood, as did the boy, seeing Baron Weyman move forward out of the shadows that lurked like spilled night around the flanks of the dining room.

Ryan also pushed back his chair, levering himself upright, looking around to make sure that everyone followed suit. Trader and Dean came equal last.

''What other prey, Baron?'' Jak asked once everyone was seated.

''You were lucky not to encounter a camp of scabbies near the sulfur springs. Not to mention the ragtag horde that has moved into the fringes of my land.''

Ryan studied Weyman, able to see him properly for the first time.

The baron was older than you'd expect for someone with a son of eleven summers. He sat slightly stooped, with powder-gray hair that hung neatly to his collar. He had a faint mustache and beard, with white eyebrows, pale blue eyes the same hue as Doc's and a pallid complexion that suggested he rarely went outdoors. He was wearing a dark maroon jacket of brushed satin over a startling white lace shirt. His pale cream linen breeches were tucked into silk slippers of crimson and gold.

He was unarmed.

''Why not lead out your sec men against them?'' Trader asked. ''Or send them out if firefights aren't in your field.''

"Since the death of my dear wife, some nine years ago, I have dedicated myself to raising Jamie, my only child. He has received the best education that Deathlands can offer. Which is something of an oxymoron."

Everyone turned to look at Doc. "Sort of contradiction in terms. Like a trustworthy mutie or a silent woman." He grinned at Mildred.

"Or a wise old man," she countered.

"Touché." He bowed.

"It is such a pleasure to have men and women of culture here at my ville," Baron Weyman said, nodding and smiling. "Is the food adequate?"

"Better than that," Ryan replied. "What we've had so far has been a real ace on the line for us."

"I eat very little and drink only water," Weyman said. "But I think it's time for the main course, Rainey. Give word. And bring a dozen of the best claret out of the cellar."

Ryan watched as the baron sipped at a bowl of clear soup, waving away the offer of the fish course, doing the same when a steaming saddle of lamb was brought in from the kitchens.

"Were you married long, Baron?" Krysty asked. "If you don't mind my..."

"Of course not. Why should I object to recalling the greatest happiness of my life? My father died young, and I became baron at the age of eighteen. There was an arranged marriage with the daughter of a neighboring baron, some miles south. Morena was then nearly forty and not blessed with either looks or temperament. We tried for children, but she miscarried thrice."

"That means she lost a baby three times," Jamie whispered to Dean, who was busy helping himself to more gravy and a spoonful of some delicious red currant jelly.

"When Morena died of a venereal disease she had contracted from one of her dalliances with a sec man, I remarried. Jamie's mother was named Nell. She had visited the ville with her father, who stayed on as a farrier. After giving me my son, she succumbed to a virulent strain of influenza that was raging from poisoned water near the hot springs. And that was that."

"I share sorrow," Jak said.

"Then I feel pity and sympathy, my friend." Weyman smiled. "It is rare that I used that word. 'Friend.' But I hope that you will at least stay long enough for us to explore that word and its layers of meaning."

"Anything we can do to repay your hospitality, Baron?" Ryan asked.

Rainey tapped on the table with the flat of his hand. "Patrol didn't find any brushwood folks, Baron. Some sign of strangers and tracks. Could be a lot of them. Mebbe Ryan Cawdor here and his friends might lend a hand with patrolling."

"Go on a recce for you?" J.B. said, glancing at Ryan. "Don't see why not."

Weyman dabbed at his bloodless lips with a pale linen napkin. "You see for yourself that I do not enjoy the best of health. When a baron becomes unwell, the word races through the ungodly and wolfish like a forest fire from treetop to treetop. So it is now. The shadows are gathering at the edges of my ville. A few bold friends would help to hold the darkness away for a while longer. Perhaps to buy a breathing space for my son to grow."

"Sword at sunset," Doc said. "Just like being a sword at sunset."

Weyman nodded thoughtfully. "A fair image, Dr. Tanner, and one that rings a distant bell in my memory. But we can safely let that pass." He leaned back with a sigh. "Such weariness! Still, I feel better on many facets of my life. A companion for my dear boy. He smiled down at Dean. "A little brightness in an arid desert of culture. And a sword at sunset."

RAINEY SHOWED THEM to their rooms.

"I saw that there was a pair of couples. So, there's a double for you and Krysty, and one for John Dix and the lady doctor. Others get to share two doubles and a single."

Trader grabbed the single for himself.

The sec man told them that they were left to their own devices. "You can do what you like," he said. "Come or go, be drunk or sober. Sleep or wake. The ville's yours. Talk about a recce patrol tomorrow."

Ryan stopped him. "We heard stories that Weyman was a bad baron. Doesn't seem that way to me."

Rainey laughed bitterly. "Like he said. The wolves gather when they scent a weakness. Weyman's not the man he was, and I know better than anyone how standards have fallen. Time'll come when some wolf's-head bastard walks in and plucks all the tender fruit from off the branches.''

RYAN SAT ON THE BED, pulling at a loose thread from the patterned coverlet. Krysty stood by the window, wiping away dusty spiderwebs from the leaded glass.

"What do you feel, lover?"

"Sadness. That above all."

Ryan nodded.

Chapter Twenty-Two

Breakfast was every bit as good as the meal they'd eaten the previous day: clam chowder that lined the stomach, followed by a fry-up of eggs and pork sausages, with a tureen brimming with crisp hash browns; a bowl of corned beef with a hot pepper sauce, as well as a huge patterned dish of grits with unsalted butter; fresh-baked bread with a range of preserves and a pitcher of cold milk.

"Could stay here some time, Dean," Ryan said, sitting opposite his son, who was tucking into a pile of hash browns, with three eggs squatting on top of it.

"That would be wonderful!" exclaimed Jamie, who'd poached the seat next to Dean.

Once again, Ryan was struck by the similarity between the two boys; both with dark curling hair and brown eyes, both with the same kind of quickness, the sort of brightness of spirit that burned like a flame.

The main difference lay in the types of education that the two boys had received.

Jamie wasn't a soft child, but he lacked the essential core of hardness that was so self-evident in Dean. He had been taught reading and writing at an early age, as well as principles of math and some knowledge of the sciences. His use of language was far more adult and sophisticated than Dean's, and he had also been taught far more history and geography.

Dean's wisdom came from the school of life and hard knocks. Ryan doubted that the baron's son had ever taken a human life, or fired a blaster in anger. If Dean cut notches on the butt of his 13-round Browning, there would certainly have been more than twenty.

Far more than twenty.

"Would you like to stay here, Dean?" Abe asked.

The boy shook his head, sullen. "No. Screw that! Stay with all of you." He sliced into the eggs, letting the lava of golden yolks flow down the side of the potato peak.

Jamie laid down his knife and fork in a perfectly symmetrical pattern.

"I would so like it if you could stay here, Dean. Even if it were only for a week or two."

"Can't."

"There's no real rush, son," Ryan said.

"We have to move on and go all over Deathlands," Dean insisted, glowering at his father.

"Nobody knows why the old United States of America came to be called Deathlands, you know," Jamie informed them, steepling his fingers together in a habit that Ryan guessed he'd probably picked up from one of his teachers. "It became a current phrase sometime during what is known as the long winters. But there is no record of who came to use it first. I believe that it is now the name for our country, all over the world."

"How come you know so much?" Dean asked.

"I was just taught things," the other boy replied, surprised. "Weren't you taught things like that?"

"Dean never had much time for training to be a scholar," Doc said, wiping a smear of milk from his mouth with his sleeve. "So don't go asking him about Manifest Destiny or Watergate or Boston Common or any of those turning points in history. All right, laddie?"

Jamie nodded. "Of course. I'm sorry if I seemed to be pompous or arrogant. Truly I am, Dean."

He turned to look at Ryan. "Can we come with you on this reconnaissance, Mr. Cawdor? I could lend Dean one of my ponies."

Ryan considered the request. If it had been Dean alone, then he would probably have allowed his son to come along. It wasn't a patrol that was likely to lead into a serious firefight, but Jamie Weyman was an unknown quantity.

Then again, Ryan didn't want to risk alienating the baron.

At that moment, Weyman himself came into the dining room, walking slowly and unsteadily, with the aid of a stick. His complexion seemed even more pale than usual.

"I am so sorry to have neglected you."

One of the serving women approached him. "Nothing for me, I think, Dorita. Though perhaps I could force down a lightly boiled egg whisked into a beaker of warm milk. Thank you."

"Father..." Jamie began.

The baron lifted his hands to his ears with an expression of distress on his face. "Quietly, child. You know how excessive noise is intolerable to my senses. I heard the discussion, and I think that this is not a party for young boys. Men of experience, only.

"Do you agree with me on this matter?" he asked Ryan.

"Yeah, I do."

"Then that is settled. Bill Rainey takes the lead of the hunters. Three of our best and most experienced men will accompany him. And you, Mr. Cawdor? How many of your party will you take along with you?"

Ryan looked around the table, knowing that most of the group would like to ride out for a morning's fresh air and exercise. "Risk of trouble," he said. "Guess I'll take the three most experienced of my men. Trader, J.B. and Jak."

"Chauvinist pig," Mildred said, not quite under her breath.

"Sorry." Ryan shrugged. "You know the rule about dividing your forces."

Trader answered. "If you just *think* about splitting your power, then don't do it. If you *have* to split your power, then cut it as near down the middle as you can."

"How come the baron doesn't get himself better breeding stock?" Trader was bouncing unhappily along on a swaybacked palomino that looked as if it had seen better days. Around fifteen years ago. It was blind in one eye and had a deep sore weeping from the left front fetlock.

Rainey was in the lead. "Time was he would. Like I said, when he started to get kind of unwell he let the reins lie loose. It happens."

J.B. had his fedora tipped back to let the morning sunlight stream down onto his sallow cheeks. "Man lets the reins lie loose opens his eyes and finds his horse has just run away with him," he said.

Trader nodded. "Wish I'd said that, John Dix."

The Armorer grinned. "Oh, you will, Trader. You will."

A HALF MILE BEHIND THEM, a couple of nimble-footed ponies were picking their way along a parallel trail, a little higher up the face of the hillside, twisting and turning among the tall pines. The air was filled with the fresh tang of juniper and piñon, the path splashed with bright puddles of sunlight among the darker shadows of the forest.

The two boys were riding quietly along, Jamie leading the way.

They had slipped away as soon as the main group had left through the gates on their recce patrol. Dean had been surprised how easy it had been for them to leave the ville. Jamie had told the careless sec man on guard that they were going out for an hour or so to exercise the ponies. The sentry had blown his nose, then opened the heavy gates for them without any further questions.

"Poor security, Jamie," he'd said when they were a few minutes into the woods.

The boy had been taken aback. "Do you truly think so? I must admit that I've never really thought about it. Father says that when I'm a few years older, then he'll get Bill Rainey to teach me about things like that."

"You don't have a blaster?"

"No." Jamie looked enviously at the big Browning Hi-Power on his companion's hip. "Can I carry that and have a shoot with it, please, Dean?"

"You greasing my pipe?"

"No. I've hardly ever seen such a beautiful piece of engineering workmanship."

"It'd break your wrist if you fired it. If you weren't ready for it."

Jamie looked wistful. "Oh, I do wish that you and your family could stay awhile with me. There's so much that you could teach me, Dean."

"*Me* teach *you!*"

"Of course."

Dean rode in silence for the next mile or so, locked into his own thoughts.

JAK'S HORSE STUMBLED over some loose rocks, nearly throwing the albino, but he kept his balance. The animal was less lucky, the accident resulting in a deep gash on one of its hind legs.

They stopped for nearly an hour until the horse seemed to be recovered.

Ryan had gone into the woods off the path to take a leak. Standing in the stillness, he was aware of the deep gouges on the bark of a nearby beech tree, where some animal had been sharpening its claws. Or its tusks. It was about the right height for a large mutie pig.

He realized suddenly how quiet the forest had become, and he stopped pissing, quickly doing up his pants and drawing the SIG-Sauer. The birds had ceased singing and vanished, and there was a sinister total silence.

Several minutes passed before the noise came creeping back again and he relaxed, rejoining the others.

Jak saw him coming and strolled over. "Hear something?" he asked.

"Sounds stopped."

"Heard it here."

"See anything, Jak?"

The youth shook his head, a stray beam of sunlight breaking through the foliage and illuminating his hair like a napalm flare. "Nothing. You?"

"No. We passed a trail turning a little while after leaving the ville. Looked like it might run in the same direction as this one. Higher up the hill."

"Think someone riding on that?"

"Mebbe." He laughed at his own fears. "Mebbe not."

"SHOULDN'T WE HAVE SEEN some sign of the main party?" Dean asked. "We've been riding for over two hours now. Must've covered twelve to fifteen miles since we left the ville. Could we've passed them?''

Jamie shook his head. "Doubt it. This trail joins the main track soon. By the old burned-out water mill. Look, you can see it through the trees."

The gloomy, isolated building was made from quarried stone, covered in dark green lichen, almost the same color as the ville's livery. The roof had fallen in years earlier, showing the jagged stumps of beams and joists beneath tumbled slates. The great iron-bound waterwheel had toppled from its mounting, lying on its side, water foaming past it in the narrow millrace.

The glass had gone from all the windows, and the dark rectangles peered suspiciously at the two boys as they heeled their nervous ponies nearer.

"I believe that it's the sound of the river that frightens the animals," Jamie said.

"Yeah," Dean agreed warily.

He peered down at the damp mud. "How come there's no tracks from their horses?" he asked.

Jamie looked down vaguely. "Are there not any?"

"You can see there aren't, you stupe! Don't you even know what horse tracks look like?"

"No. Sorry, Dean. I mean ... I'm really sorry, but I wasn't ever taught that sort of thing."

Dean shook his head in disgust. "Look, we're going to be in some seriously deep shit when we get found out. Best we can do is go and hide in that old mill and keep watch. You reckon they'll come this way?"

Jamie seemed to be on the edge of tears. "I think so. Yes."

They tethered the ponies around the back where there was a cobbled yard, slick with spray from the millrace. Dean led the way inside the ruined building.

There was a single moment when he suddenly sensed the taste of danger in the air, but it was too late. Something hit him on the side of the head, stunning him, then his blaster was snatched and a sack was thrown over his head.

The gold tooth in the mouth of the bald man gleamed in the dimness as he laughed and laughed.

Chapter Twenty-Three

Ryan reined in on the side of the hills, where the main trail wound down toward a ruined building. "That a mill?" he asked Rainey.

"Used to be," the sec boss replied. "Hasn't worked in my lifetime."

Jak was alongside and he suddenly stood in the stirrups, looking back over his shoulder.

"What?" Ryan said.

"One horse. Pushed hard. From ville."

"Only one?"

"Yeah."

"Must be some kind of message from the baron," Rainey said. "Mebbe he wants us back."

But the messenger, astride an Appaloosa gelding, was Krysty.

They waited as she galloped up to them, her horse's flanks streaked with sweat. Her own fiery hair was tangled, and there were burrs stuck in her clothes where she'd ridden hard and cut corners. The woman reined in, brushing pine needles from her thighs.

"Boys have gone," she said.

"Why've you come to tell us?" Rainey asked suspiciously. "Why not one of the sec men?" He looked at her horse. "And you got the baron's best mount."

She fought for breath. "He was showing it to me in the yard out back of the ville when the word came that the boys had taken two ponies and vanished. Weyman asked if I could ride and told me where to go. Nobody else was around and ready."

"Fireblast!" Ryan punched his right hand hard into his left palm.

"They following us?" Trader said thin-lipped. "Need their asses reddened!"

"We stopped when Jak's horse went down. Better part of an hour wasted and lost." Ryan suddenly remembered the odd stillness when he'd gone into the forest for a piss. "The trail that runs higher up," he said.

"Think they've taken that?" Rainey looked down toward the ruined mill. "Paths come together just down there. We can see from the tracks if they've come this way."

J.B. looked at Krysty. "Baron Weyman sending out any reinforcements?"

"Don't think so. He didn't seem too worried. Said it was a boyish prank."

Trader snorted. "Your son should know better, Ryan," he said. "Can't answer for that other boy."

"Can't argue, Trader." Ryan considered the options. They'd come a fair distance from the ville. If the brushwood men and women were still in the area, then they could, just possibly, be hunting out this far.

It was a worrying thought with the two boys missing in the area.

"We'll go down and take a look by the mill," Rainey decided. "You got a good tracker in your party, outlander?"

"Jak."

"Come on." He beckoned the albino to follow him down the steep track.

YOU DIDN'T NEED TO BE an expert in reading signs to see what had happened.

"Two ponies," Jak said, pointing to the clear hoof marks. "Tethered around back. Dean and other go in. Men waiting. Watching them."

"Marks are deeper," J.B. said. "Not muties. Got to be the brushwooders."

"Struggle. Not much. Not long. Eight men or so against two children. Left west. Took ponies."

Ryan knelt and looked at the trampled marks in the wet mud, seeing the way that water was still seeping into some of them. "Not all that long ago," he guessed.

"Within the hour," Jak agreed. Even in the dark interior of the wrecked building, his hair still blazed like a lamp. "Could still be around."

"They'd have hit us as we came down the trail," Trader stated. "Like blasting fish in a barrel. No, Jak. They've lifted the boys and now they're taking them all the way back to their camp. Best we get after them right away."

Rainey was out of his depth. His eyes darted nervously from face to face, the narrow mouth betraying his confusion. "Mebbe we ought to send for some reinforcements."

"Longer you wait, the less chance of getting Dean and Jamie back alive and safe." Ryan rubbed a finger down his chin, feeling the smoothness where he'd had an overdue shave before breakfast that morning.

"They could be anywhere," Rainey argued. "Brushwooders move their camp all the time."

"Not if we follow the tracks." Ryan looked the sec boss in the eye. "I don't mind much what you decide to do, Rainey. But they've likely got my only child. All I aim to do is go get him back. Quicker the better."

DEAN WAS JOLTING along on the back of a horse, his wrists tied to his ankles, under the animal's belly. The sack over his head, stinking of fish meal, made it impossible to see where they were going. But he knew that they would be heading west, knew precisely who their captors were, knew that the dangerous man called Straub rode the horse that was carrying him away into imprisonment.

Dean's head still rang from the heavy fist that had laid him low on the muddy floor of the old mill. He could taste dirt in his swollen mouth, along with a trickle of blood, and he knew that his face was masked in filth.

There had been very little conversation between the men. All the boy could tell, as he recovered his senses, was that they were in a hurry. They suspected the lads hadn't been out unaccompanied that far from the ville.

The other fact that Dean learned was that they knew that they'd captured the son of Baron Weyman.

But Straub had quickly quieted the whoops of enthusiasm, his cold, quiet voice was far more effective than the lash of a steel-tipped quirt.

"Might help us to take the ville without risking our lives," he said. "Use the son as a hostage."

When the brushwood men wanted to push the plans further along, Straub had stopped them, pointing out that Ditchdown was their notional leader and they would all have to discuss any plans with him.

The main thing was to get moving.

THE RIDERS PICKED their way westward at not much more than a brisk walking pace. Jak was in the lead, swinging low from the saddle to check on the tracks, making sure that the group they were following didn't take them by surprise.

"Two horses riding double," he said. "Means both boys alive. Wouldn't carry corpses."

Ryan had a sinking feeling in his gut that the boys might not be alive for very long.

There was no way that it could have been a planned ambush, since not even the lads themselves had known they were leaving the ville. So, it had been a lucky break for the brushwooders, one that he figured Straub would find a way of exploiting to his own advantage.

THE HORSES STOPPED, and Dean was aware of yelling and laughter all around him. Something struck him a whistling blow across the back that stung badly, but he heard Straub's voice raised in anger and the noise diminished.

The boy had been counting as best he could, through the discomfort of the jolting, with the saddle sticking painfully into his stomach.

His best guess was twelve minutes, at something between a fast walk and a trot. That meant the brushwooders' camp was around a mile and a half to two miles from the derelict mill where he and Jamie had been taken prisoner.

He felt Straub swing down, and then a sharp knife whispered through the ropes around his wrists and ankles and he was dumped unceremoniously onto the ground. The tightness of the cords had affected the circulation in his hands and feet and he sat still, blinking in bright sunlight as the stinking sack was ripped off his head.

It would have been easy to stand, but Dean stayed where he was, pretending to be dizzy and sick, keeping his eyes open for a chance to break and run.

He was surrounded by the ragtag horde of back-lane travelers. Children giggled, and one girl of twelve or thirteen tried to poke him in the balls with a long sharp stick. Dean kicked it away and was relieved to see an older woman flat-hand the girl across the side of the head, sending her staggering away, crying noisily.

Straub had disappeared into the crowd.

"These are what they call brushwooders, aren't they?" said a voice behind him.

Dean spun, seeing Jamie Weyman sitting beside him. The boy had a black eye and a cut on the side of his face. Streaks in the dirt across his cheeks told a tale of weeping, but now he seemed to be hanging on to control.

"Don't say a thing," Dean whispered.

"Do you have a plan? A dangerous induction? Oh, do say you have!"

Dean scowled fiercely at him. "This isn't some fucking game! Shut up and say nothing. And don't be surprised at anything I might say."

"What?"

"Just don't argue, whatever I say."

"Oh, all right."

"SMELL SMOKE," Jak said.

The odor of the sulfurous hot springs had been getting much stronger as they rode closer to the coast.

"Then we're near enough," Ryan said. "Stop here and we'll go ahead on foot. Leave the horses tethered."

Rainey stayed in the saddle, as did the three sec men, none of whom looked to be below fifty years old.

"I believe the baron placed me in command of this hunting party," he said.

"That was before." Ryan looked at him, trying to overcome his irritation. "You want to follow another plan, then do what you like." He paused a moment.

"But if it risks the life of my son, then you get a front seat on the last train west."

"What do you figure?" the sec boss asked. "Remember the son of my baron's out there, as well. It would chill Weyman if anything happened to the boy."

"Something's already happened," Trader said, cackling with laughter. "Question of what else happens."

"Button it, Trader," Krysty said angrily. "You're a poor judge of when to talk and when to shut up."

Ryan sighed. "Fireblast! Can't we just get something done for once without an argument? We go through the woods on foot and recce the camp. No point in even thinking about trying to make a plan till we've done that."

DITCHDOWN WAS SITTING in a padded chair beside the main campfire, which was always kept burning. The sunlight in the clearing accentuated the flash of white through his dark hair.

Straub stood at his side, as the two prisoners were hauled before him.

"Filthy little bastards," said the chief of the brush-wooders. "Filthy."

Dean rubbed at his bruised and muddied face, making a low whimpering sound. Jamie stood at his side, silent, looking fixedly at the floor.

"You got anything to say for yourselves?" Straub said. His dark, silver-flecked eyes burned at Dean, as though they were drilling into his soul and sucking out all of his secrets. The boy returned his gaze for a few seconds, when he felt a sickening void opening in his head and he lowered his own eyes.

The shaved-headed man laughed. "We have here a young hawk and a common jaybird, Ditchdown. Yet both of these puny creatures can be of use to us."

"Which is the hawk?" the brushwood leader asked. "Neither of them fit that description, Straub, do they?"

"One is the son of the baron of this ville. His name is Jamie Weyman. The other is a common little lout. I believe he might be one of the butchering party that gave us such trouble and cost us in spilled blood."

Ditchdown stood and stared at the lads, his fists clenched in anger. "I can't say I'd recognize the spawn of that one-eyed bastard. Truth is, I can't even tell these two little rats apart."

"There was a strong enough clue in what one of them carried. But ask them, Ditchdown."

"Ask them what?"

Straub toyed with the opal in his ear, barely bothering to mask his feelings. "Ask them which is Weyman and which is Cawdor. If it's not too difficult for you. One shall remain here and the other shall carry the message of what ransom we require, back to the baron. Just ask them, Ditchdown."

"I SMELL THE SMOKE," Krysty said, "and I can feel we're close. Feel the brushwooders. Sort of dull, brutish shape in my mind."

"How about the boys, lover?"

She shook her head. "Sorry, Ryan. Sorry, Bill. Nothing. But we reckon they were almost certainly alive when they were taken. Doubt they'll have had time to do much to them."

Trader hawked and spit, peering to examine the ball of phlegm. "Thought it might've turned yellow with all the sulfur in the air."

The three elderly sec men from the ville were huddled together, sharing a cigarette. None of them looked as if they were enjoying the expedition.

Jak was looking at the trampled mud of the trail that led them between the trees, toward the camp. "Pigs," he said, pointing with a long white finger at the unmistakable marks of sharp hooves. "Not long ago."

"Then let's move on," Ryan said. "Faster."

"WHICH OF YOU IS THE SON of Baron Weyman? I give you my word that he won't be harmed. Just stay and be our guest a short while. Well?"

The voice was clear and defiant. "I'm Jamie Weyman, and you're a piece of rotting shit. My father will come with all his sec men and ride you into the dirt."

Straub applauded slowly and ironically. "Brave words, little bantam. Brave words. But hollow and empty, don't you think? Now your friend will run to the ville with a message."

Chapter Twenty-Four

The boy quickly became tired.

He'd set off from the camp of the brushwooders as though his feet had been set on fire, running with his head thrown back, arms pumping.

He knew which was the trail to the ville, heading easterly. The sun, almost directly overhead, gave him a shadow that ran with him, jumping over puddles, slipping in patches of wet earth and leaf mold.

A black-masked raccoon, foraging below the tall pines, made him jump as it suddenly turned, snarling at the panting intruder into its domain.

In less than five minutes the boy was out of breath, stopping with a painful charley horse that made his thigh muscles tremble and twitch.

He put his hand down to his pocket, making sure that the folded lump of paper was still safe.

The lad knew what it said, knew the nature of the message that he carried back to the distant ville—that the eleven-year-old son of Baron Weyman was a prisoner and that his life would depend on a number of conditions.

It was time to be moving on.

RAINEY HAD BEEN CONTENT for the outlanders to take over the recce and, possibly, rescue mission, admitting that his sec force hadn't faced any serious problems for many years.

"Just the occasional poacher and one or two invasions by a few pathetic scabbies."

Jak had taken the lead, padding through the forest in almost total silence, occasionally scowling over his shoulder as someone else broke a dry branch or slipped noisily in the damp earth. The worst of the group for clumsiness were the three sec men, all of whom looked like they'd much rather have been sitting comfortably around a warm fire back in the ville.

The albino suddenly stepped off the path, crouching behind a clump of young junipers, waving with his hand for the others to hide.

"Someone coming," Ryan hissed when the sec men were painfully slow to react.

They all caught the sound of hurried, pattering feet, running straight toward them. Krysty was right at Ryan's shoulder, and she pressed her mouth to his ear, whispering, "Stumbling. Tired out."

"Only one," he breathed.

Jak allowed the runner to pass him before he ghosted out of hiding and seized the boy from behind, one arm around his throat to cut off any cry for help. Though the albino teenager only stood about five and a half feet tall and weighed in just over the hundred-pound mark, he was immensely strong, swinging the prisoner clear off the ground.

The others all emerged from cover, gathering around.

For a single, heart-stopping moment, Ryan thought that the boy who hung limply in Jak's grasp was Dean. The boy was the right sort of height, with dark curly hair.

But Rainey recognized him first. "Jamie!" he gasped. "You managed to escape. Let him go, outlander."

When Jak released him, the lad stumbled and nearly dropped to the ground, recovering himself with a visible effort. His face was pale, mud-smeared, with several bruises and cuts, his clothes filthy and torn. He was fumbling in his pocket.

"Where's Dean?" Ryan asked.

"Got him." His chest was heaving, and he looked as if he were about to pass out.

"Sit down, son," Krysty said.

Jamie gave her a grateful, wan smile and sat like a puppet with the strings cut. Trader offered him a drink from his canteen, which the boy took eagerly, gulping at the warm water. "Take it slow, lad."

"In your own time, Jamie," Ryan said, kneeling at the boy's side. "What happened?"

"Took ponies and followed you. Took high trail. Why are you behind us? We were a good distance behind you."

"Had a problem," Rainey replied. "Slowed us down by an hour. Guess you must've passed us then."

Jamie nodded. "I suppose that must be so. We reached the old mill. They were there."

"Who took you?" J.B. asked. "Scabbies? Or was it the brushwooders?"

"Brushwooders. We were knocked down and tied and hooded. Taken to their camp. A few ragged huts and a fire."

"Was Dean hurt?"

The boy shook his head. "No, Ryan. Not too badly. I think they hit him harder than they hit me."

There was something going on that Jamie hadn't told them. Ryan was conscious of the way the boy's eyes wouldn't meet anyone's face, his hands knotting and tangling in his lap, the rapid blinking, the way his tongue kept flicking out to moisten his dry lips.

Jamie hadn't yet told them the truth. Not the whole truth.

"Go on," Ryan said. "Who was there?"

"Man called Ditchdown. He had a funny white scar in his hair. And there was another one. He was in charge of the group that succeeded in capturing us. His head was shaved, and he had funny eyes that made me feel dizzy."

"Straub," Ryan said.

"They've given me a letter to take to my father. Then they let me go."

Now the raw nerve was fully exposed. Jamie had reached the point where the deceit had to stop and the truth had to stand revealed.

Trader probed first. "I don't understand, kid. Why did they let you go and keep Dean? I mean, doesn't make any sense, does it? Like throwing out the gold and keepin' the pyrites. In a manner of speaking. Well, you know what I mean."

"Show me the letter," Ryan said. "Unless there's something else you want to tell us, Jamie. Something you haven't mentioned to us yet."

The boy closed his eyes, his hands gripping each other so hard that it looked as though the white knuckles were going to break clean through the skin.

"Yes," he said finally. The single word seemed like it had been ripped out of the walls of his soul.

The others stood around him in a ragged circle. Silence crawled by.

"You expectin' us to read your mind, kid?" Trader said. "Time's passing."

"Sorry. I'm so dreadfully sorry, Mr. Cawdor. I feel as though it were all my fault."

"Go on," Ryan prompted.

Jamie was on the brink of tears as he told his story to the listeners. "It wasn't my idea," he stammered. "I swear before all the gods of land and sky that it wasn't. I didn't know that Dean was going to do that. I was speechless."

"Convenient," Trader muttered, receiving an angry glance from Krysty.

Ryan patted the boy on the shoulder. "There's times when words don't come easy."

"I argued with them."

"You did?" Ryan nodded. "Brave, even if it might not have been the brightest thing to do. Dean can probably look after himself better in that kind of trap than you can. But I admire your nerve, Jamie. What happened next?"

SHAKING LIKE AN ASPEN in a hurricane, Jamie had protested. "He isn't really the son of the baron. Can't you see that? I am."

Straub had laughed at him. "'Course you are, child. I can just see some ragged-assed brat carrying a Browning Hi-Power in top-of-the-line condition while he rides with the son of a baron who's unarmed. Highly unlikely."

"It's true." Jamie's voice leapt up the scale like a salmon going up a run of rapids. "He's the son of an outlander. Name is Dean Cawdor."

Dean had turned to him, grinning through bruised lips. "And I'm the King of Deathlands! Nice try, though. If we get out of this, Dad'll thank you for that." He looked toward Straub. "Can we get on with this. I could do with some food and a rest."

Straub had actually smiled at him, something that was more frightening than any of the man's other expressions. "Sort of spirit I expect from the son of a baron. Even if Weyman's on the downslope to nowhere."

At this moment, amid general laughter from the watching and listening brushwooders, Dean had taken a half step to bring himself beside the other boy, whispering out of the corner of his mouth. "Just fuckin' do it, Jamie. Argue and we both get chilled. Bring my father and the others. You can do it."

"Stop talking to each other," Ditchdown snapped. "Won't have it."

They both kept quiet at the threat from a fist the size of a smoked ham.

"AND THAT'S IT?" Ryan asked. "They believed that Dean was you, and they gave you the ransom demand to take to the baron. Show it to me."

Jamie fished for the note in his pockets, eventually pulling it out and giving it along to Trader, who was slightly the nearest to him.

"Waste of time givin' it to me, son," he said. "Never got on with them crawly little black spider marks. Give it to the lady to read."

The letter was crumpled, written in ink on the usual Deathlands handmade paper, though it was slightly better quality than what was usually encountered. What was surprising was the neatness of the writing, in a sort of sloping Gothic hand, impeccably spelled and punctuated.

"'To the noble and respected Baron Weyman. We hold your son, Jamie, a prisoner, but do not wish any fellness to befall him. You will be pleased to hear that we are not demanding jack from you, beyond your powers of paying. No, that is not our wish. All you have to do is return a message with this boy that you accept our terms and your son will be released unhurt. Not at once, you understand. But once you have done what we ask. That is to abandon your ville to us and disband your sec men. Once we see that done, then Jamie is a free boy again.'

"They don't want much, do they?" Krysty said. "Just everything!"

"Go on." Ryan was glancing at the sky, his mind working like a racing calculator. The brushwooders wouldn't know that he and the group were so close. It would have taken Jamie at least six or seven hours, on foot, to reach the ville, meaning there was no risk of any retaliation until after dark. They wouldn't be expecting any sort of attack within the hour—which meant their best chance. They would creep in silently and waste the camp before anyone knew they were there.

Krysty was still reading the letter.

"'In the event that you don't believe us, we will deliver to the ville, twelve hours from noon this day, the right ear of your son. Then, at such intervals, other parts of his body so as to leave him still in fair working order, but sorely mutilated. We think this is only fair. Send reply by this ragged boy at your fastest convenience.'"

Krysty shook her head. "It's signed The Levelers. Don't know what that means."

"How far's the camp, Jamie?" Ryan helped the boy to his feet. "We'll go straight in now, fast and silent. All of us. You can show us the way."

"About a mile. The trail winds and twists an awful lot, but I can find it easily."

"Good lad." Ryan patted him on the back. "Your father'll be proud of you."

"You don't mind the way I left Dean?"

"'Course not. Soon have him safe and snug with us, Jamie. Don't worry."

Trader chimed in. "Yeah. Nothing'll go wrong, kid. Not with us hitting the ace on the line."

THE ONLY THING that went wrong happened just as the hunters reached the perimeter of the camp, halfway down a steep and slippery slope.

The sky had darkened with the threat of imminent rain, sweeping in toward the mountains from the west from over the Cific Ocean.

It was perfect timing for their raid. It was obvious from a quick recce that Ryan had taken with J.B. that the brushwooders were totally off guard, not anticipating any trouble for several hours.

There had been a short, sharp shower, lasting less than three minutes, but it had been enough to dampen the grass and the mud between the trees.

Ryan was in the lead, SIG-Sauer drawn, the rest of the group strung out in a ragged skirmish line. At his order, the boy was waiting for them a couple of hundred yards in the rear, at the top of the hillside.

The only worry for Ryan was the trio of sec men with Rainey. The sharp-featured sec boss seemed the sort of man who could look after himself, but the others were slow and hesitant, clutching at their armed crossbows as though they were frightened that the bolts might fall out.

It was the fattest and oldest of them, named Micah, who lost his footing and fell crashing through the brush, yelling at the top of his voice, leaving everyone stranded halfway down.

As it hit the fan.

Chapter Twenty-Five

It was Straub who'd taken over one of the powerful AK-74s, carrying it across his shoulder on a sling of canvas webbing. Ditchdown had the other Russian automatic rifle, already in his hand.

They'd been walking around the encampment, discussing the strengths and weaknesses of their tactical position, just in case Baron Weyman decided to act contrary to his normal character and lead his sec men against them. Not that they thought there was much realistic chance of that happening.

Ryan had been absolutely correct in his assumption that they wouldn't be looking for any threat, at least until the evening. But it was unlucky that Straub had just gathered the brushwood men near the base of the wooded hillside, giving them a talk on what might happen, when a fat old man in the dark green livery of the ville came yelping through the bushes, landing almost at Straub's feet, his crossbow discharging the thrumming bolt harmlessly into the afternoon sky.

The reaction from Straub was terrifyingly fast, so quick that it was only in hindsight that Ryan realized the uncanny speed of the man.

The Kalashnikov spit out an arc of lead even before Micah had stopped rolling, spraying through the brush from left to right, which was hard luck for Al and Doug, Micah's two security colleagues who happened to be on that end of the skirmish line.

Al took two bullets through his belly, only a couple of inches apart. The double exit wounds literally blew his back apart, smashing his spine, burying fragments of the splintered vertebrae deep in the bark of a juniper just behind him. He was thrown back by the dual impacts, dying from a mixture of the massive trauma and total blood loss.

Doug was hit once. He'd been a little lower down the slope, and the tumbling round caught him in the right shoulder. It pulverized his collar bone, blowing a hole that left his arm dangling by a few bloody threads of gristle and ripped muscle. He screamed as he fell, trying to grab hold of the ruined arm with his left hand, screaming again as his falling broke the few sinews and left him holding the severed limb.

Like Al, he didn't live very long after that.

Bill Rainey had moved down the slope with greater ease, and the burst of fire from the Russian assault weapon went over his head, close enough for him to hear the high whine of its passing and actually feel the heat of the rounds as they missed him by a couple of inches.

Straub saw immediately that he was shooting high and hastily adjusted his aim as he swung the weapon across the line of men in the brush.

Ditchdown had also reacted quickly and had his own AK-74 ready, opening fire from his hip.

The rest of the brushwooders were slower.

They had a few firearms, and most were single-shot self-builds or remakes. But some had longbows, and it was only a matter of a handful of seconds before their shafts were also hissing toward the attackers.

If Micah's clumsy fall had happened nearer the bottom of the slope, Ryan could have led them all down in a bloody charge. If it had happened earlier, while they were close to the top of the steep hillside, it would have been easy to fall back to a safe defensive position and use their superior firepower to take out the brushwooders.

It was halfway house, the worst of both worlds.

Off-balance, suddenly under a murderous, raking fire, on a greasy slope of slick mud, it was hopeless.

"Get out!" Ryan shouted, his voice cracking.

He was shooting with the SIG-Sauer, managing to put down the man standing next to Straub, when he was hit by an arrow.

It struck him as he stood sideways, trying to work his way up the hill to relative safety. It entered just above the belt, driving into the muscles at the small of his back. Ryan gasped at the sudden shock of the impact and went down for a moment to his hands and knees, ducking and barely saving himself from another leaden spray from Straub's Kalashnikov.

He wasn't the only casualty.

Apart from the dead sec men, and the helpless Micah, the rest of the attackers were scourged.

J.B. took a musket ball in the left upper arm, the heavy shot passing clean through without striking bone or shredding muscle. But it knocked him over in the treacherous mud, nearly dropping the Uzi. He braced himself for a moment against a stunted tamarisk, saving himself from sliding all the way down into the brushwooders' camp.

Jak was the third casualty.

He'd been second fastest to react to the disaster, a thousandth of a second behind Ryan. The albino had seen instantly that their position was untenable, almost helpless. Their only chance was to blast away at the brushwooders and hope that it distracted them long enough to retreat up the hill to safety.

But one of the rounds from Ditchdown's AK-74 hit the dirt just below him and to the left, striking an outcrop of granite and splintering the rocks. One of the razor-edged shards caught Jak across the side of the right calf, ripping out a sizable chunk of flesh. Like J.B., he was unlucky to catch a wound, but lucky that nothing radical was affected by the injury.

"Out!" Ryan screamed again, backing away, forcing himself to carry on against the burning pain in his back, snapping off random shots through the screen of bushes.

Bullets and arrows seemed to fill the air, making it a miracle that they didn't all get to buy the farm. Their reactions had been so quick that the brushwooders were mostly firing too low, beneath their scrambling figures, dimly seen through cover.

Leaves fluttered to the ground, and the air was thick with the smell of cordite, overlaid with the tang of fresh sap from the scarred trees.

Krysty was first to the top, throwing herself flat and trying to pick off targets with her Smith & Wesson 640, though the .38, with its two-inch barrel, wasn't a good weapon once you got much above twenty-yards range. But it helped to keep their attackers moving and dodging.

Trader came second, his eyes staring wide, his lips peeled back off his teeth in a smile of pure rage, blasting away with the Armalite at his hip.

Ryan was next, Bill Rainey at his heels, the dirt-covered sec man cursing in a long, fluent tirade against the brushwooders. J.B. had gone a little way to the right, and he appeared unexpectedly over the ridge, almost catching a bullet from Krysty as she swung around to face what she had thought was an enemy.

Jak was last to reach the temporary haven of dead ground, hobbling painfully, pausing to fire back with the big satin-finish Colt Python.

Arrows hissed toward them, thudding into the trunks of the tall pines. They could hear Straub below them, shouting orders, his voice rising above the incoherent babble of yelling.

The shooting stopped.

"Hold fire," Ryan said. "What's the injury count?"

"Lost all three of my men," Rainey said. "Poor bastards didn't have a chance." His voice cracked with emotion, and there were unshed tears glistening in his eyes.

"Hit in leg," Jak stated, his voice as flat and calm as ever, stooping to bind a piece of rag around the bleeding gash in his calf. "Nothing serious."

"You know you got a shaft sticking out of your back, lover?"

Ryan grinned at Krysty. "I noticed. Leave it there until we can take some time on drawing it out."

"Best get out triple quick," the Armorer said, reloading the Uzi, holding it across his lap, blood dripping down from his arm onto the gun.

"Want that tied?" Jak asked.

"Later."

Trader lay flat, watching the activity below him. "Bald fucker's gettin' them organized. Won't take long for them to get around and behind us. Sooner we go the better."

"What about Micah?" Rainey asked. "He was alive when they took him."

"Won't be for long," Ryan replied. "Nothing to be done. Let's get out of here, best we can."

To Ryan's surprise, there was no effort made by the brushwooders to pursue them into the forest, and they reached the tethered horses safely.

"How come they aren't on our heels?" Trader threw his Armalite in the dirt, ignoring a reproachful glance from J.B.

Ryan was sitting, his shirt pulled up, while Krysty and Jak peered at the gray-feathered arrow that protruded from his back. "Only thing I can figure is that Straub's playing it real smart."

"How's that?" Trader had lain down beside his blaster.

"He reckons that our attack was a coincidence. Odds are that we hadn't met up with Jamie, so we didn't know about the ransom note. Boy wasn't with us."

Rainey was tying the bridles of two of the sec men's horses to his own saddle horn, ready to lead them back to the ville. Jamie would ride Micah's animal. "You mean he's still hoping to get the baron to leave the ville?"

"Remember he doesn't know that Jamie's with us and he's got Dean instead."

J.B. had allowed Jak to put a tight bandage around his musket wound, and he was flexing the fingers on his right hand, seeing how much movement and control he had in them. "Makes sense. Otherwise we could've had those sons of bitches swarming all over us by now."

Ryan was trying to look back over his shoulder at his own wound. "Best way's to break it and pull both ends out clean," he suggested.

Krysty nodded. "It's nicked the big muscles above your hips, but it hasn't gone deep enough to risk damaging the kidneys or liver. Just sort of pierced that roll of fat that you claim isn't even there."

"Why don't you..." He controlled himself. "Just break it in half and then pull it out, will you? And hold the wisecracks for another time."

Krysty took the slender shaft in both hands, where it had driven through the flesh, just behind the barbed hunting point. She drew in a slow, deep breath, then cracked it sharply across the middle, breaking it in two.

Ryan gasped at the jar of pain.

"Sorry, lover," she said, kissing him on the cheek.

"Get on with it."

She pulled out the section of arrow with the barbed point first, easing it carefully through the bruised and swollen flesh. Ryan bit his lip and kept still and silent, closing his eye and trying to use the meditative skills that Krysty had attempted to teach him.

"It's out. Just the flight end to go." She paused to wipe perspiration from her forehead, even though the day had become clammy and cool.

The goose feathers were damp with the misty rain that had started to fall a few minutes earlier. Krysty gripped them firmly and drew out the rest of the broken arrow in a single, smooth movement.

"Done?" Ryan asked, breath hissing from his parted lips. There was a tiny worm of crimson blood creeping down over his chin. "That it?"

The woman dropped the two ends of the bloodied shaft in the dirt. "Over."

"Thanks, lover." He kissed her, a gentle brush of the lips that became more urgent as they clung to each other.

"Should go," Trader said.

JAMIE TRIED SEVERAL TIMES to apologize to Ryan for what had happened.

"Keep telling you. Not your fault, son. We'll soon be back at your father's ville. And we can decide what to do to try and pick up the broken pieces.

"Do you have a plan, Mr. Cawdor?"

"Does a shark shit in the sea? 'Course." Ryan paused, longer than he'd intended. "'Course I have a plan."

Chapter Twenty-Six

Dean had been tied to the center pole of one of the larger tents when the rescue party arrived.

He'd been trying to do the same mental calculations as Straub, guessing that it would take Jamie until dusk to get back to the ville. At least that long. There would have to be some discussion and planning before Ryan led the assault unit that would sweep the brushwooders out of their camp and into the surrounding wasteland.

Dean guessed that Straub would be expecting an attack during the hours of darkness. But he wasn't sure whether his father might prefer to wait, then come in at them in the misty light of dawn.

What nobody had looked for was a bungled attempt at a raid, only an hour or so after the little boy with the swollen face had gone running east.

There was a desperate yell, muffled by the thick hide cover over the tent, then it sounded like all hell had broken loose outside.

Dean sat up, wincing as the rawhide thong around his throat tightened. He recognized the individual weapons—his father's SIG-Sauer, its explosions echoing and loud in the damp, humid air; the ripping sound of the Uzi; the short, sharp shocks of what he figured had to be Trader's Armalite.

The firefight lasted less than sixty seconds from beginning to the end, when Straub's voice rose over the bedlam, ordering a cease-fire from the brushwooders.

Dean waited, his body as tense as a coiled spring, unable to believe what he was hearing. From the whooping and excitement, there could only be one possible interpretation.

Unbelievably the raid seemed to have failed.

"THAT WAS YOUR FATHER'S friends and sec men," Straub said, kneeling in the shadow darkness of the tent. "Why were they out here?"

"Don't know." Dean shook his head.

"They couldn't humanly have gotten the ransom demand. I believe they were on a routine patrol and decided to chance their arm against us." He shuffled closer and took Dean's bruised jaw between long finger and thumb, squeezing hard so that the boy cried out in pain. "What do you think, Jamie Weyman?"

The beads of raw turquoise on his necklace rattled as he leaned closer. His breath was sweet and dry, like a warm cattle barn, but it still revolted Dean. He tried to turn his head, but the weird eyes bored into his.

"Don't know," he gasped.

Straub squatted back on the heels of his snake-embroidered Western boots. "I think I believe you. But when I look into the shallow well that's your puny little brain, I see ripples below the surface, boy. If I had time I would dive below the surface and explore down in those murky waters. I think you're trying to hide something from me?''

"No, sir, I'm not."

"You promise, boy?"

"On my mother's grave, sir."

Straub stood, brushing dust from his black, silver-riveted jeans. "You interest me, Jamie Weyman. I had looked to find a vapor-headed little boy and I find…" He shook his head. "What do I find? But time passes. These muddied fools wish to terminate the life of one of your sec men that we've taken prisoner. You may come and watch."

DEAN HAD BEEN LED OUT by one of the older women, his wrists tied behind him. His face still felt sore, and his teeth seemed to have become loose in his jaws. He walked out into a scene of great excitement.

A stake driven into the ground close to the main fire of the settlement. The smooth wood already bore a number of old, dark stains.

A man was tied to it, while the younger women were gleefully hacking his dark green uniform from him. They were careless with their short-bladed, pecking knives, and streaks of blood marred his pale skin.

Dean thought he might have recognized the sec man, but he couldn't be sure, as many of the ville's guards were elderly and stout.

Ditchdown was parading proudly up and down in front of the yelping mob, grinning from ear to ear, an AK-74 on his right shoulder.

Dean's attention was drawn by a pair of taunting boys to two raggled, naked corpses, lying on the village's garbage heap. It looked to his experienced eyes as though the wretched men had already been dead before the knives had done their work.

"Come and watch one of your father's proud sec men enter the long darkness," Straub called, leading Dean to stand in front of the doomed man.

"It's Micah, Master Weyman. Can you do nothing to make them spare me?" the sec guard pleaded. He had been stripped naked by the women's blades and stood quivering like a great pink-streaked white jelly, wrists and ankles bound to the stake. He had already lost control of both bladder and bowels, and was smeared with his own wastes. His eyes were like plums, protruding from their sockets in terror. They suddenly focused on the boy. "They said that you were—"

Dean saw the chasm that suddenly gaped in front of him. If the man betrayed him, then his life would be of no value to the brushwooders and they would make his passing long and painful as a revenge for fooling them.

There was a bone-hilted knife sheathed on Ditchdown's belt, and Dean kicked out at Straub, breaking free of his hold for a moment. He dived at Ditchdown and grabbed the knife, dodging the man's frantic grasp at him and launching himself straight at Micah.

The sec man opened his mouth to scream, but Dean was quicker. He stabbed the man through the heart, holding the knife point-upward, giving the blade a twist of the wrist before withdrawing it again, as his father had taught him.

The steel slid like silk between the ribs, cutting open the thudding walls of Micah's heart.

Straub grabbed at Dean, locking his fingers into his hair, yanking backward. His right hand reached for the boy's wrist and made him drop the knife.

"You little bastard," he said. But even in that moment of highest tension, Dean noticed that Straub didn't seem to be particularly angry. "Sort of spirit I'd expect from the son of a baron. Even a sad geek like Weyman."

"My father isn't a sad geek!" Dean lashed out backward, feeling his heel connect sharply with the man's shins.

The note of grudging respect vanished instantly from Straub's voice. "That hurt, you dwarf prick."

He held Dean by the collar with his left hand, slapping him across the face with the right, hard, mechanical blows that made the boy's head rock from side to side, making his ears ring, his eyes losing their focus.

Straub uttered cold, bitter words in time with each roundhouse slap. "Don't ever do that again unless you want me to flay you alive."

Dean could feel his nose beginning to bleed, more blood trickling from both ears. The pounding was so brutal that the boy felt himself beginning to slip away into darkness. He was trying to speak, to ask Straub to stop hitting him.

"Stop hitting him, Straub." His voice sounded totally unfamiliar and puzzling to him.

But the blows carried on, remorselessly.

Dean wasn't even aware that he'd become unconscious, not until he opened his eyes and stared up at the leaden afternoon sky. He felt a few spots of rain falling into his face, heard two angry voices arguing above him.

"He's our passport, Straub."

"He caused me pain. Nobody does that and walks away."

"You've beaten him to the dirt. What more do you want from him?"

Straub laughed, a sound that sent the short hairs curling at Dean's nape. "Today or tomorrow, Ditchdown? What does it matter? It is a good day to die, my brother. It is always a good day for death."

"Not now, Straub. Might be that his father wants some proof Jamie's alive."

Dean sat up, wiping his nose on his sleeve and blinking up at the two men. He looked beyond them to where the corpse of Micah was slumped in his bonds. There was surprisingly little blood spilled from the knife wound. The boy felt a pang of regret that it had been necessary to kill the helpless old man.

But it *had* been necessary.

"Get up, lad," Ditchdown said, not unkindly. "Go back to the tent and mind your own business."

Straub tapped him on the shoulder. "Your ears are bleeding, kid."

Dean shrugged away from him. "You want to pick on someone your own fucking size," he said.

"Temper, kid. Control that temper. Chilling that old guy." Straub leaned closer, his dark eyes with the whirling silver specks drilling into Dean. "I have a good idea why you did that, kid. But I'd like to hear it from your own lips."

Dean swallowed hard, tasting the salt bitterness of his own blood. He glanced past Straub to where the children of the village were amusing themselves by cutting bits of flesh off the corpse of the sec man.

"Look," he said. "You'd have let them do that while the poor bastard lived. I had to do what I could to spare him that. Loyalty's a two-way street."

He unconsciously quoted one of Trader's favorite sayings. "Chilling him was the only way I could save him from your torturing. All right?"

Straub turned around. "All right, kid."

Dean turned around. "And stop calling me 'kid,' will you? I don't like it."

AN OLD WOMAN, her face furrowed and filthy, brought him a bowl of stew a little later. As she crept into the tent, Dean saw from the fading light outside that evening was closing in.

"You chilled our prisoner," she said.

"Yeah. Best I could do."

She put down the wooden bowl and carved spoon, then spit in the greasy mixture. "Spoiled our funning," she lisped through her toothless mouth.

"Thanks for the spit."

Her face didn't change. "Wanted to piss in it, but Ditchdown stopped me."

"You're a real queen, aren't you?"

The old woman looked over her shoulder toward the entrance, and shuffled closer to him. Dean, his hands bound in front of him, readied himself to try to kick her in the throat.

"Might be the baron's son," she whispered. "Mighty and buggerin' high. But the day's comin' fast when you and all your buggerin' high-nosed kind are goin' to get brought real low. Very soon."

"That'll be the day."

She nodded, her veiled eyes peering malevolently at him. "Pretty little boy. Brave little boy. You reckon I'm ugly and old, don't you? Think I'm way below you. Wouldn't touch me with a ten-foot pole, would you?" She smiled through chapped lips. "When we got what we want from your limp-dick daddy, then Straub says we can have our funning with you."

"Go fuck a dead armadillo, you stinking slag," Dean said, just winning the battle to stop his voice from cracking.

"You'll crawl and cry and beg me to let you lick shit off my shoes," she hissed. "And that'll just be for a starter, kid."

Dean watched her go before picking up the stew and gobbling it down, regardless of her having spit in it. Food was food.

That night, alone, Dean whispered into the blackness to try to lift his sagging spirits. "Hurry up, Dad. Hurry up."

Chapter Twenty-Seven

Back in the ville, the explanations were over. The letter from the brushwooders had been read by Baron Weyman, Doc, Mildred and Abe.

The wounds of Ryan, J.B. and Jak had been bathed, treated and dressed.

Two of the older women of the ville had been told that their husbands, the sec men, were dead, and Micah's sister received the news that there was little chance that she would ever see her brother alive again.

The sun was already setting.

On the winding trail back to the ville, they had spotted a couple of the mutie pigs, heading away from the horsemen, toward a narrow side canyon that led away north, between high cliffs. Rainey had pointed to them, suggesting that it could be the place where the herd was presently living.

It was a fact that Ryan had tucked carefully away into his memory in case it might become useful in the next couple of days.

The one thing blindingly obvious was that they had only a couple of days at the outside. By then the baron would have surrendered his ville, or Ryan would have

organized a rescue party for his son. Either way, the
outlook was grim and menacing for all of them.

The baron had asked for a little while to consider his
options, wanting to spend some time with his only
child in his rooms, promising that he would meet with
the outlanders over the supper table at seven o'clock.

MEANWHILE, RYAN AND THE REST of the group also
withdrew to their own rooms. He lay on the bed, on
his side, wincing occasionally at the way the arrow
wound was pulling. Mildred had suggested that it
would help to stitch it, but Ryan had argued against it,
claiming the wound would heal more quickly unaided.

The musket ball that had gone in and out of J.B.'s
upper left arm had left a neat entry and exit wound
that was now tightly bandaged. The Armorer kept
flexing his fingers, working his shoulder, trying to find
out precisely how much damage had been done and
how it might have limited his range of movement. It
didn't seem serious.

The splinters of stone in Jak's right ankle was the
most serious of the trio of injuries. Mildred had asked
for an array of oil lamps to be provided on one of the
big scrubbed tables in the kitchens. She peered over
the white flesh, using a pair of borrowed tweezers to
pick at the tiny shards of rock. The blood had welled
from the dozen or more holes, some of them bone-
deep, but the teenager had lain quite still, not making
a sound, though he was biting his lip from the pain.

Eventually, having swilled it out with bowls of near-scalding water, using cotton swabs to pick away any remaining specks of stone, Mildred was satisfied.

"It'll do," she said.

Jak heaved a great sigh of relief as she dried the wound, then applied a length of bandage that swiftly became pink from leaking blood.

"Thanks, Mildred. Better."

But it was giving him a lot of trouble, meaning that he walked with a limp on the right side.

Trader paced around the room, slapping his hands together, fired up, ready to go again.

"That mealy prick says he'll give up the ville, then what do we do?"

Krysty sat next to Ryan, holding his hand. "Problem is that the ransom is meaningless. They think they've got his son. We all know that they haven't."

"So he'll tell us to go bite the fresh air?"

Ryan shook his head. "Lots of barons would. Not sure about Weyman. I think he'll listen a lot to Jamie. Partly his fault they've got Dean. We'll find out over supper."

J.B. stood by the window, looking out across the darkening land. "I agree. I'd lay my jack on him wanting to help us out."

"My suspicion is that the baron will do what he can to hang on to his power," Doc said, "which will probably mean having to assist us in attempting to save dear Dean. Of all the barons I've seen during my time here in Deathlands, I have to say that Weyman seems the most decent."

"Losing his power," Abe commented.

Doc smiled at the little gunner. "They say power corrupts and that absolute power corrupts absolutely. Perhaps it makes for a better class of baron if they are weakening somewhat. What think you?"

Jak had been doing kneebend exercises against the foot of the bed, wincing at the strain it put on his leg. "Waste time talking. Know soon enough."

ONE OF THE SERVING WOMEN at the supper table kept crying until she was taken away from her duties.

"Micah's daughter," Rainey said. "Lost her mother only six months ago from the flux."

Neither the baron nor his son had appeared when the first course arrived at the long refectory table, though the sec boss said that he'd received orders to get started on the meal on the understanding that Weyman and Jamie would be down to join them a little later.

The soup was a rich mix of tomatoes, leeks and potatoes, with succulent chunks of braised pork. It was perhaps a little too heavily salted for Ryan's taste, but the wholemeal bread made it more palatable.

Rainey was deeply on edge, only toying with his bowl of soup. He played with the cutlery, staring out across the room toward the shuttered windows.

He sighed suddenly and looked over at Ryan. "Well?" he said.

Ryan red the subtext in the single word. "We'll go after the brushwooders. Bring out Dean and take some blood payment for the three dead men."

"We don't have the practice. Not for a drag-them-down-and-kick-the-shit kind of firefight. Been too long. We're all too slow for Straub and his butchers."

Trader tipped up his bowl to drain its dregs. He put it down and belched his satisfaction. "Tell you what, sec man," he said. "Danger is when someone doesn't know that they're weak. You're lucky. You got all of us to ride with you and shoot with you."

"One or two of us aren't at our best," Ryan said, "but there's nothing to stop us coming along."

"Stupes." Mildred shook her head. "I know none of your wounds are seriously life-threatening, but they're all nasty enough. You all need at least two or three days rest. Make sure the infection's cleared up."

Ryan knew in his heart that the woman was right. The middle of his back was extremely sore, and he was aware that he couldn't turn or bend anywhere near as quickly and freely as he would normally.

Jak answered her first. "True, Mildred."

J.B. also nodded. "I can get by, but that's the best I can say."

Ryan looked at Trader. "Seems like the old times have just come around again," he said. "Best you take charge of the raid."

Trader nodded solemnly. "Hell, why not."

BARON WEYMAN CAME DOWN with his son at his side, when the rest of the group had almost finished the main course of smoked mutton with a mustard sauce.

He looked older and sicker, his face a dusty gray, and he leaned heavily on Jamie's shoulder as he walked to his place at the head of the table.

The serving woman offered him a choice of the soup or the meat, but he waved her away, taking only a bowl of warm milk with some of the bread crumbled into it.

But when he eventually spoke to the company, his voice was surprisingly strong. "I have talked with Jamie, and we are of one mind and one heart. Your son, Cawdor, has been trapped because of my son's foolishness."

"And because Dean was extremely brave in offering himself up as a worthy sacrifice in my place, Father. We should not lose sight of that."

Ryan was, once again, impressed at the confident way the boy spoke, and at the adult vocabulary that he used. It crossed his mind, almost for the first time, to wonder whether he was actually doing the best he could do for his own son's education. But he set the thought aside. It was something that he knew he should return to, at another time and place, providing the gods came to ride beneath their banner.

Weyman smiled at his boy. "Truly spoken. So, we shall give all the help we can to this venture. Rainey?"

"Baron?"

"How many of our men can be spared? And only the younger and fitter ones."

Rainey considered the question for the moment, his eyes half closed as he did the arithmetic. "There's no more than ten good enough for this, Baron."

"That will leave us with some force to defend the ville, will it?"

Trader answered the baron. "You don't need to be all that fit to lean against a window and fire a blaster. Different out in the forest against the brushwooders. No point in taking cripples. Just put us all at risk."

Weyman nodded slowly. "Then it's agreed. When will you go from here?"

"Midnight," Trader replied. "Enough moon to see the trail. Then I'll use your sec men as backup. Rest of us can go in an hour or so before the dawn. Time guards are slowest."

"I'm coming," Jamie announced.

Trader stared at the boy, his eyes like dark chips of Sierra ice. "Not unless I say you do, kid."

"I've been in their camp, and I know where they're holding Dean."

Ryan caught Trader's eye. "Makes sense."

The older man nodded. "Long as he does what he's told and stays where he's put."

Baron Weyman wiped his mouth with his sleeve. "Jamie will do what he is told, outlander Trader. You can be sure of that. And—" he stood, resting the palms of his hands flat on the table "—I have something to say. I will probably have to go to my bed shortly. My health and not my will dictates this. So, I may not be up when you leave on your mission."

Rainey also stood. "Best pick the men, Baron."

He looked at Trader. "Where do you want to meet? Stables?"

"Yeah. Midnight."

The lean-faced sec man bowed to his baron and walked out of the room, his boot heels ringing on the stone flags.

Weyman watched him go, then returned to his theme. "Firstly I wish you all luck. Secondly I offer you my heartfelt thanks for taking my side in this. You owe me nothing. Most outlanders would have walked on by. Or, even thrown in their lot with these brushwooders."

"Not our way," Ryan said.

"That may be so..." He clicked his fingers, waiting while one of the older women brought in several dusty wine bottles, placing them at intervals around the long table. "This is the last of a very old chardonnay, from long-lost vineyards in the valleys north and inland from here. If you would help yourselves, I should be delighted."

The baron poured a thimbleful for himself, lifting it to his lips.

"Health," Ryan said, filling his dark green goblet, "life and happiness."

"For all here," Doc echoed.

"Amen to that." The baron drained his measure of the rich, pungent wine. "Excellent," he said. "Here is to the damnation of all enemies."

"And to safe returns," Krysty whispered, touching her glass to Ryan's.

EVERYONE RETIRED to their beds to get some rest before the midnight meeting.

Alone among the friends, Doc found himself unable to sleep, the excitement of the fighting to come making him feel restless, combined with a slight overindulgence in the superb chardonnay.

He walked down to the main doors, where a sleepy young sec guard limped over to let him out into the cool night air.

There was another sec man, looking even older than Doc, carrying a single-shot musket on his shoulder, pacing beneath the shadow of the high wall.

"Who's that?"

"Doc Tanner."

"Have to speak up a little. Hearing's a tad weaker than it once was."

"Doc Tanner! One of the outlanders."

"All right, all right. No need to shout at me, Doc. Not that deaf."

Doc left the sentry and strolled quietly around the back of the ville, approaching the stable. He caught movement in the huddled darkness and stepped toward it, drawing the Le Mat. "Halt, who goes there?" he challenged.

"Friend," the small voice replied.

"Dean? That's not—"

"It's me, Doc. Jamie."

"Ah, yes. Of course it is. Forgive an old man's foolishness, my boy."

"Sure."

Somewhere behind the young lad, Doc heard the sound of a pony moving restlessly, stamping its hooves.

"Wait a moment," he said. "Wait a goshdarned moment, Jamie. Were you thinking of heading out there on your own? That's it, isn't it?"

The boy's voice was so thin it sounded as if it might snap at any moment. Doc moved closer, putting out a friendly arm, feeling Jamie shrink from him.

"You'll tell my father. Then he won't even let me come along with you."

There was a small iron bench in the yard, and Doc led the baron's son to it, sitting down beside him.

"You were planning to go ahead, were you not?"

"Yes, Doc."

"Why? No, don't answer that for a moment. Might it be that you had a thought to go to this Straub and the brushwooders? Reveal who you were and hope they would let Dean go? Could it truly be that?"

"No."

The lie was so transparent that Doc nearly laughed, just barely checking himself. "Of course, it wouldn't be, my lad. Because, assuming they believed you, they would slit the throat of young Dean within five heartbeats of your admission. And where would our plan be, then? Riddle me that, Jamie."

"Spoiled."

Doc patted him on the arm. "The thought does you nothing but credit, lad. It was an honorable and courageous intention. The shame is that nobody else will ever know of it."

"What?"

"I shall tell nobody, Jamie. Will you?"

"Suppose not."

"And you promise me on your father's honor that you will now go to your room and try to snatch some sleep? And I shall do the same."

"All right."

"Promise me," Doc said. "If you please."

"I promise."

"Good lad. One last thing. Before you scud away, I would deem it an honor to shake you by the hand, Jamie Weyman."

A small hand slipped into his, and the old man gripped it firmly. For a fraction of a second, he had a vision of his long-lost little boy, Jolyon, wondering how his life had turned out without a father.

"Thanks, Doc."

"You're most welcome."

Sitting still, he could feel the cold of the metal through his breeches, as the lithe figure of the boy vanished toward the main house.

Doc didn't bother to go to bed, contenting himself with sitting in the deserted stable yard, alone with his thoughts and his memories.

Chapter Twenty-Eight

Rainey was already there in the yard when Ryan and the others arrived at the stable. Doc was stalking around, breath feathering from his mouth in the cold, slapping his hands for warmth. The group of ten sec men stood huddled together, a few of them smoking, the glowing ends of their cigarettes like tiny beacons in the darkness.

"Horses saddled and ready," the sec boss said.

Ryan turned, counting heads, feeling a sharp twinge from the arrow wound. Everyone was there, all fully armed. J.B. had the Smith & Wesson scattergun over his back, the Uzi slung across his right shoulder.

Jak was limping heavily, his snow-white head bobbing up and down in the streaks of moonlight.

The Steyr across Ryan's shoulder moved as he set his foot into the stirrup and dealt him a painful blow on top of the bandaged injury. It took a great effort not to yelp at the stabbing pain. He waited a few moments, aware of a fresh warm wetness seeping through the dressing over the wound. The mission wasn't going to be easy.

Trader swung into the saddle, his shoulders braced, head held high. His voice rang around the cobbled

yard. "Everyone ready to ride? Then let's do it. I want
the kid up ahead with me. Rainey, bring up the rear.
Rest, find your own places." He stared at the group of
sec men. "Be careful with those crossbows. Get them
armed when we stop and leave the horses."

Ryan fell into place beside Krysty, with Doc and J.B.
just behind him. He felt strange to be riding under the
orders of Trader once again. It took him back to the
long years with the war wags, ravening across Deathlands. The thought of Trader assuming command of
the war party had raised a few doubts in his mind, but
so far the old man seemed to have it all under control.

THEY PASSED THE CANYON where they'd spotted the
wild pigs, but there was no sign of the mutie creatures. Ryan figured they were probably out in the
woods, scavenging for themselves. Something to look
out for.

The jolting of his horse was causing him a lot of
pain in that first hour's ride. He could tell from the
tightness of the Armorer's face that he, too, was suffering. Jak rode third in line behind Trader and the
boy, but his wounded ankle didn't seem to be giving
him any trouble.

"How's it going, lover?" Krysty's voice was soft in
his ear, her hand patting him on the arm.

"Gone better. Gone worse."

"Think we can bring Dean out?"

Ryan nodded, his nostrils catching the scent of piñon among the other conifers. The rain had faded

away to the south, leaving a mild dampness in the air. "Don't see why not. Brushwooders don't have the firepower we do. More numbers, but not a lot more."

"They'll be expecting trouble."

"Sure. Trader plans to circle and all go in at once. That's his idea."

"How will he use the sec men?"

"Don't know. If it was me, I'd have them come in close behind us. Pick up anyone breaking through."

Krysty's hair blazed in the moonlight like living fire. "They're a real nice bunch of guys."

"Sure. Nice guys—"

"Finish last." She laughed quietly. "I know that one, Ryan. Laughed my diapers off at it. Not sure if it's true. But I don't sense any steel in them."

"Agreed, lover. That's why close behind us is the safest place for them."

"Trader explained his plan to you?"

Ryan felt a large drop of water drip from an overhanging branch onto his face, trickling down his cheek and dropping off his chin. "Not in detail."

"Did he ever?"

"No. Never."

"Worry you, lover?"

Ryan didn't answer immediately. "No. Not really."

NOBODY HAD RECKONED on the fog.

The night had grown cooler, with chill air moving in off the ocean, mixing with the humid, steamy air over the hot springs of the scabbies' territory and swilling inland toward the brushwooders camp.

By the time it coiled in among the tall pines, it had reduced visibility to less than twenty paces.

Trader stood in the stirrups and lifted his hand to call Ryan and J.B. to join him.

"Boy reckons we're less than a mile away," he said. "Fog makes it a different sort of firefight."

"Go in close?" the Armorer suggested.

"They'll likely have guards out," Ryan said. "Could be watching, even this far from their camp."

"Brushwood bastards wouldn't come up with that," Trader said. "Too busy fucking and sleeping."

"Straub's no stupe." Ryan straightened himself, unable to restrain a sigh of pain.

"Want to go back to the ville, Ryan?" Trader asked. "We'll bring Dean out."

"Sure you will. But I sort of want to be around when you do it."

Jamie was sitting silently beside the grizzled figure of the Trader, holding the reins of his pony, listening to the discussion of what to do.

"I say we leave the sec men here with the horses and go in on foot," Trader said.

"What?" Ryan couldn't believe what he was hearing. "You mean just the sec men? Out here on their own in the fireblasted mist? Come on, Trader!"

"What's your problem, Ryan? Don't like taking orders anymore? That it?"

"'Course not. From what I've seen and heard about Straub, I reckon he's dangerous. If he's placed distant pickets, they might already know we're here."

"All the more reason for the rest of us to go direct into the camp, blasters blazing, without wasting any more time on arguing."

This was the old Trader, from the early days when Ryan and J.B. had first joined him, stone-certain in his thinking, inflexible, resisting any argument.

Later he'd been content to listen and take advice from them on tactical matters. Now, all of that seemed to have been thrown clean out of the door.

Ryan tried again. "Look, there's all sorts of things wrong with this."

Trader was deliberately ignoring him, shading his eyes as he stared ahead into the bank of roiling fog.

J.B. added his weight. "Jak's the best stalker we got. Ryan's second. They're both carrying injuries that would make it suicide to go creepy-crawling in. I can just about manage to shoot one-handed. Just about. Leaves Abe, Doc, Krysty and Mildred. None of them are that able in hand-to-hand chilling."

Trader turned slowly. "My memory's turning into gruel. I thought you said I was in charge here. Must be I was wrong about that."

Ryan closed his eye. He could feel the livid scar that seamed across the right side of his face beginning to throb with anger. Unless he kept his temper on the tightest of reins, he was capable of sliding helplessly into a crevasse of blind rage, where he had the potential of saying anything, doing anything.

J.B. tried once more. "Fog like this, we can't charge in. Finish up shooting each other. Go in slow and careful and clear them a tent at a time. All of us."

But Trader was insistent, refusing to listen to any kind of reasoned argument. "We leave the sec men here. Rest of us go in, and when the shooting starts they can follow and pick off any brushwood stragglers."

Ryan patted his horse on the side of the neck, trying to relieve his own tension. "What if Straub has men around us now? Those crossbows only give one chance to the sec men. Could get chilled. And once you run in out of the fog, blaster blazing, the first thing they might do is open up my son from throat to groin." The anger was almost beyond control. "If that happens, then the first person I waste is you, Trader."

"Oh, yeah?"

"Yeah."

The SIG-Sauer was somehow out and cocked in his hands, and the Armalite had moved around with the lazy ease of a snake, covering him.

Krysty came out of nowhere, forcing her mount in between the men. Her emerald eyes were wide and staring, green fire in the moonlight.

"Gaia! You'd rather murder each other and ruin the attack than back off and admit that either of you could be wrong." Her finger pointed at Ryan. "Back off, lover. You know how to do it."

"Trader's dog-brained wrong," he grated.

"It was agreed that I run this mission. If we were still with the war wags, Ryan, then I'd have had you held down and shot through the back of the neck for mutiny."

"You used to do the shooting yourself," Abe interrupted. "Seen you do it."

"That's right enough." J.B. let the Uzi ease down again, as the tension slithered away.

"We do it the way I said."

Ryan looked at him, breathing slowly, feeling the butchering rage passing. He had been within a ragged moment of putting a 9 mm round between Trader's eyes—assuming that the old man's AR-16 hadn't chilled him first.

"I said that we do this my way, Ryan. I want to hear what you got to say."

"I say you best not push this any further. I say that this could all go sadly wrong, Trader. I say that there could be some of the wrong blood spilled in the dirt. Understand me? That's what I say."

Trader relaxed, aware that he'd gotten his own way. "Good," he said. "Fucking good."

THE SEC MEN SEEMED HAPPY enough to rest with the horses, as a rear guard. Rainey had spoken with Trader, arguing that he should remain with them. But he'd been talked down.

"Easy enough. They wind up the cranks on those crossbows and get the bolts loaded up. They form a small perimeter, say forty yards, and watch out for trouble."

"Won't see much in this fog," J.B. stated. "Might do better to stick close and quiet."

Trader didn't even bother to argue with the Armorer. "Rest of you got your blasters ready? Make

every one an ace on the line. I'll head for where Jamie
thinks the kid's holed up. Jamie and Abe, stick close
to my side."

He looked around them, deep-set eyes lingering for
a moment on the faces of J.B. and Ryan.

Rainey held up a hesitant hand. "Trader?"

"What is it?"

"Got one question. There's women and children
down there in the camp."

"Wrong, sec man. All there is down there in the fog
is the brushwood camp. Every single person in that
camp, young or old, male or female, drunk or sober,
is an enemy to us. Understand? Every...single...
person."

THE FOG WAS singularly unpleasant.

In only a few paces the main attacking party was
already out of sight of the sec men and the horses,
though they could hear the animals whickering for
several minutes before the mist muffled the sound into
silence.

The stench of sulfur was heavy in the wreathing
clouds, and it clung to the skin and clothes, insinuat-
ing itself into the mouth and nostrils and the pores of
the skin. It was cool and clammy, like trying to breathe
through a wet kerchief.

As Jamie led Trader along the winding trail, the rest
kept close to them, walking through the dank, dripping stillness, aware of the trunks of trees that swiftly
disappeared into the fog, vanishing barely twenty feet
above their heads.

For most of the time there was no sign of life at all in the forest—though everyone stopped dead after barely five minutes, hearing the sound of something large and ungainly, blundering through the blinding mist just a little way ahead of them. Ryan was walking fourth in line behind Jamie, Trader and Abe, and he glimpsed the shape of something, which grunted and snuffled and had two tusks, one broken.

The wild mutie boar didn't scent the group of humans as they stood, paralyzed, watching its bulk disappear again toward the north of the track.

"Bit too close," Abe whispered, as they resumed walking west, toward the brushwooders' camp.

KRYSTY STUMBLED against Ryan and nearly fell. He half turned to steady her, shocked at the wide-eyed look of horror etched on her face.

"What?" he whispered.

"Oh, Earth Mother! Back. Must turn back now. Feel desperate danger behind us. Turn back now." She pushed Ryan aside, running clumsily past the others, nearly knocking over Abe.

She grabbed at Trader's sleeve. "Stop!" she hissed.

"What?" He was taken by surprise, almost hefting the Armalite to crack it against her skull.

"Must stop and go back, Trader. I can feel it. Very, *very* strong. Behind us."

"Feel what?"

Krysty stared behind her, into the dark bank of fog that was all around them like an encircling wall.

"Something's gone triple wrong, Trader. Mebbe they know we're coming. I can't tell what it is."

Ryan started to go back toward where they'd left the ten sec men, but Trader called to him.

"Goin' somewhere, Ryan?"

"You heard her. Krysty gets a feeling as strong as this one, then you take note of it."

"She doesn't know what it is, but she *feels* something might've gone wrong." Trader laughed and shook his head. "We keep going."

For a moment nobody moved.

Then the sound came from behind them, to the east, a terrible, piercing scream of soul-tearing pain and despair.

Chapter Twenty-Nine

Magnus Lette, at nineteen, was the youngest of the patrol of sec men—only by six minutes—then came his identical twin brother, Marcus. They had been with Baron Weyman since they were lads of eleven. Their mother had been a cook in the ville, but had died of pneumonia in that cold winter. As far back as Magnus and Marcus could remember, there hadn't been a father. Eudoria Lette, their mother, told changing tales of a sailor, a packman, a whaler and a shootist.

In the end, it didn't much matter.

Weyman was a good master, kind and considerate, never demanding too much from the men and women who served him. And Bill Rainey was also a decent sec boss.

Magnus and Marcus Lette were sitting together, part of a forty-yard defensive perimeter that had the horses at its center. Every man faced outward, into the fog that snaked between the tall pines. Every man had his powerful crossbow armed and ready across his lap.

The forest was dark and silent, only the ghost of a moon filtering through the mist.

"Marcus?"

"What is it, little bro?"

"Might only be little now, but baby boy Magnus is catching up to you."

It was the oldest of jokes between the identical twin brothers, but it still made both of them smile.

"What do you want, Magnus?"

"Just wondering whether we might see these wild brushwood folks. Bill says there's plenty of them."

Marcus grinned, teeth white in the silvery light. "Raggedy-assed bastards won't be no harm to us, bro. Just aim and loose a bolt at them."

The brothers blinked at the apparition that had sprung into sight from the woodland. One moment the space had been empty of life, swirling with dense fog, then, in the beating of a heart, there was a man there.

Neither Magnus nor Marcus were worried. They knew what brushwooders looked like. They were filthy, in old flea-ridden furs and torn hides, had long, lank hair and blotched skin and were better than half-way toward scabbies.

But this wasn't a brushwooder, so he obviously wasn't any threat to them.

From top to toe, the stranger looked even smarter than the baron himself.

He wore expensive Western-style stack-heeled boots in black leather with a silver snake crawling around them, and a shirt as black as midnight, and jeans to match, with lines of silver rivets. A chunky necklace of top-quality raw turquoise hung around the muscular neck, and a large opal was studded through the right ear. He was smiling at the brothers, showing the glitter of a gold tooth at the front of his mouth.

He looked to be somewhere around fifty, with a totally shaved head.

"You lost, stranger?" Magnus asked.

"Are we not all lost, friend?" The voice was pleasant to the ear. "Are we not all wanderers through that dark valley that men call life?"

"Sure we are." Marcus grinned, not quite certain of himself. "Sure we are."

The man walked closer, light on his feet for a tall man. Both the brothers had quickly noticed that he wasn't armed. All he was holding was a small disk of inlaid silver that he was spinning on the end of its long chain.

It was very eye-catching.

Magnus was drawn to it, squinting at the whirling circle that seemed to generate its own purplish light. He hadn't realized how tired he was.

"You boys look sleepy. I've just been around and talked with all your good friends. Eight of them. And they got real sleepy, as well."

Magnus glanced to his right, seeing that the next man in line, Jericho Cooder, had actually fallen asleep on watch. His crossbow lay beside him in the dirt.

Odd thing was, though it wasn't all that easy to see through the shifting fog, Jericho seemed to be sleeping with his eyes wide open.

"That's all right," the stranger said pleasantly. "Lots of men sleep with their eyes open, don't they?"

He had such a gentle, persuasive voice that Magnus found himself nodding in agreement, even though he'd never actually heard of such a thing before.

It was also strange that Magnus couldn't even remember saying anything about Jericho. Not out loud.

"Shame all of our friends aren't here. They've gone ahead to raid the camp and free the baron's son, have they?"

"Secret," Marcus whispered. "Not supposed to tell anyone the secret."

"Now then, friends, what secret would that be? Good companions don't have secrets from each other. I'd tell you any secret if I had one."

"Would you?" Magnus asked dreamily. He found his eyelids were weighing heavy, and he wanted to lie down and rest, just like Jericho. This stranger was such a kindly, good man. If he hadn't felt so tired, Magnus would've gotten up off the ground and given him a real big brotherly hug.

"Why not?" the stranger asked. "A chaste embrace? For all men are brothers who go down, go down, this lonely road. But first—" he turned to Marcus "—what's the secret about the mission? It is to rescue the son of Baron Weyman, isn't it?"

"Yes and no," Marcus replied.

Magnus shifted his position, ready to lie down, but he found he was sitting on a sharp spur of jagged rock. Though it was digging into his buttocks, he somehow couldn't be bothered to move to a more comfortable place.

He didn't feel quite so tired, and the spinning silver disk no longer held all of his attention.

"Tell me the secret," the lean stranger whispered, holding the whirling silver of metal closer to Marcus's eyes. "Tell it to me."

"Better not, big brother," Magnus said. But his voice seemed to be trapped inside his own skull. There was a silent whisper of breath from between his cold lips, adding to the coils of wreathing mist, but no sound. The stranger didn't even bother to look in his direction.

"The secret is that the son is not the son. He is a son . . . someone's son. But not the son of Baron Weyman."

The stranger's patient smile slipped and for a splinter of a second, Magnus caught sight of another face, like a grotesque mask buried beneath the skin and flesh. The odd eyes, almost black and flecked with silver, widened, showing a rim of scarlet blood around them.

"The son of the one-eyed man, Cawdor," he said, adjusting the smile back in place again. "Yes, I should have guessed. Very stupid of me." He nodded. "Ah me, but there is still plenty of time to remedy the foolish error. First, I must complete this small piece of business here."

Magnus's buttocks really hurt, the broken shard of rock probing its way into his flesh. A bizarre thought swam into his mind, that he didn't like this stranger after all.

That he wasn't really a friend.

That he meant them harm.

The dark eyes turned toward him for a moment, but Magnus's expression hadn't altered.

Marcus was acting oddly. He had reached up and opened the collar of his dark green livery shirt, running his hand absently up and down his own neck, leaning his head back to look up into the branches of the trees, making the sinews stand out, the pulse of the carotid artery clearly visible.

Magnus glanced overhead, wondering what his brother was finding so interesting, but there was nothing there.

When he looked back down again, the stranger had withdrawn something from a little velvet pouch that he wore neatly tucked away around his throat. It glittered with a pale fire in the wisps of moonlight.

It was a straight-edged razor with a carved ivory handle and the shaved-headed man had cut Marcus's throat with it, ducking slightly to avoid the cascade of arterial blood that gushed out with a frightful force, black in the silvery glow.

The crossbow fell from the dying man's lap, catching the trigger, loosing the quarrel. There was a deep thrumming sound, and the bolt thudded into a massive redwood on the far side of the clearing.

"Now, Magnus," the stranger said, smiling contentedly. "I will go and arrange a reception for the other invaders, who will walk blindly into it."

It was a nightmare.

That was the only possible answer.

The razor was moving, almost of its own accord, toward his own throat.

If it wasn't a nightmare, then this night stalker had chilled nine of Magnus's friends. Slit all of their throats so that the floor of the forest was sodden with rank, steaming puddles of fresh-spilled blood.

"No pain and no gain, Magnus," Straub whispered. "What goes around, comes around."

The pain from the stone that he was sitting on was almost unbearable. Magnus's mind had simply gone blank, knowing that he was about to be brutally murdered and not being able to do anything about it.

"Know what?" he said, his voice like the faint croak of a distant frog.

"What is it?" Straub asked, concerned as a friendly priest at a parish children's party.

"I always said I'd catch him up and get to be oldest. Now I've done it."

"Indeed, you have." Straub patted the young man on his dew-damp cheek. "Indeed, you have. Very well done."

The cold steel, honed to slice a human hair down its length, touched Magnus's skin and began the single, long, deep cut that would end his life.

Only then, woefully too late, did the teenager open his mouth and fill his lungs, giving a terrible, piercing scream.

Chapter Thirty

"We're fucked." Trader stopped dead in his tracks at the dreadful cry. "They got around us, and they're chilling the sec men."

Bill Rainey's foxy face had gone slack and loose with the shock and horror. "Can't have..." he stammered. "Can't take... them all out."

"Can and has," Ryan snapped. There was a temptation to remind his old leader that he'd warned him about just this possibility, but it was all too late for that.

"Dark night! Means they know that we're coming." J.B. had dropped to one knee, awkwardly readying the Uzi, trying to steady it one-handed.

"Could mean they know that Dean isn't me," Jamie gasped. "If they know that..."

There was a movement in the woods around them, dark shapes flitting through the dense fog, muffled shouting.

Ryan made an instant decision.

"Only one way to save my son," he said. Going in alone. Now. Rest of you, back to the ville."

The only people to argue were Trader and Krysty.

"No way, Ryan."

"I'll lose you both, lover."

He looked around the circle. Shock and dismay was on every face at the realization that their plan was in ruins.

"No choice. I'm going now. Slide in and find Dean. Bring him out. See you back at the ville sometime tomorrow. Don't try to come after me. Just fuck things up even more." He turned on his heel, then paused as another thought struck him. "Brushwooders know we're here. Get the horses if you can, but they're probably already lost. So try and circle around and move fast. Let Rainey and the kid guide you. They know the area."

"Take the greatest of care, my dear fellow," Doc said, gripping him by the shoulder.

"Thanks, Doc. Here, take my rifle with you. It'll only get in the way."

There wasn't anything else to be said.

Ryan gave Krysty a kiss on the cheek, then turned away. In passing he couldn't help noticing how Trader seemed to have aged by ten years in the past five minutes, at the realization that his fight plan had gone so appallingly wrong.

The fog wrapped itself around Ryan as he moved away.

RYAN MOVED LOW AND FAST, not worrying much about making noise. The mist and the surrounding trees would combine to muffle and distort any sounds, and there were brushwooders scurrying around him.

He had the SIG-Sauer still holstered, relying on the panga drawn in his right hand. If there was to be any chilling, it would be well to try to make it silent.

The one thing that he had on his side was the knowledge that most of the fighting men from the camp seemed to be out and about in the forest. If he could get back under cover of night and fog, and find Dean quickly enough, there was a real hope that they could get away before dawn.

He pushed aside the insistent thought that Straub, Ditchdown and the brushwooders had somehow found out that Dean wasn't the baron's son.

If they *had* found out, then he was on a mission to try to retrieve his son's corpse.

RYAN WAS TRYING TO GET the local geography clear in his mind as he ran toward the camp.

The brushwooders' settlement was in a narrow bowl, surrounded by steep hills. The only trail to the west out of it wound along a ravine, into the un- claimed territory of the scabbies, only opening up when it reached the treacherous, snaking pathway that ran through the golden wasteland of hot springs and geysers, and swamps of boiling mud.

There was the tiny seed of an idea beginning to ger- minate at the back of Ryan's mind, but it was still too small to be worth a lot of thought.

He was still thinking about the route back to the coast when he walked around a grove of stunted tam- arisks, straight into one of the brushwooders. The man was a little above average height, and he had just finished taking a leak against a redwood.

"Seen any of..." he began, turning as he laced up his pants.

Ryan didn't hesitate. He stepped in close, swinging the panga in a powerful upward cut, aiming at the brushwooder's throat.

The point struck home just below the lower ear, driving through, splintering teeth, pinning the tongue to the upper palate and continuing on.

The tip of the eighteen inches of cold steel ended up in the front part of the man's brain.

It was a brutally effective killing stroke.

The brushwooder tried to speak, but his mouth was filled with his own blood and broken teeth, the wide blade forcing his head backward.

Ryan squeezed the lower jaw so that he could withdraw the panga, but it had become jammed among the upper bones of the skull and it wouldn't come free.

The man had reached for his own knife, but the lines were down and his fingers opened and closed helplessly.

Ryan let him fall, releasing the hilt of his panga, waiting until the residual twitching and thrashing was over. Then he set his combat boot on the corpse's chest and, using both hands, tugged the blood-slick blade free.

Before wiping it on the ragged coat, he straightened and looked around him. The fog walls were just as impenetrable. Nothing human was visible, and nobody seemed aware of the instant slaughter of one of their fellows.

Yet there was a sense of bustle. Standing completely still and quiet, Ryan could sense that there were people in the forest, all oblivious to his own presence. The feeling he had was of some moving east, toward the horses and his invisible companions, and some west, back toward the village.

Which was where he was heading.

THE MOON WAS WANING, meaning that the woods became even darker, making the mist denser.

Ryan had to slow his pace, fearful of becoming totally lost, fearful of missing the brushwooders' camp altogether and blundering out into the death-trap land beyond.

There was also the very real danger that he might blunder blindly along, straight into the middle of a bunch of the hunting men.

But there was the smell of wood smoke and roasting meat, overlaying the throat-tight stink of sulfur, leading him along the right trail.

The main track was a little way north, higher up the hillside, but Ryan was following a narrower, winding path that had all the hallmarks of being made by animals rather than humans. It followed the course of a zigzag stream that ran swift and bright to Ryan's left.

His back was aching, and he stopped and stretched, feeling the stiff bandages peel stickily away from the wound and the instant warmth of leaking blood.

It had been several hours since he'd left the ville, and he was becoming thirsty. Might as well take advantage of the stream while he could.

The tinkling of the water covered any other sounds, but he stopped, head to one side, listening. For a moment he thought that he'd heard something moving on the far side of the narrow stream, where he could just see another, similar path. But the sound wasn't repeated.

He took a chance and threw himself flat on his stomach, wincing at the effect on his arrow wound. He sheathed the panga and drew the SIG-Sauer, holding it ready in his right hand. If anyone took him by surprise, it wasn't likely to be an opportunity for a swift, clean kill.

The water was utterly delicious, flowing from somewhere high up in the distant Sierras, away to the far east. It was as cold as charity and as sweet as hope.

Ryan dipped his face below the surface, drinking deeply, feeling refreshed from just a few mouthfuls.

He lifted his head, the dark curly hair dripping spangles of water back into the stream, and looked straight into the swarthy muzzle and hooked tusks of a huge mutie pig.

The beast wasn't quite as big as the boar that was called General, but it had to have weighed better than a thousand pounds of murderous hatred on the hoof. Its tiny deep-set eyes glowered at the man who had invaded its own drinking place, and its sharp hooves pawed at the bank of wet mud.

All that separated it from Ryan was less than five feet of deep, chilly stream.

Ryan didn't make any hurried, frightened movements that might have induced the pig to launch itself at him. He raised himself a little way, bringing the blaster around to cover the beast, not sure quite what effect a 9 mm round would have on a creature that size.

The pig snorted, its breath reeking with rotting meat. Ryan realized that it wasn't sure what sort of a threat he represented, and it kept lowering its head as though checking that the water was still there.

"Fuck off," Ryan whispered.

To his amazement and relief, the mutie animal did just that. It shook its huge rutting head from side to side, then backed away a few steps, as if it might be readying itself to charge. Then it simply turned and trotted ponderously away into the white fog, disappearing in seconds.

Ryan realized that he'd been holding his breath for a long time and slowly released it in a white plume into the cold predawn air.

THE EDGE OF THE CAMP was less than two hundred yards farther on, nestling in the sheer-sided valley.

There were no guards out, but Ryan could see through the clearing mist that there were men and women moving around the makeshift huts and tents.

The fire had been built up to a roaring blaze, which was one of the reasons that the fog was markedly less thick around the brushwood settlement.

Jamie had described where he thought Dean would be held prisoner. It was on the far side of the encampment, in a ragged tent with a high lodgepole from which something that looked like a human scalp was fluttering.

Ryan made his way around the perimeter, using the plentiful cover. He stopped once as three men walked quickly by, talking excitedly about the way Straub had massacred ten of the ville's sec men entirely on his own, and how they had all the horses from the raiding party.

At least that was what the snatch of conversation sounded like, though Ryan simply didn't believe that one person could take out ten armed and alert sec men. Unless he'd been armed with a first-class light machine gun. And there's been no sound of any shooting.

"Impossible," he whispered to himself.

DAWN WASN'T FAR OFF, and Ryan knew that his task would be made that much more difficult by the way the shrouding fog was leaking away.

But he was safely at the rear of what he hoped was the right tent. He'd come close to the flapping canvas, straining to catch any sound from within that would give him a clue.

But it was as silent as a tomb.

Ryan had a sudden vision of what he'd find inside—his son's corpse, naked and bloodless, hideously mutilated. It was so powerful an image that he had to kneel, fighting against the desire to throw up.

"Don't believe you."

The words were barely audible, but Ryan would have known the voice out of ten million others.

"Dean," he breathed.

There was another voice there, harsh and croaky, sounding like an old woman's. Ryan cautiously probed at the coarse material with the needle tip of his panga, boring open a tiny hole, pressing his eye to it.

A small, smoky fire and a tallow lamp gave just enough light for him to be able to see what was happening inside the tent.

Dean was sitting, hands tied in front of him, a tight strip of rawhide knotted tightly around his neck, holding him against the center pole of the tent. As far as Ryan could see, the boy hadn't been badly hurt, though there were dark shadows of bruises around his eyes.

The other person was an old crone, bent almost double. She was performing a bizarre dance in front of the helpless boy, lifting up her ragged skirt to expose herself, mocking him in a chanting, singsong voice.

"Chilled the buggerin' sec men and chilled all your buggerin' outland friends, and soon we'll be chillin' you. Ditchdown's promised me I can have some funnin' with you, laddie. Like what you see, do you? Like a ripe taste of it?"

There was no point in waiting any longer.

Every minute that passed brought the dawn a little closer, and with it the chance of returning brushwooders revealing that Dean wasn't the true son of the baron.

If he was to rescue the boy and get him away, then the last moments of darkness would be an essential friend to them. He gripped the hilt of the panga and drew the razored edge down the outer cover of the tent.

The old woman had her back to him and was too preoccupied with her taunting jig to be aware of anything happening behind her.

Ryan eased himself through the gap in the material, seeing the sudden widening of his son's eyes. But Dean knew better than to attract attention. He immediately dropped his gaze to the packed earth floor of the tent.

"Won't even look at old Rosie, eh?" the woman squawked in an eldritch screech of delight.

For a passing moment Ryan considered knocking her unconscious and tying and gagging her.

But he didn't have the time or the inclination.

He switched the steel to his left hand and stepped close to the capering figure, clubbing her hard across the nape with his right fist. There was the familiar click, and she dropped like a discarded bundle of rags.

Ryan knelt and checked her pulse, ready to open her throat. But there was no need.

He turned to his son. "All right, Dean?"

"Yeah, Dad. Better than all right now you're here."

"Hurt?"

"No. Knocked me around a bit. Worst was what that old bitch was planning."

"I can guess."

He crouched and cut the cords around the boy's wrists. Dean gasped as he rubbed hard at his hands to try to bring back the circulation. "Wow! That hurts. Watch out for the one around my neck. Real tight."

Ryan eased the tip of the blade under the rawhide, slicing through it.

"Ready? You can stand up all right?"

"Sure. Listen. That old sow had my blaster. Let's see if she's still got it."

He rummaged through her clothes, pulling out the Browning and sticking it back in his belt. As he stood, Dean deliberately kicked the corpse in the face with the toe of his combat boots.

"Wasted effort," Ryan said.

"Not when it makes you feel so good, Dad."

They moved to the back of the tent, where Ryan reached to draw aside the cut material, the movement tugging painfully at the wound in the small of his back.

"Hurt?" Dean whispered, seeing his father wince.

"Some. Not bad. Talk when we get outside. Head straight into the trees but watch out for the brush-wooders. They seem like an army out there."

Father and son slipped out of the camp and vanished silently into the misty forest beyond.

Chapter Thirty-One

Though it gave him more discomfort, Ryan led the way up along the flank of the steepest slope, above and to the north of the brushwooders' settlement. He carefully avoided the main trail back toward the ville, where armed horsemen could easily have ridden them down.

It was heavily wooded, and the recent rain made the going slippery and treacherous. But it brought them out where Ryan wanted to be, close to the side canyon that he suspected might be the home of the pack of mutie pigs.

When they'd been out of the camp for about ten minutes they both heard a piercing shriek of rage.

"Found Rosie's corpse," Dean panted, grinning happily at his father.

"Don't sound pleased."

"Think that was Straub?"

Ryan leaned his hand against the bole of a spreading sycamore, catching his own breath. "Could be. I heard brushwooders saying that Straub personally, on his own, chilled ten armed sec men. Think that's possible? I figured him for a triple creep. Something about him..."

Dean had hunkered on a rounded boulder, and he considered the question. "I felt dizzy when he stared at me, and I sort of had the feeling that he could be a seer or a doomie. Kind of reading what I was thinking. You know, Dad?"

"Yeah, I know."

"We going back to the ville?"

Ryan shook his head. "Not yet. Got an idea that just keeps on growing and growing."

RYAN WAS SURPRISED at how much the arrow had taken out of him. It hadn't been that grave a wound—he'd certainly had far worse in his life—and hadn't touched any major organs or broken any bones. The only potential damage was to the web of muscles that protected the base of the spine from harm.

But it had been a clean wound, the arrow coming out fairly easily.

"Getting older," he told himself.

He decided that it was about time to take a break from the grinding uphill climb. They were comfortingly close now to the crest of the ridge, on a deer trail that Ryan hoped would eventually bring them down again some way along the side canyon that had been his destination.

"Take five," he said.

Dean dropped on a patch of soft turf, in between a grove of alders. Now the dawn light was strengthening, and Ryan could see that the boy had been badly beaten, with congealed blood rimming both mouth and nose, as well as purple weals across his cheeks and around both eyes.

"You feel all right, son?"

"Just a few hits. Only on the surface. Right now I never felt better, Dad."

Ryan sat beside the boy, watching the pale spears of light break through the trees around them, casting long, watery shadows down the slope. It seemed amazingly still and peaceful, and it was difficult to believe that only a mile or so away, in the grove where the horses had been tethered, there had been bloody butchery done.

They'd been moving fast since the breakout, and this was their first opportunity to talk quietly together.

Ryan told the boy about the abortive raid that had ended with the deaths of the two sec men and the capture of Micah. Dean explained what had happened, and why he'd had to chill the helpless prisoner.

"Did the right thing, son."

Dean was concerned to hear about the injuries suffered by J. B. Dix, Jak and his father, though Ryan stressed that none of the wounds was life-threatening.

The failure of the night's attack surprised the boy. "Was it Trader's fault?"

"Difficult question, Dean. He and I argued about placing the backup force. But, in fairness to the bad-tempered old bastard, none of us knew that Straub had the kind of mutie power it seems he's got."

"Jamie tell you what happened?" The question dragged itself out with great reluctance.

"How you pretended to be him?"

"Yeah. It was my idea. I'm not saying that to make myself any kind of hero, Dad."

"I know that."

"Just so you know that the kid didn't turn chicken on me. He was going to own up, but I stopped him. I reckoned it was the best chance for both of us to make it."

Ryan nodded, keeping alert for any sounds of pursuit. "Turned out right."

Dean had something on his mind, but he couldn't quite steer around to it.

"You like Jamie Weyman, Dad?"

"Sure. Much tougher than you think, the first time you meet him."

Dean nodded. "I thought that. Only he's got all that...that *learning*, don't he?"

"Doesn't he? Should be 'doesn't,' not 'don't,' Dean. Krysty's always on at me for making mistakes like that."

"Think it's important, Dad?"

"Krysty says that if you can choose between getting it right and getting it wrong, then it's better to get it right. I suppose I agree with her."

Now it was coming to it.

"Jamie knows all about math and history and places and science and stuff, Dad."

"He's been well taught."

"Not like me," Dean muttered, head down, not looking up to meet his father's eye.

"No. Not like you." He moved close enough to put an arm around the boy's shoulders. "You've been taught in a different school. School of life. Sure, Jamie knows all that learning stuff, Dean. But put him in a wilderness with a knife and no shelter, and he'd die in forty-eight hours. Probably much less. You know what I mean?"

"Yeah."

"You're the most self-sufficient boy I ever met. Bet you a bucket of jack that even Jak Lauren wasn't as good as you when he was your age."

"You reckon?" Dean seemed happier at that idea.

Ryan followed the course. "You can look after yourself, Dean, anytime and anyplace. You've been in tight spots that would make someone like Jamie sit down and wait for the last train to the coast."

"Sure, but—"

"It worry you that Jamie's got such a good education, Dean? That it?"

"Suppose it is, Dad. Am I real stupe?"

"For worrying about it?"

"Yeah."

"'Course not. Everybody wants to be better than they are. I envy Mildred the way she shoots and all she knows about medicine. J.B. for his knowledge of weapons. Krysty for her wisdom. Doc for the bedrock of learning he's gotten himself. Jak for his way with knives and his tracking skills. Everyone has things they reckon they're good at. As well as things they envy others."

"I suppose so."

"You wish you were better book-learned. Jamie wishes he could do all the things you can do."

"Does he?"

"Sure he does."

"How do you know?"

Ryan shook him gently. "Hey, you doubting me, Dean? I'm telling you it's so."

"But... I mean... Do you think there'd ever be a chance of me having some sort of real learning, like him?"

"I think it's possible. I know that Krysty once talked about some kind of school where you live for a year or so. Not that far from Harmony ville, where she came from. Get yourself a real book education."

Dean nodded, eyes screwed up as he considered this totally new option in his life.

"A year?"

"Or two years. I don't know. I know that there's an awful lot of learning that a man could get. Doc sometimes says that knowledge is power, and I believe him."

"Do you, truly, Dad?"

"Yeah. We'd keep in touch. Visit. Then, afterward, it might be that me and Krysty'll have settled down someplace. And you'd come join us."

"Like Jak did?"

"Yeah."

He glanced up at his father. "And have kids?"

Ryan swallowed hard. He hadn't seen that particular question coming. "Mebbe."

"Brothers and sisters for me. I think I'd probably like that, Dad."

"If you got plenty of education, then you could pass it on to them."

Dean grinned, jumping to his feet. "Can we get back to the ville and talk to Krysty?"

"Not yet." Ryan stood and looked behind them, where the fog had thinned down to a veil of white mist, opalescent in the first light of the new day.

"Nobody's coming after us." Dean was staring intently down the trail, through the trees. "We could cut back down onto the main track and be in the ville in about four or five hours."

"We could, but we aren't. Been thinking about a sort of a plan. Been taking its own shape while we walked and talked. Now it's time to bring it out and shake it down and hold it up. See if it might work."

THEY CROSSED THE TOP of the hill, looking down the far side into another steep-sided canyon.

The trail seemed to vanish as it reached the highest point of the scarp. The hogback ridge continued northward, and it was just possible to make out where it curved round eastward in what looked like the box end of the heavily wooded valley.

"Hey," Dean squeaked, pointing with an arrow-straight finger. "Look, pigs."

Ryan looked where his son was indicating, wishing that he had the boy's keen vision. He'd been so long with only one eye that he automatically accommodated to it, having no problem with spatial concepts.

He still didn't have that same extra sharpness of sight as Dean. But he could make out movement.

Pink-gray shapes lumbered between the trees. Now he could see that there had to have once, way before the long winters, been a farm in the canyon, and it was the ancient predark orchards that had attracted the large herd of mutie animals. There were rambling apple and pear trees at the bottom of the valley, the ground below them thick with windfalls.

"Looks like it might be where they live," Dean said, dropping his voice, even though the pigs were a good quarter mile away and a thousand feet lower.

"That's what I thought."

"We can probably work our way around the top end of the canyon, then drop down into the next ravine along."

Ryan glanced sideways at his son, seeing how quickly he'd tumbled to why they'd come this difficult way. "Why do that?" he asked.

"Because it'd be triple stupe to go down where all the pigs are..." He stopped, grinning. "That's why we came this way, instead of sticking to the bottom road. Part of this special plan, isn't it, Dad?"

"Could be. Let's go slow and careful and see what we can see."

Chapter Thirty-Two

The brushwooders had taken the horses. All that was found in the abandoned clearing was a scene from a slaughterhouse.

The ten bodies lay where they'd fallen, every one with his throat neatly cut. Bill Rainey went quickly around the circle of corpses, his boots squelching in the blood-sodden grass. Already the blowflies were humming busily around the lakes of congealing crimson, sensing a feast beyond any imagining.

"This one looks like he mebbe tried to fight back a little," J.B. called, pointing down with his good right arm, the left one tucked snugly inside his jacket to ease the pain from the musket ball.

"Magnus. That's his twin brother, Marcus, lying next to him. Sweet couple of boys." The sec boss was weeping openly, holding up his carmined hands to the gray dawn sky. "You must've been sleeping, Jesus, letting this happen. Ten innocent men, butchered like little lambs."

"Best move," Jak said, limping to the far side of the clearing. "Got horses. Could follow us."

BUT THE BRUSHWOODERS didn't pursue them. Ditchdown was all for a vengeful chase, once the corpse of his aunt, Rosie, had been found with its neck snapped.

"Catch them easy," he said.

Straub shook his head. "Time for a serious change of plans," he said calmly. "Now we know the kid we held belonged to that monocular son of a bitch, Cawdor, and not the valuable son of the baron. When I finally get my hands on father and son, I'll take pains to see that they have pain. There's . . ."

"What's 'monocular' mean?" asked the leader of the brushwooders, running his hand through his damp hair.

"One-eyed."

"But why not go after them all?"

"Tracks show only one came in for the boy. Cawdor is my guess. Bet you a peanut to a honey stick the rest are hotfooting it toward the ville."

Ditchdown stamped his foot in frustration. "Then why not get after them?"

"Baron's lost thirteen of his men in the last day. He was always weak. Now we got the edge. In a day or so we can go in slow and easy and the ville's ours."

TRADER WAS FOR WAITING to see if Ryan and Dean turned up safely.

"Can't abandon friends. One of the greatest rules of living in Deathlands. Might be the number one rule."

Krysty pointed at him angrily. "Just keep your nose out of this, Trader. Ryan told you precisely what we were to do. Things've gone wrong enough as it is."

"Not Trader's fault," Abe said, the first time he'd spoken in the past hour.

"Krysty's not saying it is." Mildred looked at Doc for help. "We've learned that what Ryan says is generally the best thing to do."

"I could not agree more." Doc wiped his forehead with his swallow's-eye kerchief. "Where rank confusion offers choice, best listen to a single voice."

THE DESCENT from the ridge was more dangerous and difficult than Ryan had hoped.

The trail had vanished, running out on the bare expanse of granite and wind-washed scree that lay just over the far side, before the trees began. The loose mass of tiny stones shifted as they started to move across it, with the risk of it gathering force into a full avalanche that might dash them helplessly into the valley far below.

Where the mutie pigs were waiting.

"Run it!" Ryan called. "Follow me, like this."

The only safe way to get over the wide bed of scree was to run, taking great bounding strides, using the shingled movement of the stones to actually help you on your way, never waiting to let your feet sink deep into the sucking morass of pebbles, always keeping on the move.

It took great physical strength and agility, and Ryan was immediately aware of how much his wound was going to hinder him and slow him.

Every leaping step tugged the bandages away, opening the puckered holes wider, bringing a trickle of blood down over his buttocks and thighs.

"It's great, Dad!" Dean whooped close behind him, overtaking him. He moved ahead of his father with an easy grace, toward the end of the scree and the beginning of the dense forest of dark spiky pines.

"Slow up, Dean!" Ryan yelled. "Get down and slide on your ass to slow."

The boy heard him, waving a casual hand to acknowledge the instruction. But he found his own more effective way of slowing, zigzagging back and forth in short, tight turns, like an eager sailboat tacking up a narrow, winding channel against a strong head wind.

Ryan tried to emulate him, gasping out loud at the extra pressure it put on his back, nearly losing control and rolling helplessly.

But he fought the slide, gradually checking the frightening and exhilarating speed, reaching out and finally stopping himself by embracing the trunk of an elderly larch.

He was breathing hard, aware of his disgust at how his knees were trembling, his palms sweating, his fingers shaking.

Dean was forty or so yards to his right, punching his fist in the air in triumph.

"That was a real triple-hot pipe, Dad!" he called. "Best fun in ages."

Ryan swallowed hard, controlling his breathing before answering the boy. "Pretty good, huh?"

"How's that arrow wound, Dad?"

"Been better, thanks," he replied, trying to ignore the steady warmth of fresh blood leaking through his clothes.

"Now what?"

"Now we keep our voices down. Pigs'll have heard all that whooping. But they can't see us this high up. We move through the trees, slow and careful. I want to try and get up to the head of the canyon."

Under the spread branches, there were piles of dust-dry needles and cones, enough to start a lethally ferocious fire if you weren't really careful.

Or, if you *were* careful.

"WHAT'S THE SIGNAL, Dad?"

"I'll fire a single shot into the air. Noise should carry easily enough, even out of the box canyon."

"Might bring the brushwooders in after us if they're in the area."

"If they were going to come, they'd have been on our heels by now. Haven't seen or heard a sign of them. Could be that they're chasing after Krysty and the others. So, when you get your fire lit, watch out. You're in more danger out on the trail than me snug in the canyon here."

Dean's face was bright with an unholy delight. "Love to see their fucking faces when they first see what's coming rumbling their way."

"Don't say 'fucking,' Dean."

"Trader says it all the time."

"Trader's his own man. Always was and always will be. That's the problem between him and me since Abe brought him back to us. I'm the leader now. Trader can't settle to that. It's like him having a sand burr under his saddle. I've turned from being his trusted right-hand man for all those years to an itch that he somehow can't get to scratch."

"Will you have to fight him, Dad?"

It was a question that had been on Ryan's mind ever since the grizzled old man with the battered Armalite had reappeared in his life.

"Hope not."

"You could beat him, Dad," Dean said enthusiastically. "No worries."

"Think so?" Ryan ruffled the mat of curly hair.

"Sure. You're old, but he's even older."

THEY REACHED THE VILLE, exhausted, drained of fire and hope, a little after the middle of the day, to be greeted by a burst of weeping and anger, once their dire news had been passed on.

They held a council of war within the hour, prompted by J.B. and Krysty. Baron Weyman attended, along with his son and Bill Rainey.

Trader sat at the end of the big refectory table, blaster across his lap, staring up at the ceiling.

"We have to go back and find Ryan and Dean," J.B. insisted.

Rainey shook his head. "Don't have enough men left for that. I'll tell you straight, outlander, that I doubt we even have enough to defend the ville against an out-and-out attack. They can get up and over the walls, and we don't have the sec men to cover the defensive perimeter."

Baron Weyman was rubbing a finger along the angle of his jaw, as if he were trying to decide whether he needed to have a shave.

"In that case, I can see little point in waiting to have our throats cut by these lice-ridden mongrels. We will stand against them."

Jamie clapped his hands, leaping to his feet to declaim, "Then, Father, I will stand at your right hand and keep the bridge with you."

Despite the tenseness of the situation, Doc smiled. "You're familiar with the holding of the bridge over the Tiber, against the forces of Lars Porsena of Clusium. 'By the nine gods he swore, that the proud house of Tarquin should suffer wrong no more.' If my memory has it properly remembered. I am delighted to see that learning is not yet quite gone from Deathlands and all judgment is not yet fled to brutish beasts."

He looked around to see everyone staring at him. "My apologies, friends. But it is those same brutish beasts that confront us now. I would say only that Ryan's instructions were to wait here for him. I think that we should do that."

"What do we do if those brushwood bastards come, Doc?" Trader said, sneering. "Ask them to just wait awhile until Ryan gets back here?"

J.B. answered him. "They won't attack until dusk. But Doc's right. We should do what Ryan said. We can still cover our asses. My plan is to set out a watch on the trails from the west and north. Only way they can come at us. Soon as we get a warning, we go out and ambush them. We passed some good places for that within the last quarter mile. They won't expect that and we can use our firepower to cut them apart."

Trader patted the table approvingly. "I'll be hung, quartered and dried for the crows! You *did* learn something all those years, John Dix. Good plan."

RYAN HOPED THAT HIS PLAN was a good one.

Like a lot of plans, it seemed fine when you sat down and thought about it. When you came to try it out on the ground, you started to worry about all of the imponderables. One small slip, and the scheme was in tatters.

He adjusted the white silk scarf, with its weighted ends, around his neck. Ryan sat by the great heap of brushwood that he and Dean had dragged together. The boy would be doing the same, out in the narrow neck of the trail east, toward the ville, ready to light the wood on the signal and block off that way of escape.

Ryan's fire should panic the mutie pigs and send them stampeding out of the box canyon with only one way to go, west toward the vulnerable camp of the brushwooders.

This was one of the key moments of the plan.

If it worked, the men, women and children would totally freak when they saw what was charging at them. They had only one way to escape—back west, along the treacherous trail toward the land of the scabbies, then out into the bubbling death trap of the sulfur swamps.

Ryan's profound hope was that the terror of finding themselves in the path of the killer stampede would lead to the brushwooders fleeing, hopefully to their deaths.

The possibility that women and children might also die wasn't a factor in Ryan's plan. The quality of mercy wasn't something that you could believe in when dealing with a murderous tribe like the brushwooders.

The ending from a snippet of an old vid came to Ryan as he got ready to set his own fire. "That's Deathlands, Jake," he whispered to himself, just as General, giant among the mutie pigs, surged in to attack him.

Chapter Thirty-Three

For such a vast creature, General moved with an uncanny lightness and speed.

Ryan had been cautious, only too aware that the pigs were roaming all over the sheer-walled box canyon. The pile of dry brush and chaparral had been rustling and crackling in the northerly breeze that swirled around under the granite cliffs, helping to conceal the noise of the boar's approach.

Now Ryan was caught cold, on hands and knees, the SIG-Sauer snugly and uselessly holstered, the eighteen-inch steel panga sheathed on his other hip.

His right hand held a self-light, ready to ignite his fire. His left hand was supporting him, in the dirt.

Only at the last moment did his fighting sense save him from being slaughtered from behind.

Ryan glanced over his shoulder, seeing the imposing figure of the monstrous pig rushing at him, its head lowered, the unbroken tusk aimed at his chest. The tiny eyes, almost buried in rolls of fat and muscle, were boring into the human in front of it.

The pig was less than fifteen feet away when Ryan became aware of its presence.

He dropped the self-light and picked up a handful of dust in his left hand, throwing it into the boar's face and simultaneously hurling himself to one side.

The ground shook as the mutie beast, temporarily blinded, swerved away, hooking in his direction, the tusk brushing against the hem of Ryan's coat. It had been charging so fast that it couldn't stop immediately and blundered helplessly into the pile of dry wood and brush. It was wheezing and grunting as it turned, tossing the carefully prepared bonfire all around, stamping its hooves in rage.

The slight delay gave Ryan a moment to recover his balance, and he rolled up onto hands and knees, poised to move. His first reflex was to draw the SIG-Sauer, but he checked himself. If he opened fire at General, Dean would hear the shots and take them for his signal to light his fire.

It would be totally disastrous if the lower blaze began before Ryan had his own bonfire burning well. The pigs had to be driven down the canyon, where they'd find their path east was blocked by Dean's burning brush.

Timing was vital. If the boy lighted his fire too soon, then it would have burned well through before the herded beasts even reached him.

Ryan drew the panga instead, biting his lip as the gigantic pig finally readied itself for a second charge. It shook its head twice, trying to rid its eyes of the dust, pawing at the ground. Its jaws gaped, showing rows of savage teeth. A thread of green slime dribbled from the blunt mouth.

"Come on," Ryan whispered.

DEAN HADN'T ENJOYED his trip down the canyon. It was crawling with mutie pigs, mostly browsing among the trees, and the boy had made slow progress, dodging and waiting, his eyes constantly darting in all directions. Though he saw lifted heads and questing muzzles, none of the animals scented him and he made it safely.

Fortunately the box canyon had suffered a flash flood in the past weeks, and there was a towering pile of snagged branches of all dimension, now sun-dried, ideal for him to drag into the ravine and block the trail east. He felt in his pocket for the self-lights that his father had given him.

Dean crouched out of sight, in case the brushwooders appeared, ready to set the fire.

BARON WEYMAN RETREATED to his own private set of rooms, where he had taken out the velvet-lined trays that held his precious collection of English predark coins.

His head was lowered as he sat at a table by one of the shuttered windows, running his fingers slowly over the gold and silver lines. There were frail coins from Saxon times, from the reigns of Alcred, Osbert and Berhtwulf. A golden double leopard came from Edward III's reign; from Henry V, a half groat.

The ailing man had his eyes closed, shutting away the doubtful horrors of the last day or so, letting his beloved coins ease his uncertainties.

A dark blue silk bag held two dozen extra fine double florins from the time of Queen Victoria, and another held superb examples of soft-gleaming sovereigns.

Letting the cold metal caress his fingers, Baron Weyman was happy and contented, all of his worries forgotten for the time being.

RYAN HAD THE STEEP SLOPE of the hillside behind him and a maze of stark pine trees. There was a strong urge to turn and run, hoping to outdodge the lumbering brute, but he was only too aware that time was not on his side. By now his son would be waiting for the signal of the gunshot.

The panga was ready, perfectly balanced, an extension of Ryan's right arm.

Still General waited, working himself into a terrifying rage, his grunting growing louder. Blood flecked the twisted cord of frothing drool.

"Come on, you bastard," Ryan growled, beckoning to the monster animal, waiting for the inevitable charge, perfectly balanced on the balls of his feet, shuffling in the loose soil to make sure of his footing.

The charge was explosive, as though the mutie boar had been fired from a huge cannon.

Ryan feinted to throw more stinging sand in the pig's eyes, and General instinctively jerked his head away, altering the angle of his attack.

The boar gave the man the opening he'd hoped for, and he slashed down at the shoulder of the great monster as it lumbered past him. But the animal's skin was tough and leathery, almost jarring the panga out of Ryan's hand, leaving only a shallow cut a few inches long that wept a little purple blood.

"Fireblast!"

It was enough to provoke General to even dizzier heights of crazed ferocity. He turned, hesitating a moment, weighing up the opposition, not committing to another blind charge, taking greater care.

Since a slashing blow with the edge of the panga was likely to do nothing, except probably get him killed, Ryan had to rethink his own strategy.

The pig was a far more lethal opponent then he'd imagined, and chilling it was a triple-serious problem.

Ryan's back was to the steep path down the side of the hill, the scattered pile of brush to his left. General was directly in front of him with the ground sloping gently through dense trees to the right.

The pig came at him again, a little more slowly and cautiously, its great head swinging from side to side, ready to try to rake him with either the short or the long tusk.

Ryan saw a chance and took it, despite the appalling risk. If he missed either his footing or his grasp, then he would be down in the dirt, easy meat when the mutie creature would turn and rip him apart.

As General thundered toward him, Ryan stood slightly sideways on to the creature, waiting for the right moment.

Waiting.

He jumped high in the air, steadying himself with the left hand on the bristled shoulders, avoiding tusks and teeth, and landing astride the pig's back. Ryan gripped for his life with his thighs and knees, hanging on as the enraged animal tried to turn its head to savage its oppressor. But he was far enough away from the rending jaws to be safe. For a few hectic moments.

General tried to buck him off, running around in a tight circle, giving an almost human cry of rage.

Ryan knew it could only be a matter of seconds before the wily old boar spotted the way out and rolled on the ground, wiping him away like a mule shedding a tick.

He fought for balance, risking letting go with his left hand, holding the hilt of the long knife in both hands.

Ryan picked his spot carefully, at the juncture where the head joined onto the back, plunging in the sharp point of the blade with all his strength.

There was a momentary hesitation when Ryan feared for a second that the thick skin had diverted the blow. Then he felt the steel penetrate through, deep into the wedge of muscle, finally reaching the delicate spinal cord.

It was hilt-deep, but he still tried to drive it in those extra fractions of an inch.

General skidded to a shuddering halt, front legs braced, nearly throwing Ryan over its head. It gave a strange, groaning cry, like an old man stricken with a heart attack. Ryan felt its gigantic body start to shake and quiver, as if it were suffering an ague.

He drew out the panga and drove it in again, pushing the hilt with both hands, feeling the steel nick on bone.

Like a brain-shot horse in an abattoir yard, General slumped suddenly onto his knees, snout gouging a furrow in the packed leaf mold. Then he rolled onto his side, legs kicking helplessly, enabling Ryan to step quite safely off, withdrawing the steel.

Feeling that he was being watched, Ryan spun, seeing at least a dozen of the mutie pigs staring at him from the edge of the woods, only a few yards away.

"Time to move," he said, sheathing the panga and drawing the SIG-Sauer. He reached for the self-light that he'd dropped on the ground.

Ryan realized that the pigs weren't looking at him. Their attention was fixed on their dying leader. General wasn't going gently into the good night. His hooves were scratching in the dirt, fighting for purchase, and he kept lifting his head, eyes red-rimmed, seeking the creature that had slain him. The monstrous bulk was convulsing, actually driving it along like a vast pink slug, toward Ryan. Bright blood trickled from the muzzle and streamed from the open, panting jaws.

The self-light blazed into life, its yellow flame hardly visible. Ryan thrust it into the pile of tiny twigs that he'd prepared, gathering the dried branches that the boar had scattered.

There was a wisp of smoke, then the scarlet glow of a fire that gathered momentum fast under the light breeze.

The herd of pigs had already grown in numbers to thirty, a few of them showing signs of restlessness at the scent of the flames.

Moments later, the fire was burning fiercely, tongues of red and yellow racing across the carpet of dead needles, igniting the chaparral and mesquite with explosions of flame.

Ryan straightened, checking that the course of the fire was right, along the canyon, toward the pigs. Some had already turned away and were starting to move restlessly down through the close-set pines trees at something between a fast walk and a lumbering trot.

It was burning more quickly than he'd anticipated, making it time to give Dean the gunshot signal to start his own bonfire before the entire herd of pigs gave way to panic and fled out of the box canyon.

General was snarling and grunting, more blood tumbling in gobbets from its open jaws. The boar could see that the fire was going to surround him and burn him alive.

Ryan saw that as well.

"All right," he said, aiming the SIG-Sauer just behind the mutie boar's left ear and squeezing the trigger. The crack of the heavy handblaster echoed from the granite walls. The pig's skull jerked and a tremor ran through its body.

A moment later it was quite still, the flames already licking at its mountainous carcass, singeing the bristles.

And Ryan was off and running.

Chapter Thirty-Four

Krysty had been resting on the double bed in the room that she'd been sharing with Ryan. She suddenly got up and walked to the window that faced west, peering through the slats in the shutters. Doc had been sitting with her, the friends talking about when the brush-wooders might put in an appearance. And when Ryan would return to them.

"What is wrong, my dear lady? Are you having one of your feelings?"

She nodded, pushing back an errant curl of her bright red sentient hair. "Something like that."

"How does it work? Do you see it or hear it? I find such an ability quite fascinating."

"Like hearing the sound of a bell, very far off. Sometimes the bell's bright and silver. Sometimes it's more like the tolling at a funeral. I don't mean that I can really hear a bell. Just that it's the nearest I can explain it."

"What can you see?"

"Over in the direction of the sea. Looks to be about fifteen miles or so away. Can't tell easily. Fog's coming back again. But . . . it looks like smoke."

IT WAS WORKING.

Ryan felt his heart leap with excitement and delight as he ran as fast as he dared down the slope of the canyon, weaving and dodging between the trees.

The main flow of the fire was to his left, raging through the conifers, igniting the underbrush, flames reaching into the lower branches of the pines, bursting from tree to tree. The smoke was still relatively thin, rising in a boiling column, darkening the blue sky.

Ahead of him he could hear the constant squealing of the herd of mutie pigs, driven into a wild panic by the pursuing flames. Every now and then Ryan would glimpse some of the animals, scampering at speed, moving faster than he was.

For a moment he stopped, breathing heavily, wiping sweat from his forehead, moving the patch to clear it from the puckered socket of his missing left eye. He squinted through the drifting smoke to try to see whether Dean had heard the signal and had managed to set his own fire going, but he couldn't make it out from where he was.

Ryan continued to run toward the main trail.

NOW EVERYONE, including Bill Rainey, was in the bedroom with Doc and Krysty, crowding around the window. Trader turned away first. "I say that's two separate fires," he shouted. "It's two fucking fires."

Jak nodded in agreement. "Yeah," he said quietly. "Two fires."

DEAN WAS WAVING HIS ARMS, whooping and jumping up and down in a cloud of choking gray dust, cheering on the stampeding pigs ahead of him.

He saw his father emerging from the billowing smoke and the shifting threads of fog.

"See 'em go!"

The boy had his retrieved Browning in his right hand, ready to encourage any stragglers among the animals.

His fire was burning well, completely blocking the trail to the east, forcing the mutie creatures to funnel down the ravine to the west.

"Which way we goin', Dad?"

There was a temptation to withdraw to the ville, skirting the flames by climbing above them, but that would mean missing out on the final act of the drama. When you had a good plan that seemed to be working, you wanted to see it all the way through.

"After the pigs," he replied, jerking his thumb toward the camp of the brushwooders.

"Think they'll run when they see the stampede coming?"

"Won't have much choice," Ryan told him.

MOST OF THE MEN AND WOMEN in the camp had celebrated their earlier victory by consuming large quantities of home brew, and were rotten drunk. Some had been sick, and others had passed out. One or two had been copulating openly. Children wandered around, helping themselves from the caldrons of food that were beginning to burn over open fires.

Ditchdown and Straub were sitting together at the western edge of the village, sipping at a jug of home brew. The leader of the brushwooders was three parts drunk, belching as he took another pull on the jug.

"We hit them tonight?" he mumbled.

Straub was three parts sober. He looked around at the squalid scene of debauchery. "If we can sober them up in time. Way that they look right now, I wouldn't back them against a handful of angry rabbits."

"They'll be fine and jim-dandy when the time comes, old friend. You see."

Straub sniffed at the air, his forehead wrinkling. "What's that?" he asked, standing, uncoiling himself from the dirt with a pantherish grace.

"Usual stink of sulfur," Ditchdown replied unconcernedly. "Fog's coming back, as well. Wind must be westerly for the smell to be—"

"Stupe!"

"What?"

"Wind's northerly, veering easterly. Freshening. It's not the sulfur. It's wood smoke. Look. There's a fire burning toward the ville."

Ditchdown set the jug down, where it fell over, its contents gurgling into the thirsty soil. With an effort he staggered to his feet, peering toward the narrow canyon that bore the trail east, blinking owlishly. "By the gods! You're right, Straub, old comrade." He ran his fingers through his tousled hair, brushing the white scar.

Straub was licking his lips with his long, reptilian tongue. "Been no lightning to set a fire. It's a trick from that one-eyed whoreson, Cawdor. But what good does a fire do?" He cocked his head to one side, his silver-spangled eyes opening wide as his keen hearing caught the first sound of pounding hooves, overlaid with a high-pitched squealing.

He relaxed, half smiling. "Of course," he whispered. "The mutie pigs."

RYAN AND HIS SON RAN behind the pigs, losing distance to them, following the trampled trail along the canyon. They passed three or four animals, dead or dying, all hideously mangled by the hooves of the other panicked animals.

"Close now?" Dean called, glancing back over his shoulder for his father to catch up with him.

"Yeah. Don't get ahead. Fog's thickening again. Some of the brushwooders might manage to get around the herd and come this way. Keep ready."

An almost invisible path snaked off to the right, only a foot or so wide, leading to a bluff that overlooked the brushwooders' settlement.

"There," Ryan said. "Get a grandstand view from up there."

THEY HAD NO TIME to collect any possessions, no time to gather any viable defenses against the raging torrent of ferocious animals.

Ditchdown staggered around the camp, yelling at the top of his voice to rouse the brushwooders, hesitating by the main fire, his AK-74 on his shoulder, unfired.

"Straub!" he shouted. "Where are you? Use your skills and save us all."

But the shaved-headed man was nowhere to be seen.

The place was in a turmoil of panic, with women scooping up bawling brats, carrying them under their arms, dashing here and there, staring wildly and hopelessly at the steep hills that cupped the camp.

One or two of the more drink-sodden men couldn't be roused from their stupor, and their relatives left them sleeping to face their fate.

"Straub! You bastard! Save us!"

DEAN SCRAMBLED UP the trail like an agile mountain goat, crouching on the lip of the dead ground, beckoning to his father, who was panting along a few yards behind.

"Pigs are nearly there!"

Ryan dropped flat on the top of the bluff, staring down through the wreathing bank of mist that was creeping silently inland from the ocean.

It was the best seat in the house.

Below him and to his left, the vanguard of the stampede was pouring through the ravine like a gray-pink tidal wave, dust rising around the unstoppable column.

They were now within a hundred yards of the edges of the brushwood settlement, where the lords of chaos held total sway.

Like ants scurrying around when their castle has been destroyed, the inhabitants of the settlement were dashing in all directions. Above the sound of the pounding hooves of the giant mutie creatures, Ryan could clearly hear the noise of screaming, high and thin, and futile.

DITCHDOWN WAS STANDING still, a fixed point in the milling idiocy of the confusion. He held his blaster at the hip, staring toward the place where he knew that the pigs would be appearing.

He ignored the yelling and screams from all around him, steadying the powerful blaster, wishing that the vanished Straub was still somewhere around him, so that he could have chilled the outland bastard.

No time for that.

If there had been a few minutes of warning, then it might have been possible to guide some of the settlement up into the sheer hills around them.

Now the only hope was to run west, toward the ocean. But that meant the territory of the scabbies, then into the yellow land of boiling mud.

Ditchdown just didn't feel much like taking up either of those options.

"That's enough," he said quietly.

The pigs were already at the outskirts of the village, hundreds of them, most of them weighing well over the five-hundred-pound mark, tusks gleaming through the dust. They charged clear across the camp, their attention burning toward the trail that continued out the far side, barreling straight through anything that was in their way.

RYAN'S ATTENTION WAS on the white streak that ran through Ditchdown's dark hair, blazing like a beacon in the cloudy, misty gloom.

There was the brief muzzle-flash from the Kalashnikov, and several of the leading boars went toppling over in a tangle of hooves. But it was like trying to stop a crumbling dam with your finger and thumb.

"He's not trying to run, Dad."

"I see it."

"Why?"

"Times that you have to stop running, Dean. For better or worse."

"Don't see Straub."

"Nor me."

The leading pigs were beginning to emerge from the other side of the camp, hot on the heels of those brushwooders who'd taken the option of running. Behind them they left ruined tents and splintered huts.

And the dead and dying.

Because of the whirling dervish of dust and the deepening fog, it was difficult to make out the full details, but it looked as though there weren't going to be many survivors in the settlement.

Nor any settlement to survive.

A young woman, carrying a child, was knocked sideways by a huge sow, vanishing under the trampling herd.

An old gray-haired man was tossed high in the air, his body spinning, arms and legs flailing, his guts spilling out of him in greasy cartwheeling loops, before he too was absorbed into the dust and fog.

Ryan watched Ditchdown meet his doom with an extraordinary calm, still holding the blaster, staring defiantly at the mutie pigs, standing upright until he crumpled before the tidal wall of rampaging flesh.

As the cloud of dust began to clear, it was possible to see the mangled bodies, one or two of the slower pigs pausing from the stampede to begin their snuffling, rutting feed off the smears of blood and broken bones and mashed flesh that had once been the wild brushwooders.

Ryan stood, wincing at the stabbing pain from the arrow wound, an injury that he'd managed to forget during the adrenaline rush of the deathly battle with General and then the lighting of the fires.

It had been a plan fraught with all sorts of perils and chances for spectacular failure, failure that would probably have meant their deaths as well as the destruction of the ville. But Dean had done his part perfectly, and it had worked.

The brushwooders were scattered and destroyed. Though the unseen final act was played out a mile or so farther to the west, past the territory of the scabbies, among the lethal geysers and sucking swamps of scalding, bubbling, golden mud, Ryan knew that precious few from the ragged camp would live to see the sun set that evening.

Though he would have been a little happier to have seen the man called Straub meet his own doom.

"That it, Dad?" Dean also stood, adjusting the heavy handblaster in his belt.

"That's about as much 'it' as you can ever get. Yeah, it's done."

"Baron Weyman and Jamie're safe?"

"For a while. Until next time."

"Will there be a next time, Dad?"

Ryan smiled at his son. "There's always a next time, son. Always."

He turned away from the scene of murderous desolation, ignoring the feasting mutie pigs, leading the boy along the ridge, eastward, skirting the fire, back to the ville and their friends.

Chapter Thirty-Five

The events of the past few days had put a great strain on the frail physique of Baron Weyman, and he was only able to bid farewell to the outlanders from his bed. Bill Rainey stood by the shuttered window, and Jamie sat in a small armchair by the side of the fireplace, where a pile of weathered apple logs burned bright and clean.

The baron was pale, wearing a thick woolen shawl around his shoulders, but he seemed cheerful enough.

"Well, Ryan Cawdor... and all of you outlander friends, it is time to say goodbye and to thank you all, yet again, for everything that you've done."

He smiled across at his son. "What would you say, dear boy?"

"That parting is such sweet sorrow, Father."

Doc Tanner beamed at Jamie.

Mildred nodded. "Even I know that. *Romeo and Juliet,* isn't it?"

Jamie blushed. "Yes, it is."

He looked at Ryan. "Forgive my asking, and I know that I've asked you this a lot of times in the past few days, ever since you came back from scorching the brushwooders' camp..."

"But can Dean stay here with you for a while?" Ryan completed. "And the answer's still the same. I'd be happy enough, but the decision is my son's. Not mine."

"Thanks," Dean muttered, eyes fixed resolutely on his feet. "But we all stay together."

Trader slapped him on the shoulder. "Nothing's forever, boy. Time comes when everyone has to move on. Fucking better or worse. Way life is."

Dean swallowed hard. "I know that's true, Trader. And me and Dad've talked some about... about making changes. But not yet, not now. Got to go a little farther down the line. But I like being here and I like you, Jamie. Be good if we could sort of meet again."

"Farther down the line?" Jamie grinned, then got up and offered his hand to Dean.

The two boys shook, watched approvingly by the others.

Baron Weyman broke the silence, coughing into a white linen kerchief. "Forgive me. Time passes and you must be gone. You're sure you don't want an escort to the coast?"

Ryan shook his head. "Appreciate the offer, Baron. But I think we can handle any raggle brushwood remainder that might've made it through the mutie pigs and the scabbies and the sulfur swamps. Thanks, anyway."

THEY HAD their armament, clothes washed and patched, wounds treated and rebandaged.

Rainey and a couple of sec men rode with them as far as the remains of the camp, stopping there to lead back the string of horses that the friends had borrowed. It was late morning when they finally parted company, after the briefest of farewells, and headed west on foot, toward the ocean and the raft. There was far too much death between them and the solemn-faced sec boss for any more cordial goodbyes.

Trader walked with Ryan.

"Don't know which is the worse stink," he commented. "Sulfur all around us in this bastard fog, or the smell of those bodies rotting away back there."

"You and me've smelled more bodies than sulfur over the years, Trader," Ryan said.

The older man shrugged the Armalite to a more comfortable position on his shoulder. "Ain't that the truth, Brother Cawdor? Sure have seen too much chilling."

"Likely see plenty more." Behind them, the vultures that had been scared off into the misty sky came flapping down again on their wide, leathery wings. There hadn't been that much left of the brushwood dead after the pigs and the carrion eaters had taken their pleasure of them.

There were only a few pathetic tangled piles of gnawed bone and sinew between the wrecked camp and the beginning of the sulfur pools and hot springs.

"FOG'S THICKENING a lot, lover."

"Yeah. Wind's freshening, as well. Blowing dead

behind us, from the Sierras. Could be some seriously bad weather to come. Sky's black as an Apache tear.''

Krysty's hair was curled tightly around her nape against the miserable, damp weather.

"Least we can get on the raft, paddle across the strait and make the jump. Reckon we should be at the coast in about fifteen minutes.''

They had come through the seething, blighted terrain without serious harm to any of them. Jak's ankle was still giving him trouble, and he had once stumbled over some loose stones and nearly fallen into one of the boiling springs. But his amazing reflexes had saved him.

The whole region still carried the sickly smell of overbroiled meat.

Much of it was pork, with several of the smaller basins of scalding mud choked with the corpses of the stampeded herd of pigs, the meat already tumbling from the white bones. There was also evidence that more of the brushwooders had perished in that bleak and dreadful place.

The lower half of a woman's body lay on the winding path, several chomping bites ripped from the thighs. The upper half of the corpse was immersed in brightly boiling, salted water.

It wasn't possible to tell any difference between boiled pork and boiled human.

Doc chose that place to offer an academic lecture on how cannibals in the South Seas used to call human flesh "long pig" because of its alleged similarity in terms of texture, smell and flavor.

JAK EXAMINED THE TRAIL once they were through the hot springs. "Some pigs got past safe," he said. "Some came back."

"Brushwooders?" J.B. asked.

"Some. Also bare feet. Scabbies? One man in Western boots. Straub?"

Ryan wasn't that worried. He had never imagined that his plan would involve the deaths of all of the ferocious mutie pigs or all of the brushwood tribe.

But it was enough to know that the twin threats had been thoroughly diluted.

By the time they reached the rocky beach, the weather had deteriorated. There was the unusual combination of a howling wind and a thick fog that swirled about them.

Krysty shuddered. "Like to get away fast," she said quietly to Ryan. "Don't care for this much."

"Me neither. Raft was over here."

There had been the worry that someone, or something, might have found the fragile, ramshackle craft and destroyed it.

But it was where they'd left it.

"Wood's gotten sodden," Abe said, peering at it. "Floats lower in the sea than before."

Abe was understating the problem.

There was barely any freeboard above the lapping waves.

"Two trips?" Mildred queried.

"Make it one," Trader argued. "Bastard impossible journey to try and run a ferry service. Look at that fucking riptide running out there."

Ryan had to agree with his former leader.

Through the patches of fog, they could see the way the ocean was tearing past them, with oil whirlpools and ragged stretches of white, tumbling water. The mist concealed the redoubt.

"Once we're off, there won't be any coming back," Ryan said. "Current'll pluck us off, and we'll have to paddle like smoke. Be risky."

They all stood and looked at the raft, barely afloat, tethered to a jagged spur of rock at Trader's feet.

"Go for it," Dean said. "That's my vote."

"Why can we not detour along the coast to that other craft that needed a bit of mending?" Doc asked.

"Take too much time," Ryan replied. "And we might finish up in a nest of scabbies."

"I say let's take a chance," Krysty offered. "Got a bad feeling about staying here."

Jak stared out into the fog, the wind blowing his silken white hair around him like a torn veil of snow. "Go," he said, lips hardly moving.

"Three to one so far," Krysty said, turning to the Armorer. "What do you reckon?"

"Sea's triple bad. We could wait until this evening, or even until tomorrow morning."

"I vote with John," Mildred said. "I agree with you, Ryan. Once we've pushed off there's no way we could get back to shore with this tide running."

"Three all. Abe?"

"Stay," the gunner replied, tugging nervously at his mustache. "Definitely stay. I'm not that good at swimming. But I reckon I'd be terrific at drowning."

"I vote for chancing it," Ryan said. "If we keep balanced, we could make it across to the island."

He turned to Trader. "Well, seems you have the casting vote."

The old man looked at him, half smiling. "You and John Dix were the sons I never had. You know that?"

"Sure." Ryan sniffed, realizing at that moment how much he owed Trader, how different his life would have been, probably a deal shorter, if it hadn't been for the survivalist ways of the grizzled man standing in front of him.

"I say we try for it. Man never opens the door, he never gets to know what's behind it. I've always wondered about what lies behind that door. Could be a good way of finding out. Yeah, fucking go for it."

"Five for and four against," Ryan said. "Means we go for it. No point waiting. Everyone on. Slow and careful. Keep balance or she'll go over."

Dean went first, followed by Jak, the albino still clumsy. J.B. climbed cautiously on board, reaching to help Mildred. Even with only four of them settled on board, the raft was already almost under water.

Doc nearly fell into the weed-wracked breakers, his sword stick snagging in some of the tangled cordage. "By the Three Kennedys! I sympathize with your sentiments, Abe, my dear chap. For a moment there I was more nearly drowning than waving."

Krysty stepped on, finding a place for herself, taking up one of the makeshift paddles.

Only Abe, Ryan and Trader remained on the shore.

The little gunner hopped on, his weight pushing the raft a little farther below the surface of the sea. He clung to the water-logged timber like a monkey, on the landward side of the craft.

"You next, Ryan," Trader said quietly.

"Age goes before beauty, Trader."

"Give me your hand."

Slightly puzzled, Ryan offered his right hand to Trader, wincing at the power in the old man's grip.

"Now get on."

Ryan picked his moment, waiting until the sullen raft was on the crest of a wave, then stepping beside Krysty, turning to face Trader, who had loosened the rope and was holding it coiled in his right hand.

"Nothing's forever, Ryan," Trader shouted, hurling the rope onto the raft, simultaneously giving it a hard push with his boot, sending it spinning out into the strait.

Everyone was thunderstruck. For once, Abe was the quickest to react.

Feeling the first tug of the current starting to suck the raft away from the shore, the little gunner gave an inarticulate shout and threw himself over the side, splashing the few dangerous feet to the rocks, where Trader stooped to help him, dripping wet, from the water.

"Get back!" Doc called. "We must—" He stopped speaking abruptly as he realized that it was already way, way too late.

They were already swinging into the main channel, thirty or forty yards from the mist-shrouded promontory of sea-slick boulders.

"Paddle!" Ryan bellowed. "Fireblast! They've given us a better chance. Don't let's piss it away. Paddle till your backs break. Keep her straight for the redoubt."

The fog wrapped itself around them, the wind tearing at the raft, trying to lure it off course.

Ryan glanced back once, seeing Trader, the shorter figure of Abe at his side. The older man lifted the familiar Armalite once above his head in a valedictory salute.

That was almost the end, the mist shutting down visibility, the surging water needing all of Ryan's concentration.

"NEARLY THERE," J.B. gasped. Effectively one-armed, the Armorer had done what he could. But it had been a desperately close thing. Now the raft was well below the water, but the jaws of the current had relaxed their grip, and Ryan knew they were going to make it.

He looked back one last time. The gusting wind suddenly tugged back the white fog, like a curtain across a huge window, revealing the shore.

There were the jumbled rocks, and Trader and Abe, standing side by side, facing away from the ocean.

Surrounding them was a menacing circle of men, looking, as far as Ryan could make out, like a mix of brushwood survivors and some capering scabbies.

And at the front, leading them, was the unmistakable figure of Straub.

There wasn't a thing that could be done.

As the raft grounded near the entrance to the redoubt, Ryan whispered, "No, Trader. Nothing's forever."

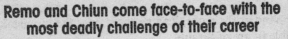

TAKE 'EM FREE

4 action-packed novels plus a mystery bonus

NO RISK
NO OBLIGATION TO BUY